THE
SCORE

The Russian Guns, Book Three

Bethany-Kris

Published by Bethany-Kris

www.bethanykris.com

ISBN 10: 0-9947909-1-0
ISBN 13: 978-0-9947909-1-0
eISBN 10: 0-9937797-1-8
eISBN 13: 978-0-9937797-1-8

Cover Design © Jay Aheer
Editor: Elle Leigh

This is work of fiction. Characters, names, places, corporations, organizations, institutions, locales, and so forth are all the product of the author's imagination, or if real, used fictitiously. Any resemblance to a person, living or dead, is entirely coincidental.

For A. Inspiration and obsession are fine lines walked by authors. Thank you for taking me through the journey of both..

CONTENTS

CHAPTER ONE 7
CHAPTER TWO 21
CHAPTER THREE 32
CHAPTER FOUR 44
CHAPTER FIVE 58
CHAPTER SIX 70
CHAPTER SEVEN 87
CHAPTER EIGHT 102
CHAPTER NINE 118
CHAPTER TEN 131
CHAPTER ELEVEN 147
CHAPTER TWELVE 158
CHAPTER THIRTEEN 168
CHAPTER FOURTEEN 176
CHAPTER FIFTEEN 188
CHAPTER SIXTEEN 200
CHAPTER SEVENTEEN 211
CHAPTER EIGHTEEN 221
CHAPTER NINETEEN 238
CHAPTER TWENTY 251
CHAPTER TWENTY-ONE 261
EPILOGUE 268

Chapter One

"Mr. Avdonin?"

Anton glanced up over the pictures he'd spread out over his desk. "Come in."

The new server at Seven Lights entered Anton's spacious office with hesitance. It was her first time being allowed inside the space. Given the Bratva business that took place in the office, it wasn't often, especially during the club's business hours, that anyone but him or one of his men were permitted in.

"Yes?" Anton asked, making the pictures of the new possible shipment of guns from Mexico scarce with a quick swipe of his hand. "What can I do for you, Natalie?"

The young girl raised the serving tray in her hand as an explanation. A tumbler of vodka rested in the middle. "A friend wanted to send up his regards to the owner."

Anton sighed and rubbed his forehead. "What kind of friend?"

"Huh?"

"Old, or young? Russian, or English? What kind of friend, sweetheart?"

Natalie just looked confused. Anton shouldn't have been surprised. Even though her uncle was affiliated with the Russian mafia, she was sheltered from it growing up. Or at least, that's what he understood. Even so, the girl should have understood what Anton meant.

"Is the friend *Bratva*?" Anton asked pointedly.

Finally, Natalie seemed to get it. "Oh! Um, no. I don't think so. Maybe just someone you know from Brighton Beach or something, because when he asked if you were around, he didn't ask about the office like the other guys do."

Well done, Anton thought. Perhaps Natalie would work out as a server for Seven Lights after all.

"Thank you. Leave the drink, but refuse anymore, and I'm not interested in having guests. Is that clear?"

Natalie nodded before plucking up the tumbler from the tray and placing it on a stand. "Also, your wife called about an hour ago. I guess she couldn't get through to your office or—"

What time was it, again?

"Shit!"

Anton was such an idiot. A couple of unexpected guys showed up earlier and out of respect, he hadn't turn them away. Then, he got caught up dealing with the new shipment prospect. Everything on his desk that wasn't needed was swiped into an opened drawer. A simple look at his watch told him he'd missed the late dinner Viviana wanted them to have together. It was her birthday, for Christ's sake.

"Vine's gonna kill the fuck out of me," Anton mumbled as he grabbed the suit jacket off the back of his chair.

Natalie barely managed to move out of his way. "Should I have told you earlier?"

Anton paused at the doorway, turning to give the girl a sharp stare. "If my wife calls this club looking for me because she can't get through to me herself, then yes. I don't care if the fucking mayor of New York is dancing on my goddamn toes. You come up here and get me. Understood?"

"Yes, sir."

"Good."

Anton made it home in record time. The house was dark and quiet instead of filled with the usual loudness of his wife, son, and their live-in maid, Clarissa. Of course, it was a little after midnight. Everyone was likely asleep.

Damn, that just made Anton's guilt rise tenfold.

Making his way through the bottom floor, the cleanliness of the kitchen happened to catch his eye. There wasn't a thing out of place to say Viviana had cooked the dinner, let alone eaten it. Upstairs, light was seeping out from underneath the door to his son's bedroom, leaving a streak of color through the dark hallway.

Quietly, Anton slipped down the space to listen to the quiet murmurs coming from the bedroom.

"Shh, it's sleep time, Demyan," he heard Viviana whisper.

"But, Ma—"

"Papa will be home soon, and then he'll read you the train story. Sound good?"

At least his wife didn't sound too angry. That boded well for him.

Anton pushed the door open with a grin, peeking in to wink at his instantly alert son. It never failed to surprise Anton how much Demyan looked like him. From the blue of his eyes to the black of his hair. Even the quirks and mannerisms of his child seemed to come directly from him.

And he loved it.

"Papa!"

Their German shepherd Rocco barely reacted but for the quiet thumps of his tail hitting the wood floors.

"The train story, huh?" Anton asked, stepping into the bedroom.

"Please?" Demyan pleaded.

With a sigh, Viviana moved from the bed. Anton couldn't help but notice she was fully dressed and ready for bed herself.

"He's up a bit late," Anton noted to his wife as she passed.

"His father missed his bedtime. This usually happens, Anton."

Ouch. "I'm sorry, baby. Stuff came up and—"

"Later," Viviana said before leaving the room.

Focusing his attention on his son instead of the bitter bite his wife's tone held, Anton crawled into the small single bed. Instantly, Demyan seemed calmer, happier.

"Were you giving Ma a hard time?" Anton asked as he grabbed the book off the small bed stand.

Demyan shook his head with wide eyes. "No way, Papa. I is always good for Ma."

Anton held back the snort of disbelief that his young son wouldn't understand. Always good was a bit of a stretch for

Demyan. The child was a hell raiser in more ways than one. He gave his parents a run for their money, and that attitude of his made a daily appearance.

"Demyan," Anton warned. "If you're lying to me ..."

Twinkling, tired blue eyes stared up at Anton with familiar mischief. It was clear he wasn't going to get anything from his son tonight, but they'd definitely be having a chat about his nighttime behavior in the morning.

"Let's read your story, little man."

Demyan grinned into his blanket, satisfied. "Okay."

Forty minutes and a bit of bribery later, Anton left his sleeping boy to find his wife. In their bedroom, Viviana was hidden under blankets, the soft glow of a lamp giving her the needed light to read the novel in her hands.

"What are you reading?" Anton asked as he began the process of removing his jacket and dress shirt. "Anything good?"

Viviana smirked over the black cover of the book. "The Godfather."

"Seriously?"

"As a heart attack."

"Is it accurate in the fact sense?" Anton climbed into his side of the bed, pushing away the blankets. The sight of naked, creamy skin resting against Egyptian cotton sheets had his breath catching hard in his throat. "Damn, baby ... you look like ... God, I don't even know."

"Accurate enough," Viviana replied. "I only know the ins and outs of some things regarding the Cosa Nostra, so I can't really say for sure. It's mostly fictional, though the author did base a character or two on some real life organized crime figures."

Wait, were they still talking about her book? Screw that.

"*Viviana.*"

"Hmm?"

Anton swallowed the saliva gathering in his mouth as his gaze roamed over pert breasts and the swell of her hips. Beauty in the purest form. That was his sweet wife. She was sexy without even needing to try and the only thing on earth that could make him hard enough to pound fucking concrete.

"Are you angry with me for being late?" Anton asked, his tone husky.

"When I called, the new girl did manage to tell me you were busy, so I chatted with Jen for a while. She mentioned you had a few visitors show up, so I knew you were probably distracted."

"I am sorry, Vine. I didn't mean to miss dinner, and I really needed to give an okay for a shipment tonight." Even though he hadn't been able to give that go-ahead. It didn't even matter. Viviana took precedence, as she always had. The rest could and would wait. "But you didn't answer my question. Are you angry with me? I'd understand."

Viviana tossed him a coy glance through dark lashes. "No."

Just to be sure ... "No?"

"Oh, no. But I do think you owe me something special."

"Absolutely, birthday girl."

• • •

"Happy anniversary, Vine. I've been waiting to tell you that for days."

It'd been three years since Anton and Viviana Avdonin married. While the first year had definitely been the most difficult and dangerous for the Russian mafia boss and his pretty wife, the following two were filled with a quiet, loving happiness. The growth of their child, the beginning of their family, and the true start to their life.

There was nothing to step in their way, now.

Their actual anniversary was the day before Viviana's birthday, but Anton always took the week leading up to her day to celebrate that. Then, after Viviana's birthday, they celebrated the anniversary of their marriage. Sure, it was different, but they never were traditional. The emotional meaning was still there. It didn't make a difference what day they celebrated it, really.

It was also nearly Christmas, being the twenty-second of December, but it was one holiday Anton didn't celebrate, so neither did Viviana. Anton was Jewish, but he didn't celebrate his religious holidays, either. It just wasn't his thing, and Christmas had never been celebrated in his home.

"Mmm, happy anniversary to you, too," Viviana said softly.

The faint flutter of her lashes followed a relieved, contented sigh when Anton kissed a path along the smooth contour of her stomach. His wife wasn't particularly athletic, but she worked damn hard to get her figure back to the perfect feminine form after their son Demyan was born almost two and a half years ago. Damn, Anton was happy with Viviana's body the way it was, but he couldn't deny how utterly fucking beautiful she was fit, trim, and toned, too.

"Are you nearly ready for another?" Anton asked. "A little girl this time, maybe?"

Viviana gave a breathy laugh in response, her hand coming down to run through her husband's dark hair. When his teeth nipped lightly to her outer thigh, her fingers tightened their grip to an almost painful point, but it was still so fucking good.

"Oh, don't start with that again, Anton. It's too early for your nonsense."

Anton grinned against her sweet smelling, silky skin. "It's never too early if it gets me what I want, baby."

"To whose detriment?" she asked with a cock of her brow.

Their gazes met over the comforter tangled around their bodies, each holding a challenge. Anton wasn't ready to let his desire for another child go, and he knew Viviana was hesitant about having another while Demyan was still a toddler. He'd been trying to convince her to have another baby since their son's first birthday.

Yes, he knew she was exhausted. So was he, really. Demyan was a peculiar child. Their son seemed to keep at least one of them running from early morning to late at night. He didn't give them a damned break. But, Anton was sure a sibling would help to settle his son, somehow.

Sure, Viviana had her excuses. All were valid enough for a while. She wanted to wait until their son was off the bottle after he was weaned from breastfeeding. Then, it was after he was potty trained. Now, it was looking like they'd be waiting until Demyan was in elementary school.

That was a no-go. Anton was not waiting that long for another child.

"Come on, Vine." He pleaded with soft pecks landing down to her hip before trailing up her side to punctuate his words and want. "Just be serious and consider it, please. If he had someone to play with—"

"Daycare, playdates, and park time. He has more than enough interaction with children his age. Demyan has friends. Nice try, Anton."

Nope, Anton still couldn't let it go. Using the tips of his fingers to trail up and down her sides, he kept her thin T-shirt bunched up around her breasts. Viviana shivered under his innocent touches. If Anton learned anything about his wife, it was that she loved to be touched. Anytime, all the time, whenever the hell he could … Yeah, Viviana wanted it.

Anton was not above using that to get what he wanted from her. "He's two. That's the worst time, right? He's already half way through it. You have to realize he's smart, too, so he gets bored easily. He needs something new to keep his overactive mind distracted."

Leaning up, Anton loomed over Viviana's form, thoroughly enjoying the view of her staring back through thick lashes and hooded eyes. Using one thumb, he traced a line over her plump lips, feeling her kiss the digit softly.

"Please just think about it?"

Viviana sighed. "You're serious about this, huh?"

Anton nodded. "More than serious. I want another child with you. Soon, preferably. You keep putting it off and I don't understand why. It's not like we don't have the means.

Your bookstore is doing fine, you have somebody to take care of it if needed, and everything business-wise on my side has been quiet. I mean, I know Demyan gives us a run for our money some days—"

"And nights," Viviana added, a yawn giving proper due to her point.

Anton agreed, but after almost three years of this with their son, weren't they used to no sleep by now? "Why not?"

"You keep using Demyan like he's the only reason I say no."

Anton's brow furrowed. "Isn't he?"

"No. You just assumed."

"Well, what else am I supposed to think, Vine? You won't even talk about it beyond telling me no and leaving it at that."

She huffed, refusing to meet his gaze. "I would love to have another child."

Happiness and triumph swelled in Anton. Despite the loudness, messiness, and crankiness of other children, he didn't mind a bit when it came to his son. Really, he loved seeing Viviana growing, glowing, and ripe with pregnancy. Filled with his child, and so much more beautiful because of it.

"But we had a tough time the first go-round," Viviana continued quietly. "A lot was going on with Jersey and us. We were lucky to make it out of some of those situations alive. I'm not saying me being pregnant was the catalyst to it all, but I don't want to go through it again. The diabetes is another matter. I have a better chance of getting it again. That was hard for me, Anton."

"I know it was," he said reassuringly. "We know this time around, so it can be monitored and your sugars can be controlled from the start to prevent the use of insulin."

"You're really, *really* serious."

Anton pushed himself away from Viviana's form before sitting cross-legged in the messy sheets. Taking his time to think about what he wanted to say instead of just blurting it out like he usually would seemed like the better way to go about it all. Sitting up also gave him access to see their bedroom.

A few of Demyan's toys had managed to make their way inside, scattered in a haphazard circle in the corner where he played while watching his mother put away clothes. The master bath door was wide open, the towel Viviana used to dry off their son after his bedtime bath the night before still hanging off the hook on the door.

Their son was everywhere in their home. There wasn't a spot Demyan left untouched by something of his, physical or otherwise. He was so attached to his parents, rarely leaving their sides. Anton loved that; he didn't want to give it up or intrude on his son's time or claim he had, but he wanted to see more.

Another baby, another little being to leave his or her marks on their life.

"Yeah, Vine, I'm serious," Anton finally said. "I'm thirty. I don't want to wait another couple of years. We had to wait far too long as it was to start our life together. You're—"

"Twenty-eight and *one* day," Viviana interrupted coolly, shooting him a look.

There was nothing Viviana hated more than someone pointing out her age. It wasn't how old she was that bothered her, but how close to thirty she getting. Anton knew that, but he wasn't bringing up her age to irk her. Anton didn't care if she was thirty or forty or eighty, so long as Viviana was beside him every morning.

"Exactly. So, the way you've been putting it off, we're looking at maybe when you're thirty for another baby." Anton shrugged, raking his fingers through his hair. "We both know after thirty, there comes a whole bunch of other issues with pregnancy. You're concerned about diabetes, but what about the other stuff? The longer we wait, the more prevalent the rest becomes. Controlling your sugars could very well be the least of our problems.

"Just meet me halfway here," Anton said. "Anything."

"I did. I told you I would love to have another child."

"But that's not a yes for sure, let alone a promise for anytime soon, Vine."

"You're right."

Viviana fixed her shirt, ignoring her husband's watchful gaze as she slipped out of their bed. If it was any other morning, Anton would have tugged her back into bed and kept her there with slow kisses and tantalizing touches until she was begging like only she could for his love and want. But it wasn't any other morning and he'd brought up a touchy subject for them both.

Maybe he shouldn't have.

"Listen, I'm sorry," Anton started to say.

Viviana shrugged as she opened up a dresser drawer and began pawing through her clothes. "Don't be. I know you want another baby, and I do, too. It's just …"

"What?" he asked.

"We can handle another child, I know. Demyan would be so happy to have a brother or sister, which is great. Children after thirty wasn't in my plans, but thanks for pointing it out to me again."

Anton flinched. "Vine."

"I know all of these things, Anton."

"But?" he prodded.

"But nothing."

Every inch of Anton that wasn't awake fully before suddenly was. Whipping around to stare at his wife with wide eyes, a slow smile crept over his lips. Was she saying what he thought she was? God, he fucking hoped so. "Yeah?"

Viviana rolled her eyes. "You're so unobservant sometimes, Anton."

Well, he disagreed there. Nothing about his family flew under Anton's radar. They were the most important things in his life. "No, I'm not."

"A little bit, especially when the Bratva is keeping you away from home like they have been lately."

Unfortunately, that was truer than Anton wanted to admit. Ever since the mess with the New Jersey Bratva two and a half years earlier, his own guys had to be doubly careful over everything and anything they did. Taking out the Jersey boss ended up being a hell of a lot messier than any of them intended it to be, and the feds were so far down their throats that a lot of their dealings were just barely scraping by unnoticed.

But, wasn't that always the mafia way?

Until the feds found a bigger fish to fry, they'd be on Anton's ass like dogs looking for something to bite into. Being the boss of an organized crime family, he knew the risks he took. He also understood his responsibilities. Sometimes they had to come first, whether he wanted them to or not.

For instance, spending later nights at his club in Brighton Beach to keep the attention on him while his guys slipped by the ever watchful eye of the feds. Anton also felt the need to be constantly on his men, now. They couldn't afford mistakes and he was the one left guaranteeing no one made any. No one would take him away from Viviana or Demyan. Not one of his guys screwing up. Not Anton overlooking a fuck up. Certainly not the FBI.

Viviana dropped her choice in clothing on the bed. "You have been gone a lot more than normal. Four nights this week I've put Demyan to bed without you. Sure, you're always here before morning, and when you're home, we have all of your attention. I'm not disputing that at all. I'm just saying that if you want another child, something has to give. Promise me I won't be eating supper alone every day of the week. Tell me you'll be here to read Demyan his bedtime story. Say you'll make every doctor appointment."

"I didn't realize I've been letting you down so much lately."

Viviana blinked back, surprised. "I didn't mean it like that."

"Didn't you? If you feel like I'm lacking with you or our son—"

Before Anton could say another word, Viviana was

climbing over their bed. She crossed the space between them in a flash, forgetting about the clothes she'd tossed to the bed and the morning routine she kept for their son. Instead, Anton found her falling into his lap, her thighs straddling his as her fingers fisted into his T-shirt.

Soft, warm lips pressed to Anton's. He drew his wife closer into his body by wrapping his arms around her lower back and holding tight. For a long, silent moment, they stayed just like that with their foreheads pressed together and lips moving a slow, languid beat. Something heated and sinful built in Anton's groin. Maybe it was the way Viviana's hips were shifting on his waist, creating just enough friction to wake his body up all over again. Or, maybe it was the gentle breath of air she blew against his mouth when she finally pulled away.

"Never," Viviana told him quietly, her gaze sharp and fierce. "You don't let me down. You can't. I just want you here more, that's all. I know you've got a crap load of stuff going on, but can't you let a little bit go, for us? Demyan asks for you when he wakes up in the night and I'm so tired of telling him you'll be here in the morning. Be here at night, too, Anton. I don't want to feel like I'm doing this alone, okay?"

Anton nodded, wishing the thickness that had built in his throat would disappear. "I'll take him with me today. Let him spend time outside of the house with me, or whatever."

"We have that dinner reservation, too."

"I know. I made it for us," Anton said with a smirk. "Just be ready by seven, Vine."

"Any requests?" she asked, a coy gleam lighting up her eyes.

Anton's hands slipped down lower to grab roughly on her backside. Viviana's legs tightened to his waist as her bottom lip found its way between her teeth. There was no hiding the hard length of his erection pressing to the cotton of her panties.

"No, you've always got that handled just fine, baby, but I

might send something along for you to have."

Viviana hummed low. "About the rest ..."

"Another baby, you mean. I'll stop pressuring you about it, if that's really what you want, Vine."

"Unobservant," she repeated, punctuating her words with a kiss to his mouth.

No, Anton wasn't as inattentive as she thought. Viviana might have presumed he was so busy with everyone else that he was forgetting about her, but that certainly wasn't the case. She was, and always would be, the first thing he considered when he woke up in the morning and the last thing he wondered about before bed. It didn't matter when those times happened to come, especially if he was late getting home, or early getting up, Viviana still owned them.

Anton grazed his nose along the apple of his wife's cheek as he said, "Two weeks ago you cancelled your appointment at the clinic."

Viviana stilled in his embrace, her brown eyes flicking down to meet his smug stare. That appointment was for her birth control shot. Ever since she missed the one that led to the pregnancy for Demyan, Viviana was always on the ball about keeping up her shot. She only missed the shot by a couple of days and was still able to conceive within weeks afterwards.

"Instead, you brought Demyan to the club so we could have lunch together. You're not the only one who keeps track of those things, Viviana."

"You've been so busy ..."

"Mmhmm," Anton agreed, reaching up to cup her cheek. "But I still know what my priorities are. Sometimes they get a little skewed and end up mixing up with the rest of the stuff, but they're still there. I don't ever forget about you, or him."

"Promise?"

Anton brushed the bangs that had fallen down over her eyes out of the way so he could see what was really behind that question. "Do I need to?"

Another puff of air blew against his mouth. "No, of

course not."

"I show more than I tell, and I obviously haven't been doing that a lot, either. I haven't had time to sit down lately so you could tell me about the appointment, I know. I'm sorry. It won't happen again."

This time, Viviana didn't ask for a promise. "Okay."

"So …" Anton trailed off with a suggestive lift of his brow, allowing his hands to clasp tight to Viviana's ass again. "Are we a go for at least one more?"

Viviana smirked playfully. "We're certainly going to *try*."

Chapter Two

"Do you think—"

Erik's question was cut off as Demyan barrelled into the office at Seven Lights with his self-appointed best friend in tow. Rocco, their always faithful German shepherd, rarely left the boy's side, even taking to sleeping in his bedroom beside his little bed.

"Papa! He got the car. He *got* it!"

Rocco barked, resting himself down proudly beside Demyan. As was their favorite game to play, Demyan would hide a toy somewhere, and the pup would go and find it. Perhaps the bomb that nearly killed Viviana and their dog hadn't nullified all of Rocco's scenting ability as much as they thought, considering he found the toy nearly every damned time.

"That's great, little man," Anton said, turning back to Erik. "Do I think what, now?"

"Should we put off that export—"

"But, *Papa* ..."

"Demyan, I'm busy. Don't interrupt. It's rude."

"But—"

"Demyan!"

The indignant blue eyes of his toddler son glared up at Anton. When the boy rose his dark eyebrow, just like his father would when someone irked him, Anton held back his chuckles and a grin. It never failed to astound Anton how much Demyan acted and looked just like him. From his mannerisms, to his attitude, to his appearance, he could have been his little twin.

Sometimes, it was annoying as hell.

Other times, it was cute as shit.

Anton knew he and Viviana were in for a world of trouble when puberty hit. Just thinking about how he acted all those years ago was a scary prospect. He'd surely given his parents enough trouble and headaches to last them more than a lifetime. Anton dabbled in everything and anything he could get his hands into, chased every pretty face that caught his eye, and barely kept his head above water all the while.

Thank fucking God they still had a few more years before that storm came with Demyan.

Sighing, Anton went back to his son. "What, buddy?"

"What's intewup ... intewup ..."

"*Interrupting*, child," Erik said, shooting Anton a smile. "It means coming in on something you shouldn't."

Demyan huffed. "But, Papa, I got to pee."

"I have to," Anton corrected. "Not got, have, Demyan. And you know where the bathroom is."

With another baleful look tossed over his small shoulder, Demyan disappeared out of the office with Rocco on his heels.

"You know," Erik said, "he's just like you."

Anton grinned. "Thank you."

"That's not a compliment, asshole."

"Oh, I know."

"I'd be very afraid of that child, Anton," Erik said teasingly. "He's only two—"

"And a half."

Erik snorted like that didn't make a difference. "He's taller than everybody his age, talking like he's four-years-old, and you've even got him potty trained, for Christ's sake."

"Nah, that was all Vine," Anton replied. "The moment he showed interest in taking a leak standing up, she had him all but trained."

Thank fuck, Anton added silently. He hated changing diapers, but he did it.

"Does he point when he tells you no like a smartass, too?"

Anton's head jerked up from the paper he was reading. "What?"

Yes, Demyan did that. At least once a day he tried to pull that nonsense on somebody. Viviana thought it was cuter than nothing else, but Anton couldn't figure out who taught Demyan that ridiculous shit. They assumed it was because he was two and all toddlers did that kind of thing.

Didn't they?

"You used to do that to Daniil all the time. Picked that up from Nicoli, you did. They never did break you of it, either. Hell, you still do it."

"Really?" Anton asked.

Erik nodded, pulling a cigar from the inside of his suit jacket. "Yeah."

"Huh."

A wave of sadness washed over Anton as he considered his dead father. Surely Daniil would have enjoyed Demyan and the likeness he shared with his own son. Anton's mother Sasha still told Demyan stories of his grandfather every chance she could, though he was still too young to fully understand.

With a sigh, Anton said, "No smoking while Demyan is in the club."

Erik scowled. "But it didn't kill you."

Anton pointed his finger at his friend. "The answer is still no."

"See, right *there*."

"Oh, shut up," Anton muttered under his breath.

Whether he liked it or not, Anton knew the truth of the matter was simple. Demyan was reflecting him. Just like Anton had for those around him. But, unlike his father and step-grandfather had while he was growing up, Anton tried to keep his son away from the family business as much as possible.

At just two-years-old, it already seemed like that was becoming a losing battle.

"Just like you he is," Erik said quietly, glancing up over the cigar he was cutting. "The little prince."

"I'd like to keep him as just my boy for a while longer."

Erik shrugged. "Sometimes, you don't get the choice."

Those were dangerous, familiar words. Something Anton

had once told his wife. It was a truth he didn't want to face anytime soon.

"He's just a kid, Erik. He doesn't even understand all of this."

"Yep, and so were you."

• • •

The note smelled like roses. Fitting, considering it was written on a pink parchment with golden roses embossed in the corners.

Do not open, it read.

Viviana's curiosity was killing her. She knew better than to open the gift before Anton wanted her to, though. Half of his pleasure was giving her something, the other half was watching her unwrap his presents. Damn man. He could have just brought it home himself, but no. Instead, he sent it home with one of his bulls so she could stare at it for hours and wonder.

"What did he do, now?" Clarissa asked, observing the velvet case resting the kitchen counter.

"I'm not sure."

"Weren't you two just going to dinner?"

Viviana nodded slowly, contemplating. "Yep."

"Jewelry, then?"

"Probably not," Viviana replied. "Diamond earrings yesterday morning for my birthday. Anton isn't one to do a repeat."

No, he was liable to go bigger and better. Something that would make her heart pound and her breath stutter. Money wasn't an issue for her and Anton, and he never went cheap with anything he bought. Sometimes Viviana wondered how much money he spent on her, but she learned it was better not to ask and just appreciate the time and effort he put into his gifts. That way, she wasn't so frightened to wear things like those pearls that were nearly a million dollars in her jewelry box upstairs.

Damn man, she thought again.

"Could be something to match," Clarissa suggested. "It's big enough to be that."

"Too big. He knows I'd never wear something gaudy."

Clarissa offered Viviana a smile that said she was on her own. "I think that husband of yours enjoys torturing you like he does."

Well, after missing a good portion of her birthday yesterday and not coming home until after midnight, Anton was due for a show like this. "I did tell him he owed me something special."

"Good luck. You better start getting ready, Vine. It'll take your mind off that box."

Sure it would.

Viviana took her sweet time getting ready for dinner. Make-up, while she rarely needed to wear it, was used to accentuate her dark eyes and create the smoky look her husband seemed to love so much. A deep, crimson red balm popped her lips with the same color that she used to rosy up her cheeks. Carefully, she hid the tiredness and nerves with strokes of concealer and brushes of bronzer.

Being that it was December, Viviana was choosy about her choice in shoes and a dress. The mid-thigh, white sweater dress that was suggestive enough to be considered sexy, but appropriate enough to be worn in a high-class restaurant and the white leather pumps were fine, so long as she didn't have to walk through snow. The black thigh-high stockings lined with lace at the top would be enough to give her husband a hint of the garments she wore underneath the heavy dress and heels.

Knowing Anton, she wouldn't have to hint at anything.

Just as Viviana was putting the finishing touches on her messy chignon, her cell phone buzzed with a text.

The pearls. You know which ones. Wear them. There will be a car to pick you up in five. Bring the box.

Viviana stared at the phone, confused. Where was Demyan? She was sure Anton would bring their son home so he could stay with Clarissa. Also, Anton was supposed to pick her up so they could go to the restaurant together.

What in the hell was he up to?

She sent him back a text to ask about their son, but Anton didn't respond.

Sticking her head out of the master bathroom, Viviana called, "Clarissa?"

Oddly, there was no response from her, either.

Viviana unlocked the jewelry case and grabbed the pearls in question, ignoring the queasy feeling in her stomach over the dollar price of the jewels she held. If she lost them, or worse, someone accidentally broke one of the strands, her heart would surely break. They had been a gift from Anton for the birth of their son.

After the pearls were secured around her throat, Viviana made her way through the house, grabbing one of the darker mink coats from the hallway closet. Again, she called out for Clarissa to tell the maid she was leaving, but no one answered her back. A quick check of the bottom floor told her the back entrance was locked and Clarissa was missing. Had she said she was going out, too? Viviana didn't think so. Clarissa didn't have many friends, given her past and lack of trust in outsiders. She didn't have a great deal of places to go, honestly.

Grabbing the velvet box and slipping on the soft, heavy coat, Viviana opened the front door and nearly fell out onto the front step.

The car that should have by all intents been just a regular car to pick her up, was anything but. Sleek and black, it sported strong lines and sexy curves. The chrome lining the doors and wheels surely cost the same as a small car. Red lines trimmed the bottom of the vehicle, giving it the sporty, expensive effect those cars were known for.

Only on scarce occasions had Viviana seen a vehicle like the one at the end of the driveway, and she was pretty sure it was only on the television.

The Bugatti was a high-performance car and luxury on

every level. It didn't just catch eyes and turn heads, it screamed at passersby. You couldn't find a car like it, in Viviana's opinion. She loved her Bentley like nothing else, but this was ... *whoa*.

She was so stuck staring at the black piece of metal art in front of her that she didn't even notice the man standing beside the car.

"Mrs. Avdonin?"

Viviana seriously needed to get a damned grip. "Huh? Oh, yes, that's me."

The man waved at the passenger side of the car. "After you, Mrs."

He didn't have to tell Viviana a second time.

• • •

"I'll take that, now."

Viviana passed the velvet box to her husband's waiting hands, all the while giving him a good one-over. He looked fucking gorgeous in his suit that hugged every strong line of his body with a perfect fit. The white tie and handkerchief in his suit pocket had her curious.

"How'd you know I would wear white?"

"I didn't," Anton admitted with a roguish smirk. "Clarissa let me know when I called her, and I dressed accordingly."

"Your ridiculous need to keep a dozen suits at the club, hmm?"

"You never know."

Viviana stared at her favorite restaurant behind them. The little Italian place was cozy and comfortable in a quiet part of the city. The food was great and the atmosphere was always romantic, but never overdone. It certainly wasn't high society and Viviana suddenly felt overdressed.

Anton seemed to pick up on her unspoken question. "No other cars but ours, baby. It's just us here tonight. "

"Yeah?"

"Yeah," he said with a nod. "There's only one server, the

cook, and the owner inside. He was nice enough to give us the run of the place for a couple of hours. They'll open for normal business later, and by then, we'll be long gone."

"Huh." Viviana didn't know what to say. "Where's Demyan?"

"With Clarissa at my mother's," Anton answered. "I didn't want you waking up the house when we got home."

Say what?

"The car, Mr. Avdonin?"

The driver who had escorted Viviana from their home in Brighton Beach to the restaurant was waiting patiently with the keys to the beautiful machine. "Should I take it back to the storage?"

Anton chuckled. "No, but thank you, Pav." A simple toss of his hand and a second set of keys flew through the air. Pav caught them without missing a beat and threw back the set for the Bugatti. "Take my SUV, drop it off tomorrow at the club. Sound good?"

"Absolutely, sir."

The driver didn't wait for anything more to be said before making himself scarce. Viviana eyed Anton suspiciously.

"That's a Bugatti," she said. "Since when do we drive around in a Bugatti?"

"That it is. Beautiful car, isn't it? First time I've seen it taken out of storage in five years."

Viviana was positive her tongue stuck to the roof of her mouth. "What?"

"I've never had the right … night, I guess, to drive it. I love this car."

Well, she understood why. "It's yours."

Anton shrugged, his blue eyes raking down Viviana's body shamelessly to the black stockings. A lift of his dark eyebrow gave her the indication he liked what he saw. "Hmm, yes. Ours, of course, but I bought it. I told you once that I liked fast cars."

"It's certainly fast."

"If you're a good girl, maybe I'll let you drive it home."

Viviana's laughter fell into the cold air like wind chimes. "Hell, I've got no chance, do I?"

"That depends on what you consider to be good, baby. You know how I like you bad."

• • •

Anton reveled in the feeling of Viviana's lips encompassing his fingers. The wet heat of her mouth and tongue as it licked along his skin, taking with it the remaining bits of a sweet pastry he'd been feeding her had all the blood in his body going straight to one place. Her mouth closed tighter to his digits, teeth scraping along his knuckles, and her eyes closed as she moaned.

"Good?" he asked, willing away the thickness in his throat.

Viviana released his fingers with a wink. "Very. Thank you."

It wasn't often he got the chance to have his wife like this—relaxed, willing to be adored, pleased, and so unknowing as to his plans. That was the best part for Anton. Everything he planned for the night would be a complete surprise to Viviana.

"Did I tell you how beautiful you look?"

Viviana smiled, allowing his hand to travel up under the skirt of her dress, resting just above her knee. "Yes, but go on and do it again, or we both know it'll eat at you."

"Damn right."

God, she looked amazing. All white, like innocence, but those spiked heels and black stockings gave away just enough taste of sin to get the adrenaline pumping. No, Anton never needed to worry about Viviana's choice in clothing, or how she prettied herself up for him.

"Beautiful is a goddamned understatement," Anton murmured.

"I try," Viviana replied coyly.

"You don't need to."

The server made her way into the private dining area,

staying to the darkness of the shadows until Viviana and Anton were finished with dessert. While the server began cleaning off the table one final time, Viviana pulled out her cell phone for the third time.

Anton's sigh was loaded. "I swear to God, if you're calling about Demyan again, Vine."

Guiltily, the phone was slid back under the table. "I am not."

"He's fine, baby, I promise. If anything, he's giving Mom a good reminder of what I was like at that age. Like a blast from the past."

"She already dealt with you once. I imagine it was enough."

Anton grinned salaciously. "And I'm your problem now, huh?"

"Sasha knows I manage you just fine, Anton."

"Manage me?"

"Controls. Wears the pants. Rules the roost. What do you want to call it?" she shot back. "Or dare I ask your opinion?"

Yeah, Anton knew what battles to pick. This wasn't one of them. "No, I think we both know you're the only queen ruling me, Vine."

Viviana patted his cheek. "Damn right. So, are you going to let me open the mysterious box, or what?"

Anton chuckled lowly. He knew that was bothering her. "Not yet."

"I know you're only doing this to torture me, Anton."

"No, I'm doing it because you don't need the gift, yet."

Viviana's eyes narrowed in curiosity, but she said nothing. Instead, her hand wandered over to his leg under the table as she plucked up the wine glass from the table with her free hand. While taking a sip of the red liquid, her hand slid higher up the inside of his thigh. Anton responded to the suggestive touch by sliding his hand higher under her dress until the heat between her thighs was dancing along his fingertips. Those stockings she wore had nothing on the lace he could feel covering her sex.

Viviana squeaked into her glass when he stroked her through her panties. "Anton!"

"You started it," he murmured.

"Well, stop it. I wasn't doing anything."

Sure. That's why her hand was still attached to his thigh, so close to his groin that Anton's cock was beginning to twitch to life under his dress pants. If Viviana moved her hand a millimeter, she'd feel exactly what she was doing.

"Tease," Anton said under his breath, squeezing her warm thigh again.

"Remove your hand, Anton."

Anton did, but he smirked all the while. "No problem, baby. Besides, it's too early for you to be screaming my name, and I'd hate to scar the poor staff with the things I'd like to do to you."

The red blush that stained Viviana's cheeks was pretty close in color to the wine in her glass. Her hand on his thigh jerked away, embarrassment coloring up the noise she made under her breath.

Battle won, Anton thought smugly.

It was all about picking the right ones.

Chapter Three

"Anton, we can't possibly—"

"Ah, ah, ah," Anton interrupted in a teasing manner. "Do I ever uproot us without making sure every little thing is taken care of?"

Viviana huffed, crossing her arms and staring into the hangar at the private jet. Anton bought the plane a couple of years earlier. On the back wing of the jet, he'd had a similar style tribal design to his own tattoo painted in thick, black strokes.

The hired pilot and one flight attendant stood at the bottom of the stairs leading up to the jet. Anton was paying them well for the time they were spending away from their own families during the holiday season, and for keeping quiet about the passengers they were flying out of the country.

While Viviana continued to stare at the jet inside the private hangar, Anton pulled out a rolling luggage from the trunk. It earned him another pointed look from his wife.

"Did you pack clothes for me?" she asked.

Anton was a man, but not a stupid one. "No. Clarissa did yesterday when you were busy. She's sneaky sometimes."

"But you said everyone was out of the house because you asked for them to be."

Anton smirked wickedly. "I lied. I couldn't have you even considering the possibility that we would be flying somewhere. Besides, Demyan is taken care of. We're not going to be at the house, so Clarissa isn't needed there, either. She was more than happy to spend some time with Ma. We're only going to be gone four days. I promise everything is fine here, even the bookstore."

Viviana's bottom lip disappeared between her teeth. "Where are we going, then?"

"You can open your box, now," Anton said instead.

She'd been holding onto that black box ever since he handed it back in the Bugatti after dinner. Viviana wasted no time unfastening the silver latch and flipping open the lid. There, resting in black velvet, was a set of house keys. Her genuine surprise was almost cute.

"Keys, for what?"

Anton's chest suddenly felt tight, constricting with the fast pace of his heartbeats. "Where was the first place I fell in love with you, Vine?"

The sound of her breath catching was audible. "We can't leave the States."

"Yes, we can. The paperwork I have and the passports I paid a pretty dime for say differently. They also have a different last name from ours, but that's not really important. No one will know. The people hired for this flight were also employed because of their ability to keep quiet."

"Barbados, really?" Viviana asked quietly.

"Not just Barbados. That two storey beach house, the one you snuck through to get to me ... yeah, that one."

Viviana's brow furrowed as she stared at the keys. "But you have keys."

"No, you do, baby."

Finally, she seemed to understand. "You bought me the beach house?"

"Barely managed to. It's a hot piece of property over there. Hell, I couldn't walk away from it when I got word it was going on the market."

"Too many memories," Viviana whispered.

"Mmhmm. My thoughts exactly. So, you ready?"

Viviana could only nod.

• • •

The outside of the beach house in Bridgetown, Barbados was just like Anton remembered it all those years ago. From the gated front entrance with the white stone walkway, to the pale yellow color of the siding. Even the big bay windows on the top and bottom floor, allowing all the beautiful Barbados sunlight in without even needing to turn on a light bulb in the daytime, were still as clear and open as they'd always been.

Back then, when he was eighteen and stupid, he thought the place looked warm and inviting. Now, it felt the same, but a hell of a lot more sentimental, too.

They left New York around ten at night, and arrived in Bridgetown just after three in the morning. Viviana refused to sleep on the plane. Anton could see the exhaustion Viviana was feeling, but she was insistent on not finding a bed to sleep in just yet. They certainly had plenty of beds to choose from; the house came fully furnished.

Viviana wanted to walk through the halls of the home before they did anything else. Using the tips of her fingers, she grazed the walls, staying silent and remembering. So many things were the same in the house, and a dozen more were entirely different. A decade would do that to just about anything.

But the walls knew. They heard things others hadn't. The window in the far bedroom on the bottom floor had reflected the innocent beauty of a sixteen-year-old girl Anton fell in love with and the strange courage she'd found in an eighteen-year-old him. Maybe if the sun was out, and he looked out the back where the beach led to the ocean, he'd get that feeling all over again. That first one when he saw who Viviana was, not who he thought she would be.

Anton followed behind silently, too, watching his wife pull the pins from her hair, letting it fall out of the chignon into waves down her back. Then, she was reaching back to tug at the zipper of her white dress. The thick fabric that was surely too warm for Barbados weather slipped off her shoulders like water, falling around her waist before dropping to pool at her heels. Viviana stepped out and over the forgotten dress without even looking back at it.

Anton wasn't looking at the dress anymore, either.

"Vine ..." he started to say, his voice husky and throat thick.

Viviana didn't pay him any mind.

"What are you doing, baby?"

Still, nothing.

Fuck, she looked good. The olive tone of her skin melted in with those black stockings she wore, right up to the garter belt and clasps keeping the lace trim snug around her thighs. The black lace covering all the curves and edges of her sweetest spots hinted at sex and sin. Viviana's hips swayed when she walked. A natural back and forth motion that always fucking mesmerized Anton like nothing else.

She was sexy as hell.

Anton yanked at the buttons of his dress shirt, pulling the offending clothing off and leaving it wherever in the heck it fell. The same thing happened to his socks, shoes, and belt. It didn't matter that he was tired, too, and that they'd probably sleep their first day of vacation away. No, it didn't matter a bit what with the way Viviana walked, and those stockings he wanted to pull down her mile-long legs with his teeth.

"I want you," Viviana said demurely.

Something wicked twisted in Anton's stomach, shooting straight down to his cock.

"Here," she added, her hand grazing the wall again. As Viviana passed a bathroom in the bottom floor hallway, she said, "There ..."

Jesus.

"Vine, then you need to stop walking away from me."

She didn't.

Now, Anton just wanted to get a reaction out of his wife. If she could tease him, it was only fair. "I should have fucked you on the jet, Viviana. Join the club, and all that jazz." There was no hiding the shiver crawling up Viviana's spine. The little minx didn't say a word, though. Still, he got a reaction. "Would you have liked that?"

Viviana turned to glance over her shoulder, her heated brown eyes boring into Anton's with a fire. Then, her thumbs hooked into the lace garter and the hem of her panties. Anton's throaty growl stopped her from pulling the fabric down. She had also come to the end of the hallway.

"Don't," Anton ordered. "I want to take those off myself."

The sexiest smile curved her sweet mouth. "With what?"

"My teeth while I bury my fingers into that tight pussy of yours."

Viviana moaned low. The sound reverberated straight to Anton's aching dick.

"Oh, God."

"Oh, I'll have you crying that out a dozen times over," Anton murmured as he came to stand behind his wife.

Skimming one hand over Viviana's shoulder, he pulled the straps of her bra down at the same time his mouth landed at the junction of her shoulder. The heat of his breath washed over her skin as he kissed a path along the side of her neck, to the back, where he began ghosting down the middle of her spine.

With every kiss, Anton could taste the sex already on her body. With every taste, Viviana's skin bloomed with goosebumps. There was something he loved about the way she reacted to anything and everything he did. From her shivers to the way her breath picked up at the graze of his thumb along her hip.

"Let's start with here, baby." Anton was down to his knees, kissing the dimples at her lower back. The faint smell of her sex was just a hint in the air. He planned on getting her smelling so damned good by the time he was done. "Right here in this hallway, against this wall."

"Fuck."

"That's the plan, Vine."

Viviana sighed when Anton's teeth caught the hem of her garter. He took his time dragging the flimsy fabric down before snapping the plastic clips attached to the stockings. Anton let the garter fall to her feet, enjoying the view of his wife's perfect ass covered in black lace.

"It's not the same, you know," Viviana said quietly.

Anton hummed a sound as he tugged down her panties.

Viviana stepped out of the panties at his urging. "The house, or us?"

"Both, I guess."

"It's still the same in a lot of ways, too."

"It is," she agreed. "I was so terrified coming down here that night. Roman never laid a hand on me or my brother, but I think he would have for that."

"No way, crazy girl. Me, likely. Never you."

"I was way too young to be doing the things I did. Stupid, though I wanted you."

Anton stood, peppering his kisses back up her spine, and stopping at her shoulder again. He made quick work of unclasping the bra at her back, leaving her in nothing but her heels and stockings. Just like he wanted her.

"Maybe you were too young back then," Anton finally replied, splaying both hands out to her back.

He slipped one hand further down to skim over her ass and in between her thighs. Already, Viviana was wet, throbbing and almost swollen in her need. As his fingers spread her fleshy folds, he reveled in the slick heat coating his hand. Fuck, her juices were like honey to him.

"But you're not now, baby."

Viviana's breath caught as he pushed her to the wall with the hand pressing to her back and thrust two fingers into her clenching pussy with the other. Anton nuzzled his face into the back of her neck, loving the silky waves of her hair and the scent of him beginning to mix in with her rose perfume. Nipping at the sensitive skin behind her ear, Anton listened to the soft moans that matched the rhythm of his fingers.

"And that's why it's not the same," she whimpered.

"Time to make some new memories, Viviana."

Anton unsnapped the button on his pants, letting them pool at his ankles. Viviana's fingers widened to the wall as he freed his erection from the confines of his boxer-briefs. The length of his cock rested heavily at the crack of her ass, leaking a streak of pearly pre-cum along her skin.

Damn it, he loved the sight of his come on her body.

"I need to love you good, Viviana," Anton murmured into her hair. "Feel how hard you've made me. It hurts, for Christ's sake."

That wasn't a lie. His cock was so rigid and swollen, it needed to be buried into her pussy as soon as he could possibly fucking get it there. The heels she wore put her at a perfect height, or just about. Anton removed his playing fingers from her sex to slide them along the inside of her thigh. Then, he was grabbing tight and lifting her leg high to give him the access he needed.

Using his hand to guide his cock, Anton slid home with a groan. He just wasn't sure which one of them the sound came from the loudest. It could have been him, because all he felt was her wet heat wrapping around every inch of his cock like damp, warm silk. Or it could have been Viviana, because she took all of him in without even a moment of hesitation from her body.

Now, every muscle in her tight channel was holding him vise-tight.

"Fuck," Anton muttered through clenched teeth. He pressed his forehead to her back, feeling the hand holding her leg up begin to shake. Sometimes their sex took his breath away, and sometimes it yanked away his thoughts. This was doing both. "God, that's good. So fucking good, baby."

Viviana's cheek had pressed to the wall, giving him a beautiful view of the pleasure singing over her features while she moaned out something intelligible. Slowly, he pulled out to the tip before sliding right back in.

"What was that, Viviana? *Louder.*"

"Oh shit, yeah," was the only thing she managed to say.

Anton knew it had to be the position he held her in. With her leg high, he had her opened and stretched, filled fucking full of him. She didn't have much room to move, either, pinned to the wall like she was. Looking down, Anton could also see she was practically on her toes in heels.

Yeah, he was pretty goddamned sure she was feeling every inch of him everywhere.

"Hold on, baby," he ordered.

Viviana's breathy laugh caught in her mouth and instead, turned to a throaty moan. With one hand holding her leg up, and the other grasping her hip, Anton started a rhythm that was just as much teasing as it was punishing. Like the rising noises falling from Viviana, the sounds of their meeting slaps of skin echoed in the darkened hallway.

She was so soaked, the juices of her pussy coating his cock and already slicking up his balls. Anton loved her like that, and the smell of her sex was heady and thick in the air. Viviana rested her cheek to the wall, gritted her teeth, and bit out a stream of obscenities that only made Anton fuck her harder.

The grip he had on her body was likely going to leave imprints of his fingertips that would stay for days. He'd enjoy kissing them when she woke up tomorrow and then making more.

A slight shift in his hips, a little raise in her leg, and Anton hit a whole new spot that made Viviana gasp out a broken cry of his name.

"God, yeah ... *there.*"

"There, you sure?"

"Fuckin' right there," Viviana breathed. "Oh, I'm coming ..."

Viviana shook and cursed through her orgasm, her inner muscles flexing and fluttering. The sensation milked Anton's cock to a finish, taking him right over the edge with his wife. Anton wanted her to feel his come filling and coating her, so he gave her one last hard thrust and held her ass tight to his groin as he came.

"Fuck, oh fuck, yeah," Viviana chanted.

She all but crumpled into his embrace when he finally stepped back to pull out of her warm body and released her leg. Sweat had slicked up his skin something awful. Viviana couldn't seem to catch her breath or complete a sentence. Anton rubbed the sting she must have felt in her thigh out with his hand, feeling his hot come trickling down the inside of her leg. All the while, he kissed a path on her shoulders.

"Love you, baby," Anton said.

Viviana blinked out of her haze. "Mmm, love you. Best anniversary gift ever."

Yeah, it wasn't going to be easy to top this one.

• • •

When Anton thought about Barbados now, he wasn't transported back to a different time. Now, he thought about the heat, the taste of sweat on his wife's skin, keeping her close in crystal blue, cold water and sand everywhere. He thought about the pile of white blankets on the floor in the middle of the living room because they couldn't pick a goddamn bed. The way the bay windows streaked rays of sunlight over every inch and curve of his wife curled up in those blankets.

It still had that living, breathing kind of feel to it in his heart, of course.

It was still so beautiful.

It just wasn't the same. It was better.

Anton rested back on the white leather couch, taking a drink of his too-hot coffee and ignoring the way his T-shirt stuck to his skin. The air conditioner system in the house needed repaired. For the last three days, he'd been taking inventory of things that needed updated or fixed in some way, and that was one of them.

Viviana didn't complain, though. It probably helped she barely wore a damned thing and when she did, it was usually a bikini. Anton wasn't complaining about that, either.

They barely left the house except to go and get the few supplies they would need for their four-day stay. Occasionally Anton found his wife outside in the back, walking across the beach or sitting in the ocean with salt waved hair and a smile, ordering him in the water, too.

Really, they didn't need to leave and without saying it to each other, this trip was essentially the honeymoon they didn't have before. Anton knew he owed his wife one, so he was giving it to her in the tenfold now.

Viviana still used the house phone to call about Demyan at least four times a day. Anton figured she couldn't help it, being the boy's mother and all. It didn't matter if their son had a village of people to care for him—which he kind of did, an entire brotherhood worth of men to help raise the little prince—no one was going to do it as well as she did.

A quiet groan drew Anton's attention to the pile of blankets on the floor. Hell, it was so hot the night before, Viviana jumped in a cold shower and then promptly fell asleep still wet in the blankets. Viviana stretched in her makeshift bed, her sun kissed skin looking so damned good in that mountain of white. It was well into the afternoon, and their last day on the island, so he'd let her sleep until she was ready to get up.

"Morning," Viviana said, rolling to her back and giving him the sweetest view of her tits.

"More like afternoon, baby."

"Really?"

Anton nodded, smiling. "Didn't want to bother you by getting you up earlier."

They'd fly back to New York in the middle of the night. It was safer for him to arrive that way. Less likely to draw attention.

"Did you run this morning?" Viviana asked, turning on her side and propping her chin up on her hand.

"Nope. Too busy."

"Doing what?"

"Watching you."

Viviana's tinkling laughter was muffled when she turned into the blankets again. "Whatever, Anton."

"It's the best way to spend a morning." Brown eyes peeked up over the sea of white and Anton knew what she was going to ask before she did. "Yes, I called about Demyan an hour ago. Ma's going to take him to the indoor park to meet up with Ivan's girls."

"That's good."

Anton cocked a brow. "You're still going to call, aren't you?"

"Probably. I miss him, that's all."

"I know you do, baby."

Viviana did another stretch, mewling a soft noise, and hooking her leg over the blankets so all her curves were on display. She reminded him of a kitten in the morning. Sweet and soft, with tiny claws that rarely ever hurt. A familiar heat began coiling in Anton's gut.

They'd loved more than enough over the last couple of days. Touched more than he'd ever remembered. Fucked in every place he could have her. But, there was one thing he hadn't done, or rather, hadn't told her. He'd been reminded of that earlier in the morning while he stared at the smooth contour of her stomach that led down to the bareness of her sex.

"Vine?"

"Hmm, what, Anton?"

Setting the coffee aside, he tugged off his shirt and dropped his shorts, crawling through the blankets to meet his wife's gaze through all the white. Gently, but firmly, he pushed her to her back, using his knees to widen her legs open for him to seat himself between her thighs. They always fit so well together like this, no matter which way he liked her the best.

A thickness built in his throat, but he cleared it away. "I want a baby."

Viviana's brow furrowed. "I know. I thought we already talked about this."

Anton shook his head, spreading her wider, tracing his thumbs along her sensitive folds. Sure they talked about it. Viviana stopped her shot, he didn't use condoms. They couldn't really try any more than they already were, but that wasn't what he meant, either.

Viviana shifted her hips upward, seeking him. She opened so well for him, taking his member in short thrusts that filled her quickly. With each one, he could see she woke up a little more, her head tilting back into the blankets to expose her neck.

"No, Vine. I know we did. That's not what I meant. I want a baby."

Finally, she seemed to understand. It wasn't about what they had already agreed, it was what he wanted to do *now*.

Breathless and seeming spun, Viviana whispered, "Okay."

Chapter Four

Anton was glad to see the near end of January finally arrive. The hustle and bustle of the holidays he didn't celebrate were finally over. Everyone else was getting back to their normal routine instead of the craziness Christmas and New Year brought with them.

Demyan plopped himself on the couch, settling in with the cup of juice his mother had given him. Once he was snuggled into his father's side, he seemed content to stay still and focus on the television.

"The car one?" he asked his father.

Anton nodded and started the movie of his son's choice. "Yeah, little man. Let's watch that."

Watching children's cartoons wasn't his favorite thing to do, but his son enjoyed it. This was the first Friday night he'd spent at home in a long time. Too damn long, really, so he wasn't about to make Demyan watch something more grown up that would bore the kid.

Viviana walked through the living room with her book in hand, sitting down in a lounger and giving her husband a wink topped off with a brilliant smile. She was happy to have him home on a Friday night, too. Things had been so good between them since they arrived home from Barbados three weeks ago.

Anton was dying to know if she picked up any pregnancy tests. They'd been trying for their second child for a month. Actually, a month and a half if he took into account the two weeks she'd been off her shot before telling him. If Anton considered how fast she conceived Demyan after forgetting her birth control shot the last time, he was hoping this time wouldn't be any different. Viviana was a fertile woman, thank God. Beyond all that, he was pretty damned sure his wife was late this month, but he was too pussyfoot to ask.

Yeah, his curiosity was a killer.

"Vine?"

"Hmm?"

"How're you feeling?" he asked.

Viviana looked up over her book with glittering eyes. "Fine. Why?"

Anton shrugged and turned back to the cartoon. "Just curious."

"Sure you are."

The teasing lilt in her tone didn't escape his notice. Had Viviana already taken the steps to find out if they'd conceived or not? He was away from the house most of the week doing business and back at a later time than normal, so she very well could have picked something up at the store, or made an appointment at the clinic.

"Do you have something you want to tell me?"

"Not yet," she replied sweetly. "But soon, maybe."

That was enough for Anton. God, he so wanted to see her growing with his child again. "Yeah?"

Viviana grinned knowingly. "*Maybe*, Anton. Stop worrying about it."

"Papa?"

"What Demyan?" Anton asked, glancing down at his ever curious child.

"Shhh, be quiet."

Damn kid.

"All right, little man. Papa will shut up."

"Yeah, shut up," Demyan muttered.

Anton didn't correct Demyan, mostly because he'd been the one to say it first. He had a feeling that was going to be the story of his life when it came to his son.

● ● ●

Anton rushed out of the bathroom with a toothbrush still stuck in his mouth to catch the ringing cell phone he'd left in his jeans pocket. Viviana raised a brow at him from their bed, obviously recognizing the ring. It was his work cell phone, the one his men used to call him if something needed attention and it was Bratva related.

"Yeah?" he mumbled into the phone.

"Boss, you busy?"

Anton recognized Boris's voice instantly. Boris was one of his oldest brigadiers, or captains, and one of his very best.

"Why?" Anton asked, pulling the toothbrush out of his mouth and turning his back on his glaring wife.

"Remember those fucking gangbangers that were poking their noses in mine and Viktor's streets?"

Some of Anton's men had been having issues with a few local gang members. Anton wasn't sure if the young kids were actually members of the gang, or simply trying to be. Problem was, they were dangerous, moving in on the Bratva's dealers, causing shit, and stealing. It just wasn't okay or acceptable. Anton tried to let it go, stay out of view of the police, but sometimes it didn't work that way. He had a feeling this was one of those times.

"Sure. What about it?"

"They tried a goddamn drive by on one of Viktor's guys tonight. Clipped him good."

Anton cursed under his breath. "And?"

"Some of Viktor's guys retaliated. Let's just say it's finished. But we were left with the vehicle, you know? There were twenty bricks in the back. Twenty. A few pounds apiece. You need to get down to the club and handle this product. Check it, whatever. Decide on who you want to handle it from here."

Crap. This was one of the perks, and downfalls, of Anton's position. When things were picked up that weren't already theirs, or stolen, for lack of a better term, like the drugs Boris was dancing around, Anton was the only one allowed to handle distributing the products. That way no one could say a fucking word about the profit turned on it because the boss decided, not anyone else.

"Just a second," Anton muttered into the phone. Holding

his hand over the receiver, he turned to Viviana. "Baby, I need to handle something."

Viviana's pretty lips drew a thin line. "You promised to stay home with me tonight."

"I'm sorry, really. Something came up. I have to handle it tonight, get it out of my hands. The less time I have with it, the better. I won't stay at the club late tomorrow night, okay?"

"It's that important?" Viviana asked doubtfully.

"Yeah, it kind of is."

There wasn't just the matter of keeping the peace between the men who picked up the drugs, but also the gang that would be looking for their product. Like Anton said, the less time it was in his hands, the better.

Then, he had another thought and winced internally about it. "I'll probably have to stay a little while, also," Anton added quieter.

"Why?"

"The guys will want to celebrate."

As ridiculous as it was, they'd want to see Anton there celebrating as well. He'd been trying hard to keep his promise to his wife of being home more often and keeping the Bratva business as his day job. That wasn't exactly realistic, and Viviana knew that because sometimes shit like this came up. Still, Anton felt like crap over it.

"I'm sorry, Vine. I won't be partying, just a drink or two to show face."

Viviana still didn't look pleased. "Fine, whatever."

Anton went back to the phone, frowning. "Yeah, Boris, I'll be there in twenty or so."

"Gotcha, Boss."

With the phone call ended, Anton went about gathering something appropriate for him to wear at the club, tossing his toothbrush back into the bathroom in the process. Viviana stayed silent while he pulled on a pair of dark slacks and a white dress shirt. Then, he dropped a kiss to his wife's forehead and turned to leave.

"Nothing bad, right?" Viviana asked quietly from behind him.

"Nothing dangerous for me," Anton replied. "Just business I have to handle because it's me. I'll be back in a couple of hours at the most, baby."

"Thanks for putting Demyan to bed."

Anton smiled. "Always."

"Be here to wake him up in the morning, too, Anton."

Anton made it to the club in decent time. Parking his car around the back, he called in to the bar for one of the servers to let him in through the rear exit. Natalie was the server who greeted him on the other side of the door with wave.

"Hey, Boss."

Anton held back his frown. Where did that come from? "Just Anton, Natalie."

"Sure," the girl drawled with a smile. "I let the guys up into the office. They were pretty insistent about it."

"That's fine."

Despite the club only being open for a short while, Anton could tell walking through the main floor that they were already at their fire code limit for the number of bodies inside the building. It wasn't unusual, and more often than not, the club could handle another fifty people above the limit before complaints were made, but he wasn't comfortable with it tonight. The last thing he needed was the cops showing up.

"Natalie, go to the front and let security know they're to refuse entrance until some people clear out."

"Not a problem, Anton."

In his office, Anton found more men than he expected to. Boris, Viktor, one of their associates who Anton suspected had been involved in the run in with the gang, Erik, Ivan, and Rory.

"Jesus, are we having a party, or what?" Anton asked, closing his office door.

"Already here," Rory said, fiddling with his phone. "Keeping an eye on Jen, Boss."

Ivan jerked his thumb in Erik's direction. "Dumbass

wanted a drink."

"Fuck you," Erik replied blithely. "You'd need one, too."

"Issues I need to know about?" Anton asked his old friend.

"Not unless they involve my wife," Erik said.

Ah, yeah. Anton chose to stay away from that nonsense.

Ivan, on the other hand, did not. "That's what you get for marrying someone half your age."

Erik rested back to the couch with a scowl.

"All right," Anton said, turning to Boris. "Where is it?"

Boris pulled a flat, cellophane wrapped brick from an inside pocket of his coat and tossed it to Anton's desk with a thump.

Anton was positive he'd been told twenty bricks earlier. "And the rest?"

"In Viktor's trunk. I didn't think you'd want it inside the club tonight," Boris explained.

Anton nodded. His men knew him well. "No, you're right. I don't. Get this out of here as soon as we're done, also, to be safe."

There was a small pocketknife in the desk Anton pulled out. Flicking open the blade, he cut a small line on the side of the brick. Shaking the rectangular package, yellowish-grey crystalline white power spilled to the table. Odorless, a small bit of the power on the tip of his pocket knife all but disappeared in a glass of water.

Instantly, Anton knew this wasn't his drug of choice to handle and sell.

But just to be sure, he wet his pinky at the tip, dabbed at the powder, and slid the substance along his tongue. If it were cocaine, it would have created a numbing sensation, being the natural anesthetic-like drug coke was. This powder, however, simply tasted bitter and ill. Anton wanted it off his tongue and out of his mouth.

Turning to Ivan, he waved for the drink in the man's hand. "Give me that."

"Not blow?" Ivan asked while Anton downed the glass of

vodka. "You know you didn't need to taste that to know for sure. There's a dozen meth-heads that would have gladly—"

"Shut up," Anton said, handing back the glass. "It's methamphetamine. Of course it is. The gangbangers around here seem to have a problem fucking around with crack or this shit, and I don't want it on my streets. They must enjoy the risk of blowing themselves up to make speed. Fuck that leaves an awful taste in the mouth."

"Meth is cheap and fast to produce," Viktor put in. "It's more addictive than most of the higher end product on the streets right now."

"And dangerous," Anton replied. "Which is why we don't produce it."

"You enjoyed speed once or twice, Boss," Erik pointed out from the couch.

"I enjoyed dropping it, sure," Anton replied. "You wouldn't catch me cooking in a meth lab to make it, though."

"You know," Ivan said, leering, "... they say this is better to fuck on than cocaine."

Anton scoffed under his breath. "Yeah, I'd have to respectfully disagree. There's nothing like fucking on coke. But I'm not in the mood to talk about my previous exploits."

There was nothing like fucking sober and being able to remember the next morning, either, but Anton didn't bother to mention that.

Done with the direction the conversation had taken, Anton turned to his brigadiers. "Which one of you has boys able to get rid of twenty bricks of this within a couple of days?"

Viktor stayed quiet while Boris raised a hand. "Me, Boss. Well, they've got the contacts to get it into the right place, given we don't usually deal in this."

Yeah, that was exactly the problem.

"Work for you to have Boris's guys handling it, Viktor?" Anton asked.

Viktor shrugged. "Sure."

"Forty percent to Boris for handling it. Sixty to Viktor for getting it. I want ten from both of your cut because it's in my territory. Simple math, make it work. I want my cash by the end of the month, and it's not a part of your regular tribute." Anton turned to the young kid, maybe only twenty-two, who'd stayed silent in the corner. "And you, who are you?"

"Joshua," the boy mumbled. "One of Viktor's boys."

Yes, Anton figured that. Every brigadier essentially controlled a brigade of men who ran the streets, handled the products, and paid their captain. If they were lucky, quick, and smart, they could move up the ranks. It wasn't easy, it often took a long while to get off the streets, but it happened if the man showed potential.

"Your friend who got shot, is he okay?" Anton asked.

Joshua shook his head.

"Sorry to hear that, but that's dealing on the streets when you've got enemies, kid. Do you use?"

"Not meth."

"Chemical at all?" Anton pressed.

The kid nodded. "Not serious use, it's mostly recreational. You can't expect to turn a profit if you're only selling to feed an addiction."

Joshua was a smart kid, but he could get a hell of a lot smarter.

Anton flicked his knife closed and tossed it back into the drawer. "Well, I suggest if you want to stand in my office for a different reason someday, you don't ever touch a chemical again. Got it?"

"Got it ... Boss, is it?"

Most street thugs never got the chance to stand in the same room with the head of the family. They heard them talked about enough, sure, but meeting them was a whole other ballgame.

Anton smirked at the kid. "It is to you."

"Boss, then," Joshua said quickly.

"All right." Anton leaned over his desk and pressed the conference button to call own to the bar. "Now, let's get some drinks. On the house."

• • •

Anton rested back in the booth. The calmness sweeping his senses barely registered as unusual, but somehow, he knew it was. He was never this relaxed inside a venue with well over two-hundred drunken bodies moving around him.

"Boss?"

Drumming his fingers to the tabletop, Anton was vaguely aware of the heat that bloomed under his fingertips at every tap and moved up his digits. Fuck, that sensation was great. He rapped his fingers again just to feel it spread.

"Boss?" someone asked again.

Anton wasn't in the mood to talk. The spotlights rounding the moving wave of people were far too interesting and had caught his eye well over a half an hour ago. Melting into his seat and watching the rhythmic movement of the rays, he almost felt dreamlike. As if he had no weight. Like there was no substance to his self, or the things around him.

Maybe his thoughts, though.

Those had to be real.

"Jesus, Boss, look at me," Rory snapped.

Anton glared in his bull's direction, aggravated that his mood was being interrupted. "What?"

"How much of that shit did you swallow?"

"What?"

"The meth, how much of it did—"

"Shut up," Anton ordered, turning back to look at the lights again.

Rory didn't make sense, Anton decided. He'd merely tasted less than a pinch of the meth and washed it back with a drink. It certainly wasn't enough to make him fly, or get his mind jumbled up. Anton might not have used anything strong in a long while, but a blow of powder wasn't going to get his mouth sticky like wet cotton, or make him crave a joint something fierce.

No, he was just drunk.

"I need to go lay down," Anton muttered under his breath, the decision coming as quick as the last thoughts had gone. No worries. No cares. He was tired, unbothered, and his nerves felt really, really good. "Yeah, in my office."

Rory's brow furrowed across the booth. "Want me to take you home?"

"I want to lay the fuck down."

"Boss, look at me," Rory repeated.

Anton waved him off, already leaving the table.

It seemed like a blink and Anton was in his office.

A blink.

Staring at the large decorative clock on the wall, he tried to figure out what time it was. That was a massive failure. Between the time it said it was, the time Anton was sure he'd arrived, and the time in-between, he couldn't possibly put it all together. How had he been here three and a half hours already?

That was his first inclination something wasn't right.

Where was that time?

Blankness, that's where it was. Nowhere.

Ten more minutes passed while he stared at the clock.

Wasn't he supposed to be home with …?

Anton's thought process cut off at the quiet click of the office door shutting closed.

"Boss?"

That feminine voice was nothing like Rory's. Anton turned on his heel to face Natalie. Leaning back on his desk, he pressed his palms into the edge to steady the sudden swaying, feeling that glorious heat travel through his skin and nerves again.

Anton pressed harder to make it repeat. It did.

"Anton," he said gruffly. "That's my name."

"I can call you that," Natalie replied sweetly.

Something was wrong here. Anton knew it. Like the color of her eyes and hair. Or the way her jasmine perfume soaked the room when it should have been the scent of roses instead. There was something else unexpected crawling through

Anton's awakening nervous system, too. Arousal. He was turned on, and he didn't have a fucking clue why.

"You need to leave," Anton heard himself say, but it wasn't very firm.

Natalie took another step closer and Anton felt his own try to take a step back because of it. Oddly, he knew he wasn't in control of this situation. Certainly not of the woman five feet away, who usually followed directions well, kept her head out of trouble, and left him alone. Thinking he was in control of his own body was goddamn joke, given the only thing his cock was considering was something warm and wet.

Not hers, though. Not Natalie.

Anton wanted a dark haired beauty with brown eyes, a pretty mouth, and rose scented skin he could get lost in.

Not Natalie.

No.

Anton blinked out of his haze, glancing from Natalie to the clock. "What time did I get here?"

"Ten-thirty."

Her voice was soft, he noticed. Not silky like his wife's. But soft.

Not soft enough, something whispered.

Natalie took another step forward and Anton noticed the heels she wore. Silver strappy things with spikes that had to be hell for working in the club after hours of walking the floor. Unfortunately, those heels were attached to a pair of legs that traveled all the way up to a tight, short dress showcasing the sexy curves of a young woman. She had a sway when she moved, not a natural one, but a learned one.

Anton nearly choked on the spit gathering in his mouth. What in the fuck was wrong with him?

Natalie's voice distracted him from taking the thought further. "Are you as bad as they say, Anton?"

"Hmm?"

"You ..."

Natalie was right in front of him then. Anton had no idea how she got there that quickly. The sensation of being caged crept in and he sidestepped the female. The brush of her fingertips along his exposed skin where he rolled up his shirt sleeves earlier sent a burst of sparks along every nerve in his limb.

God, it felt fucking amazing. And *wrong*.

"Jesus," Anton whispered, jerking away.

Natalie's face tipped sideways. "You okay?"

"Fine. Why are you here?" Anton asked.

"I wanted to talk. The club is starting to clear out, so I had a few minutes."

The club was clearing out already? Again, time had gone somewhere and Anton didn't know it passed.

The cotton sensation was back in his mouth. "I need a drink of water."

No more liquor. He didn't need that at all.

Natalie handed him a glass of clear liquid that was resting on his desk. Anton downed the room temperature water, barely realizing what he had just done. A couple of hours before, he'd slipped at least a half a teaspoon or more of drugs into that water to watch how quickly it would dissolve.

Too late now.

His mouth was still dry.

Shit.

"Anton …"

Where was Rory? That offer of going home certainly sounded good right now.

"Anton."

Viviana's quiet tenor in his mind asking him to be there in the morning to wake up their son reminded him of where he needed to be right now. Where he wanted to be …

"Anton?"

A hand landed to the middle of his chest. The heat from Natalie's unexpected touch and what was already moving over his skin sent Anton moving backwards instantly. When the back of his legs hit the couch, Anton found himself seated.

Then, she was on him. Straddling his waist, hands moving.

It was much too fast, and Anton couldn't process the feelings with his thoughts, and his thoughts with the feelings.

"Are you?" he heard her ask again. "Did you?"

Buttons on his shirt were snapped open. Fingers trailed up his chest, over his neck. Something hot spilled along his cheek. Anton's fingers were digging into her sides, but he wasn't entirely sure if it was to try to move her off him, or keep her there.

He certainly liked the way her hips ground into the length of his erection, but disgust was rolling heavy, too.

Not right, he knew. So wrong.

"What?" Anton rasped.

"Those people they said you killed."

"Who says that?"

"People. I wondered," Natalie mused above him. "You hear talk, but you don't really know. Did you do that?"

"To some," Anton muttered. "Men who didn't deserve breath."

Anton was aware he needed to stop talking, but the filter between his brain and his mouth wasn't working. Just like the filter between his mind and his cock. They weren't in agreement, either.

"Sonny?" Natalie asked softly.

"He tried to kill my wife," Anton answered. "I made sure he didn't try again."

Something screamed at him to shut up.

"And what's his name ... Sergei?"

Anton chuckled lowly. "Someone else did that. I just helped."

"His daughter?" Natalie whispered, coming down dangerously close to Anton's face.

"That was me," Anton said.

A hand was at his groin, then, pulling at the button, sliding down the zipper. Wetness flicked at his neck, sending something new pulsing and racing through his blood and cock.

"Say yes," Natalie said gently. "Tell me yes, Anton."

She didn't say his name right. It didn't fall over his senses like liquid gold, or send him spinning. Again he was reminded of how wrong she was with her light colored eyes and jasmine scent.

Fuck, he wished his body would understand that, too.

"Stop touching me," Anton breathed. "No!"

With a sudden strength that seemed to return with no warning, Anton shoved the female off his lap. Natalie landed to the hardwood floor of his office with a thump, her legs sprawling out underneath her as her face morphed into a mask of surprise.

"Don't you fucking come anywhere near me."

Anton wasn't sure if she'd heard him. Time was jumping again.

Chapter Five

There was a god-awful pulsing in the back of Anton's skull. Nausea rolled through his middle like a wrecking ball intent on killing him. That feeling was only increased when he turned in the bed and groaned, wanting to bury his face into something sweet-smelling and soft, like his wife.

Anton only met cold sheets instead of Viviana's warmth.

Instantly, his eyes popped open, unfocused and unsure. The morning light filtering into the master bedroom of their home burned his vision, making his headache that much worse. Struggling to figure out exactly why he felt like shit and where in the hell his wife was, Anton rolled over to his back and pressed his palms to his forehead.

"Oh God, I feel like death. Holy he—"

"Rough night?"

With a dry mouth and bleary eyes, Anton chanced a glance in the direction of where Viviana's annoyed voice had come from. Standing in the entrance of their bedroom, her hip pressed to the doorjamb and a cup of coffee in hand, his wife looked pissed.

Somehow, Anton knew he needed to apologize. He didn't know for what, but the stale taste in his mouth mixed with the hangover he seemed to be experiencing was a pretty good indicator he'd done something he shouldn't have.

"Vine—"

"Oh, it's not *the wife* today?" Viviana asked, cocking a brow.

Anton flinched. Had he called her that? "Where's Dem—"

"*Sleeping,*" she interrupted. "It's still early, Anton."

"I should … move, or something."

"Three in the morning, really? I can't even believe you! If it hadn't been for that new girl answering the phone at the club, I would have thought you were fucking *dead*."

Anton blinked at the bright white ceiling, guilt and queasiness filling him up to the brim. The memories he tried to reach from the night before were hazy at best, but he could remember being at his club in Brighton Beach. A few of his guys had showed up and they drank a bit, but that wasn't anything new.

"I don't know what happened."

"Well, your pupils were the size of a dimes, if that helps any. Thank God for Rory driving you home. That was a selfish move, Anton. And coming home stoned, drunk, and stupid? That's nothing like you."

"I'm sorry," Anton said softly. He wasn't going to make excuses, because clearly he fucked up, but he really wished he could remember why or at least how it had happened. "Vine, really, I don't know … Did I say anything?"

"Other than telling Rory that the wife would handle it? No." A heavy sigh fell into the room. The sound felt like a loaded gun pointed directly at his chest. Viviana had never seemed so totally overwhelmed or angry at him before, not like this. "Anton, I just … After last night, I can't do this."

The beating heart in his chest might as well have stopped altogether. "What?"

Something was tossed to the bed and Anton didn't miss the fleeting disgust that flitted over Viviana's pretty face. Pushing himself up in the bed, he grappled for the dress shirt that now lay forgotten where she threw it. At first he assumed she gave it to him to put on, but a simple glance at the article of clothing told him that wasn't the case.

Smelling like it'd been washed in a brewery with the faintest smudge of sparkly, red gloss at the collar, the dress shirt might as well have been a bomb ready to blow. Anton choked on the air in his throat. Sure, it was his shirt, no doubt about it. That gloss on the collar, though, meant something else entirely.

"No way," he said, dropping the shirt like it'd burned him. "No fucking way, Vine. I wouldn't ever—"

"Pick it up and smell it," she whispered, anguish filling up the brown eyes that met his unflinchingly. "Smells like a *whore*, Anton. Smells just like she was all over you, and the fact that I had to take it off of you last night to get you into bed … Why would you ever do that to me?"

Anton hurt all over. It wasn't just a physical pain from the hangover, but an emotional one. Simply looking at his wife, her heart so open and broken on her sleeve, he fucking damn well ached. What had he done? Surely there wasn't any way he would do *that* to Viviana. It just wasn't possible. He couldn't even *think* the word, let alone consider it as a real possibility. They'd been married three years and not once had he strayed from his wife.

There were opportunities, sure. Considering his profession as a high ranking boss in the Russian mafia, mixed in with his many businesses that had beautiful women roaming in and out by the dozens, Anton was surrounded by those kinds of opportunities. Drugs, illegalities, and women were a common thing in his day-to-day life, but never … no. Anton could not even consider it.

"Vine, I swear to God," Anton said, swallowing the lump in his throat. "You know—"

Viviana shook her head, the coffee cup in her hands trembling. "I don't *know* anything."

"You know *me*," he insisted.

"The man I know doesn't come home stoned out of his mind with a pint of vodka in his hand. He doesn't worry me half to death, degrade me when he gets home, or forgets that he has a two-and-a-half-year-old son sleeping down the hall. This man …" Viviana said with a flick of her wrist in his direction. "Who in the hell is this man? Not one I need, or want, honestly."

Before Anton could say another word, the sound of tiny feet pattering down the hallway stopped him. Usually the approach of his son in the morning only served to warm his soul, but today it felt foreboding. Demyan never witnessed his parents' disagreements. Children had a habit of blaming themselves, and Viviana and Anton kept their issues quiet and behind closed doors.

"Papa!"

Anton just managed to hide the dress shirt he didn't want to look at for a second longer before his son was tumbling into the bedroom. Viviana reached down to tousle the boy's raven black hair, but Demyan only had eyes for his father. Slipping across the hardwood floor in his socked feet, tiny white teeth shone as he grinned happily at the sight of his father awake and waiting.

"Hey, little man. Get up here."

Anton reached down to grab Demyan around the waist before pulling him up into the bed. Tickling his son, the high pitch squeals and childish laughter filled the room. Anton took the moment with his son to enjoy the innocent happiness of a child, but a heaviness still hung thick in the air.

"Did you use the bathroom?" Anton asked Demyan.

The huffing, pink cheeked boy shook his head. "Nope."

In a flash, Anton set his son to the floor. "Go do it and we'll have some breakfast." Once Demyan was out of the bedroom, Anton forced himself to move and get up from the bed, ignoring the pounding headache that made him want to puke. Viviana closed the door to shelter their conversation. "Vine—"

"No, I need you to listen to me for a minute, Anton. I am so angry with you. Even if something serious didn't happen, you still allowed a woman to touch you, to get close enough to you that she left behind her smell and her lipstick. Goddamn it, you promised me you wouldn't ever stray from our marriage, and I stupidly believed you.

"I can't do this," she repeated lowly.

Before Anton could say a word, Viviana kicked at a black duffle bag sitting on the floor that he hadn't noticed before.

"What is that?"

Viviana wouldn't meet his gaze. "It's a bag, for you. You need to go somewhere else for a little while, okay?"

"But, Vine—"

"Be here in the morning for Demyan, and if you want, at

night to put him to bed, but in-between, you can't be here, Anton. I need to think, and I can't do that with you nearby. All I want to do is scream at you, or hurt you. He can't see that, so you need to give me some time."

"This is my house, too," Anton whispered. "You're just going to kick me out of our fucking home?"

Viviana nodded jerkily and tears slipped from the corners of her eyes, though she didn't make a move to wipe away the wetness. "I told you, I need to think about some things."

"Things," he said, spitting out the word. "You mean us."

"That's one, yeah."

Fucking hell, why did she sound so indifferent and cold about it all?

"Well what the fuck else is there but us, huh?" Anton's shout practically reverberated in the room. He didn't miss the second flood of tears that fell from Viviana or the way her hand, still holding the coffee cup, had wrapped around her midsection as she folded in on herself. "I'm sorry," he rushed to say. "Baby, I didn't mean to yell."

"Don't ... God, just don't, Anton. I won't keep you from this house, or your son. On the other hand, you need to leave me alone when you are here. That's all I'm asking."

Viviana still hadn't removed her arm from her stomach. Anton's gaze was drawn in on the protective nature of the hold and the way she just wouldn't look at him. That wasn't his wife standing there, frightened and weakened. Viviana was the strongest damned woman he knew, and somehow—by him—she'd been broken.

"I didn't do anything, Vine. I wouldn't—*couldn't*."

But he couldn't remember for sure.

However, in the back of his hazy memory, Anton could feel the weight of someone on his lap, and the breath spilling on his neck. Blonde and blue-eyed with a sweetened voice, the female wasn't his wife. She didn't feel right. Nothing about her was.

No way, Anton thought brokenly.

He just *couldn't*.

"Please," Anton begged when Viviana refused to speak. "What aren't you saying?"

Viviana finally regarded him with shining wetness in an anguished stare. "I'm pregnant."

Oh God, his heart stopped. Anton wanted to be happy at her confession, but the absolute pain marring her features kept him from feeling anything but a deep, settling ache. "What?"

"I was a couple of days late, so the day before yesterday I stopped at the store and got a test just out of curiosity. I wasn't sure if it would happen so quickly like it did for Demyan when I came off the shot. I should have known better, of course it would. The home test came back positive, but I wanted to be sure so yesterday I went into the clinic. They confirmed it."

Anton's mouth was so dry he could barely speak. "Pregnant."

"Yeah. And I still need you to leave, Anton. Especially now."

• • •

Anton stared at the blank screen of his phone, lost and confused. The three texts he sent to his wife had all gone unanswered, although they'd all been about them, and not their son as Viviana requested. The heart inside his chest was aching and breaking in ways he couldn't even begin to describe. It was as if someone had taken his entire soul and ripped it apart before burying it deeper than he could try to dig.

At least Viviana had allowed him to take Demyan with him for the day. His little boy was keeping him sane with mindless chatter and constant business at the club. Anton, however, was still feeling like hell, but he was doing all he could to hide it from his son.

"Did you talk to Rory about last night?"

Anton glanced up at his lawyer's voice.

"Yeah," he croaked out.

"And?"

Demyan, playing in the corner with Rocco and his matchbox cars, didn't seem to be paying attention to the conversation, or his father's broken tone. The boy had done remarkably well all morning, despite the obvious frustration and hurt between his parents.

"And nothing," Anton answered faintly. "Said Natalie seemed like she was pulling down her dress and I was fixing up the buttons on my shirt. She made a big deal about getting out of there, and Rory said I was completely blitzed right out of it, but—"

"That sounds bad, man."

Yeah, Anton was aware. "Shit, Ivan, I can't even remember. I don't think I can count the amount of times I've drank enough to black out on one hand, and the hangover I've got is fucking ridiculous."

"I don't think you drank a heck of a lot, but you were slamming back on the bourbon pretty fast," Ivan noted. "Maybe more than we thought. It happens."

"Not to me," Anton insisted. "My drinks have always been watered down, especially when I have Bratva in this club."

"It's not like you, I agree." The lawyer nodded, shooting a look at the little boy in the corner. "Where are you going to stay?"

"Here for a while. I can go home for whatever I need, so I might as well."

"And what about you-know-who?" Ivan asked with a cant of his head towards Demyan.

"Keep him with me when I can. Make sure he sees me around enough to know I didn't leave. There's not much else I can do."

"Kids blame themselves for shit like this, Anton."

But not his boy. Anton wouldn't allow that.

"We'll figure it out," Anton muttered. "Somehow. Right now he doesn't know the difference. Surely we can keep him from noticing for a little while."

"That Papa, the one person besides his mother who is his absolute everything in this world, isn't waiting for him every morning like he had every other day of his life?" Ivan asked sarcastically.

A lump lodged painfully in Anton's throat. "We'll make it work, like I said. My son ... It doesn't matter, Ivan, he's *my* boy. She wouldn't keep him from me, because he's all of me and she knows it. Even if whatever this is between her and I right now keeps up like it is, then we'll figure something else out for him."

"You're taking this well," Ivan said frankly. "As good as can be expected for you, I guess."

"I'm breaking apart inside," Anton admitted. "That woman is my whole life and has been since I was eighteen. I've never loved anybody like I love her. I've broken every damn rule for her and would again in a heartbeat. I'm supposed to just accept that I stepped out on her because I drank too much liquor? Like fuck. Something doesn't feel right here."

Ivan hummed noncommittally. "If all else fails, you could pull rank, Anton. She's your wife and he's your son. Divorce isn't an acceptable route if you don't want it to be. I know you've always been a little cleaner cut than others is our business, especially where Viviana is concerned, but you're more than capable of playing dirty if you need to."

"Jesus. That's ..."

"It was just a suggestion. An option you can use if you want. I'm not saying I would, but I'm not you, either."

"Even if ... It doesn't matter how much I love her, I still couldn't do that." Anton felt his molars practically crack beneath his jaw as he grinded his teeth. The thought of forcing a reconciliation on his wife just because he said so didn't quite feel right for him. "This isn't twenty or thirty years ago, Ivan. She has choices. I won't take them from her because I fucked up. She's not a piece of property."

"Others wouldn't feel that way."

Anton scowled, the action causing his aching head to

pound harder. "They're not me."

"What about Natalie, have you tried talking to her?" Ivan asked.

"Absolutely not," Anton growled, glaring at his friend. "The last thing I need is to be near that woman again, Ivan."

"She'll be in the club tonight working."

Anton flinched, disgust filling him to the brim. This whole situation was horrible, and he felt dirty with ten grimy fingers pointing straight at his guilty chest.

"Well, aside from firing her, there's not much I can—"

Anton didn't get to finish his sentence. A loud bang and shouted orders rang out in the downstairs of the club. The tinkling sounds of canisters popping along the empty floor echoed up to their spot. There was no denying what was happening downstairs.

"Fuck," Ivan muttered.

Instantly, Anton was off his office chair, ignoring the gun he knew was in the desk, and the information of a shipment, never mind the laptop he should have tried to somehow destroy. No, instead, the only thing he could think of was the little boy on the floor with wide blue eyes and terrified, reaching for his father.

"Papa?" Demyan cried.

"Shhh, little man," Anton whispered.

In his arms, he held his son tighter and turned his back to the door of the office. It seemed like only milliseconds, but his mind was running a million miles a minute. Anton couldn't begin to understand why the officials would be raiding his club. His guys certainly hadn't been given any indication and they'd all been pretty quiet.

Demyan's shaking increased as the shouts down below became louder. "It's okay, Demyan, it's okay. Papa's here."

The sounds of a dozen or more pairs of boots pounding up the metal staircase ratcheted up Anton's nerves to a breaking point.

"Anton ..." Ivan started to say. "Anton, give me your son!"

The hardest thing Anton ever had to do, next to walking out of his house that morning knowing his wife's heart was breaking, was hand his trembling, scared, and crying son off to another man. It was safer for Demyan, though.

No doubt, they weren't there for Ivan.

Anton watched Ivan curl a fighting Demyan into his chest as he got to his knees on the floor and automatically put his hands behind his head. The less threatening he seemed at their entrance, the less likely they were to cause him harm, never mind his son seeing it.

"Demyan, it's okay," Anton repeated when the first kick to the door landed with a solid thump. The second and third only followed louder, harder. "Hide his face, Ivan!"

When the door finally broke, it wasn't a second before Anton found himself face down on the floor, his son's cries overtaking all other sounds. Cuffs tightened around his wrists to an almost painful point, but Anton refused to show it. A boot landed hard between his shoulder blades, keeping him pinned to the floor even though he wasn't fighting.

"*Papa!*"

"Anton Daniil Avdonin, you're under arrest for the murder of Sonny Carducci, Tatiana Belov, Sergei Belov ..."

Anton tuned the words out and focused on his son, instead.

• • •

"Vine!"

Frantically, Viviana turned in every direction she could look searching for the familiar voice calling for her. FBI agents had swarmed her home less than an hour earlier when she was getting ready to leave for the bookstore. Everything they held dear in their home, from photographs, to knickknacks, to their son's toys, were thrown about and strewn so carelessly.

There was nothing clean or nice about this search.

Viviana felt intruded on in the worst way.

"Sasha, I'm in the kitchen," Viviana called back.

"Ma'am, I'm sorry, but you're not permitted inside during—"

"*Zatknis', idi na khuy*," Sasha spat. "Get out of my way, you fucking fool, so I can take my grandson in to his mother!"

Despite the seriousness of the situation, Viviana snorted. In all her years of knowing her mother-in-law, Viviana hadn't once heard Sasha tell someone to shut up so venomously, never mind the colorful words she used to do it with.

When a furious Sasha rounded the corner to enter the kitchen with a confused, frightened looking Demyan, Viviana's heart broke a little more. From what she understood, thanks to the very short call with Ivan, her son had been there to see his father arrested. The team that went in on them at the club hadn't been particularly nice about it, either.

"Ma!" Demyan wailed and reached with grabbing hands for Viviana.

"I'm sorry, Vine. I would have gotten him here sooner, but the traffic is awful and they've got roadblocks set up down the street," Sasha said as she gave her daughter-in-law an awkward, one-armed hug.

"It's okay, really."

"Here, take him. I think he's hungry, tired, and in desperate need of a nap."

Viviana hadn't been able to go to the club to pick Demyan up because of the goddamn agents searching her house. No way would it be acceptable for them to be inside the residence without her or Anton's presence.

Demyan calmed the moment he could bury his tiny head into his mother's neck. As was his favorite thing to do when he was overwhelmed, he grasped tightly to the free strands of his mother's hair and turned silent.

"What about Anton?" Viviana asked, keeping her tone calm for her son's sake.

"Ivan will be with him as much as he can. Arraignment will be in a day or so. The best we can hope for is a bond."

"On murder charges," Viviana said dimly.

With everything that had happened over the last night and day, Viviana didn't want to see her husband behind bars. They had too much that needed to be said, whether it was from anger, or not. And no matter what, she loved Anton.

Always. Even if it fucking hurt.

"What am I going to do?"

Sasha nodded, sadness coloring up her familiar blue eyes. "Faith, Vine. You have to find it, sweetheart. I know you don't pray, but you should now."

Chapter Six

"Did you want me to be there for supper tonight?" Anton asked.

Viviana sighed into the phone as her son ran past the front counter of her bookstore. "Sure," she replied after a long moment.

"Vine, if you don't want me there …"

"No," she rushed to say. "It's not that, Anton. I'm just tired today is all and not in the mood to argue, all right?"

"All right, baby. Whatever you need."

The rush of sadness that flooded her veins from the comforting sentiment didn't help the ache burrowing deep in her chest. It had been two weeks since the arrest that literally turned their world and life upside down. The prosecuting attorney on the case had studiously argued Anton's flight risk at his arraignment, but Ivan was just as strong in the courtroom.

Without a passport, no real means to leave the country as their bank accounts had been frozen, and Anton's lack of leaving the state unless he needed to, flight risk was a bit of an exaggeration. As far as they knew.

Luckily, the judge agreed. For an eight-hundred-thousand dollar bond.

Anton was also forced to wear an ankle bracelet, just to keep track of him, apparently.

Any and all interview attempts with Viviana ended horribly. She all out refused to speak about her husband or any of his possible dealings with the officials. She wasn't required to anyway, being his wife. That didn't mean they were making it easy on her, though. Beyond that, there were reporters showing up outside their home, at her bookstore, and hell, even when she went to the grocery store. High profile was an understatement. Anton's upcoming trial was being called the one to watch.

The stress was seriously eating away at Viviana one day at a time.

She was still refusing to allow Anton to come back home, too, and it killed her more and more. Anton insisted repeatedly that even though he couldn't remember all the events of that night, there was no way he had slept with the woman. Natalie. Just thinking about it made Viviana sick to her stomach.

She loved her husband, but forgiveness was not as easy as it would seem.

"Come to dinner," Viviana finally said. "We should talk, and we could put Demyan to bed. He'll like that."

"Okay. Five good?"

"Perfect, Anton."

"I'll see you at five, then, baby."

"Five," she agreed.

After hanging up the phone, Viviana rested up on the stool and willed away the heaviness settling in her stomach. Like a dead weight, it had been there for days it seemed. She was so tired, too, but that wasn't anything new. The slight cramping she seemed to be experiencing was worrisome, but because she'd also had a similar issue early in Demyan's pregnancy, Viviana assumed this was the same thing. It would pass.

At least the morning sickness had yet to begin.

"Ma," Demyan said, making another round around the counter. "Is Papa coming?"

Just his speed alone made Viviana dizzy.

"Demyan, take a break for a moment, okay?"

Damn it, all of the sudden, Viviana didn't feel so well. The ache in her back increased. She'd been ignoring it for most of the morning, given the fact that she toted around a two-and-a-half-year-old on her hip for the greater part of her days. Especially when he was feeling clingy.

"Ma?" Demyan asked.

Demyan had come to stand in front of Viviana, looking up

at her with his little brow furrowed. When had he gotten so close?

Thirsty, Viviana tried to stand from the stool only to find her vision swimming with colors and her head pounding. Something was wrong. So, so wrong. Dread filled up Viviana's heart. When she stood, shakily and swaying, the ache turned into a cramp so severe it caused her to double over with a groan. Again, Demyan called her name, but he didn't sound so close the second time, and his voice was unsure.

While her mouth felt dry and parched, Viviana's jean covered thighs felt sticky, warm, and wet.

Oh, God.

Reaching for the cell phone she'd tossed to the counter earlier was useless. The light-headedness and spinning vision kept her focus from staying still. The ground felt like it was swaying under her feet.

"Demyan ..." Even her voice was faint, the realization of what might be happening to her body and her baby was catching up and slamming down on her like a wrecking ball. "Demyan, call Papa."

At his young age, Demyan could recite the most important phone numbers he needed to know off by heart. He was also able to dial them, too.

"Ma?"

A wave of pain washed over Viviana from her head to her toes. The force of the feeling had bile rising in her throat and air gasping out of her lungs. Terrified, she clutched at her midsection and shook her head.

Why? What had she done to deserve this?

"Call Papa," Viviana repeated through clenched teeth. "Now, Demyan!"

She didn't have to tell him again, though, because he already had.

"Papa, Ma's got a booboo."

Not her baby—*Anton's* baby.

Another cramping pain stabbed through her womb with

killing force. Viviana clasped her hands to the counter like it was a lifeline, and cried.

•••

Besides the soft beeps, the room Viviana woke up to was quiet with dimmed lighting and an antiseptic smell. The sheets wrapped tight around her midsection and lower half were scratchy and thin. Nothing like the soft, comforting sheets of her own bed. Immediately, she knew she was in the hospital.

Blinking away the hazy aftereffects of waking up, Viviana smacked the dryness from her mouth. Even though her body was weak and tired, it was also tender and sore all over. When she tried to move her hand to wipe at her eyes, a stinging pain followed the action, making her yelp.

"Viviana … hey, baby. Careful, you've got an IV in that hand."

Anton's soothing, familiar dark tenor sent Viviana spinning into a fresh round of tears.

"I'm sorry," she whispered, her voice cracking on every single word. "I'm so sorry, Anton. I didn't mean to—"

"No, no, no," he chanted. "God, Vine, just *no*."

Anton's concerned features colored Viviana's vision when she turned her head. Tears spilled further at the pain and sadness etching lines into his strong face. Quiet, hiccupping sobs bubbled up from her chest and fell into the room as everything caught up to her all at once.

She'd done him so wrong, she knew. The baby he'd pleaded with her for over and over again. The one he wanted so badly for them and their son. She *lost* his child. What use was she to him if she couldn't even care well enough for his baby to carry it?

What was wrong with her?

Viviana was empty. The heaviness that plagued her all week was gone, but so was something else, too.

"I'm sorry," Viviana repeated.

She didn't know what else to say.

"Vine, listen to me. It's not your fault," Anton insisted firmly. "It isn't, baby. Things happen, that's all."

"But, I—"

"But nothing. God, I love you so fucking much, you don't even know. I wish you would have told me something was wrong so you didn't have to do that alone. And Demyan, he just ..." Anton trailed off, sucking in a harsh breath before rubbing a hand over his drawn face. "He's going to stay with Sasha for a little while."

"No, I want him with *me*," Viviana said.

Especially now, she needed and wanted her son.

"Vine, stop. It's only for a couple of days, enough to get you settled and then we'll bring him home. I'll stay with him at Mom's, so he will have one of us at least. They've got the club on lockdown and there's no real timeline of when we'll be permitted to open it up again, so I need a place to sleep, too."

What? He wasn't coming home, either?

Before Viviana could ask, the door to her hospital room opened. An older man wearing blue scrubs and holding a chart in his hand gave a small knock on the door before Anton waved him in. He was introduced as the doctor who had been on call when Viviana was brought in through the emergency room, and he simply wanted to check on her before she was granted release.

Viviana felt distant from the man as he talked. Things were explained the best they could be. She'd been dehydrated and anemic. It wasn't uncommon and usually the anemia wouldn't be caught until the first round of blood work, but Viviana had been too early for that, yet. One in three pregnancies ended in miscarriage, though most women were so early in the pregnancy that they wouldn't even realize and instead, mistake it for their period. She'd also just come off birth control, and some studies showed that could possibly cause an early termination, too, while other studies disagreed. There were too many variables to be sure about anything.

As Anton told her, the doctor said the same: things happen. Sometimes the reasons are clear, and sometimes, they're not. It could have been her body's way of reacting to the sudden stresses in her life, or maybe it was nature's way of terminating an unhealthy pregnancy. The anemia and dehydration hadn't helped, but it certainly wasn't the only cause.

The dizziness and fainting, however, could have been her mind's way of reacting to the shock. As if it had been trying to protect her because she was already overwhelmed enough. And while it might have seemed like she bled a great deal, the *D&C* the hospital preformed to be sure everything was gone …

Viviana didn't want to hear any more after that.

Nothing, the doctor told her. Over and over.

You did nothing to cause this, sweetheart.

The worst part? Viviana didn't believe him.

• • •

"Why won't you stay?" Viviana dared to ask.

Anton froze at the door of their home, letting the jacket he was putting on slide off his arm. "Excuse me?"

A week earlier, she'd been released from the hospital. Demyan had been home with her for a couple of days, but he was doing well and with him closer, Viviana felt better for a moment. Anton came like he always did, to have breakfast with Demyan, take him with him for most of the day, and then he spent a great deal of the night with him, too.

But, then he left.

He kept leaving. Every fucking time.

The conversations between Anton and Viviana were short, without any real depth. He didn't push her to talk, he didn't question her about her day, and beyond their son, he didn't have much to say, either, it seemed.

Had she done this? Had losing his child pushed him away?

"You keep leaving. Why?"

"I …" Anton struggled for words, his gaze darting from hers to the wall. "You asked me to leave you be, Vine. You asked me to *leave*, so I did. You wanted time to think. I'm only doing what you wanted from me. If you want something different, you need to tell me that, too."

"That was before, though." She couldn't even say before what. It was already real enough and she didn't want to confirm it further by repeating it constantly. Their communication skills were seriously lacking lately. "You won't even come close enough to touch me. I didn't mean to hurt you, Anton. I'm sorry I lost—"

"Stop saying that!" Anton threw his hands up into the air, frustration writing heavy lines over the action. "Stop apologizing for something that was completely out of our control. I keep fucking telling you that it's not your fault. I never thought it was. Why can't you hear me when I tell you this? I'm trying to listen for you every day, to speak to you somehow, but you hear nothing from me.

"You want to play the blame game, baby? How about the fact that the morning you told me you were pregnant, you also had to ask me to leave our home. I did that. Or when you needed me, you didn't feel like you could tell me. Then, we've got the arrest, this fucking trial, and everything else that just kept slamming you down over and over. That was all me, Viviana. I did that to you. So no, don't tell me you're sorry. But I wish just once, you'd let me apologize to *you*."

Tears betrayed Viviana, falling down trembling cheeks to land on her dry lips. The hands she'd hidden from his view by wrapping them into her chest were shaking. The heart that beat only for the man across from her was breaking apart all over again.

Why would he possibly blame himself?

"Anton, you didn't do anything."

"Didn't I?" he asked sharply. "It doesn't matter how many times I tell you I didn't touch that girl willingly, you don't believe me. And what's fucking worse, I don't blame you. Because if it were me in your spot, I'd have done the same.

Just when I thought maybe we would work it out, I turn around and get myself arrested. What have I done for you, really, Vine?

"Hurt you, baby. Over and over. I'm scared of hurting you, Vine, of pushing you away more than I already have. All I seem to do lately is hurt you, and you've hurt enough. You're my whole world—you and that boy. I breathe for you. My heart beats, and breaks, and bleeds only for you. I can't keep hurting you, so I let you push me away. It's easier than watching you struggle to love me."

"Not for me," Viviana whispered. "It's not."

"You're so quiet, sometimes. You won't even look at me, and it's killing me. All I want to do is hug you, hold you, care for you ... *anything*. I need to and I can't because you won't let me. I'm dying here. Tell me what you need from me and I'll do it. Just fucking *tell me*."

Without even thinking about it, Viviana blurted, "I need you here."

Anton waved his hands at the hall and shrugged. "I'm here. I've been here every day, no matter what."

Viviana nodded because she knew it was true. "I need you closer."

Three short steps later and Viviana was staring into teary blue eyes. "What else, Vine?"

"I need you to want me, Anton. To talk to me, to touch me, and to be here when I wake up, and when I go to sleep. I don't want to feel like this is my fault, but I do. I don't want to think you blame me, but I can't help it. I need to not be strong right now and for that to be okay with you. I'm so sick of trying not to cry and of being alone. I don't want to be alone. I need you."

"I can do that," Anton murmured. "Anything you want."

"Come home. Stay with me, please. Love me."

Because he was the only one who could do that so fiercely, so wholly. Viviana felt lost without Anton.

Viviana didn't need to say another thing. The coat was forgotten, hung up with the rest. Anton kicked both shoes off and tossed his Mercedes keys into the glass bowl on the stand. Then, he turned back to his wife with an opened palm, waiting. Viviana met his hand instantly, feeling the calming heat of his flesh siphoning into hers.

She let him lead her through their home, up to their room. It had been so long since they had been together, alone, in that space. Without a word, Anton began tugging at the sweater Viviana wore, pulling the heavy fabric off her frame to expose that she wore nothing underneath.

"Anton, we can't," Viviana said, remembering the doctor's orders about waiting until the bleeding had stopped.

Anton shook his head, fingering the hem of the yoga shorts she wore. "Shush, baby. I don't need that and neither do you. Just … let me hold you, huh? That's what you need."

So, she did just that. Anton pulled off his own clothes until he stood in nothing but boxer-briefs. Slowly, like he was making sure she still wanted his touch, he reached out for her hands, weaving their fingers tightly together. Then, he was stepping closer, pulling Viviana into his naked chest until every inch of their exposed skin was touching.

Warm—he was so warm. Like a blanket that covered, hid, and protected every bare nerve she had left. It ached, but it was so good, too.

Viviana listened to the shuddering exhale Anton released as he hugged her tighter.

"I'm sorry, Vine," he said into her hair.

Strangely, she needed to hear that more than anything else.

• • •

Anton was never more relieved than when the feds finally took the tape off Seven Lights. They wouldn't be able to do any Bratva business there for a while, but Anton still felt like he was missing his left hand without his club and office.

"Good to be back," Ivan noted, kicking his feet up over the arm of the couch.

Anton agreed with a grunt, still surveying the damage the

bastards had caused his office. "Where are Boris and Erik today?"

"Laying low. Keeping their noses clean and making sure everyone else is doing the same."

"Fucking bastards. This whole doorjamb needs to be replaced," Anton said.

"That's nothing, Anton. All of this can be fixed quick enough. Sit down and relax for a minute, would you?"

That was the last goddamn thing Anton wanted to do. Even though he was enjoying having his club back to himself, he really just wanted to be home with his wife and son. Viviana was doing better a month after losing their second child in some aspects, and in others, she seemed to be moving backwards.

It felt like a losing battle.

"How's Vine?" Ivan asked softly.

Anton flinched internally. Ivan was with him the day Demyan called and followed him to the bookstore when Anton rushed over there. They couldn't exactly hide what had happened from their good friend, not that he would have, of course. Most others didn't know, except for Anton's mother.

"I don't want to talk about it, Ivan. Just leave it alone, it's private. That's how we want to handle it."

"I'm not asking about the miscarriage, I'm asking about her for you. My friend. It's been a month, man. Is the depression any better?"

Anton's snort was derisive. "Depends on what you mean, I guess."

"Well, you're home," Ivan noted.

Thank fucking God for that, Anton thought. "She needs me. I need her. It works."

"So why do you look like somebody just kicked your puppy?"

"I don't know what else to do to help her, that's all. She's hurting, but she talks. She's depressed, but she gets up, works, takes care of Demyan and does all she needs to do." Anton shrugged, feeling a heavy weight on his shoulders. "I mean, it sucks. You don't even get the time to enjoy having something before it's taken away. The doctors can be so fucking callous, too. Telling her she can try for another when her cycle comes back, because it will help with the loss. Really? That's kind of fucking ridiculous, I think. Just here, keep trying for another and everything will be better. But what do I know? It wasn't me who lost the baby."

"But you did, in a way," Ivan added gently. "It was your child, too. One you wanted."

Anton didn't like to think of it that way. It wasn't so black and white. "I didn't bleed for weeks after, Ivan. I didn't lay in our bed blaming and hating my body for betraying me. I didn't cry like she did, or grieve. Does that make me awful, that even though I understand why she feels like she does, I can't hurt over it like she did?"

"No, it makes you human. Everyone feels things differently. You're the kind of man who handles your own emotional pain by taking care of those around you that you love. There's nothing wrong with that."

Anton stayed silent, absorbing his friend's words.

"Are you two ... you know, sharing a bed, or just sharing a home?"

"Way to be vague," Anton muttered under his breath.

"Did you want me to ask if you're fuck—"

"Don't be an idiot, Ivan. And no, we're not. She had to wait a while, anyway. That time has passed, but I don't think Vine's quite ready for anything physical."

Or maybe she was. Anton didn't know. They shared a bed, sure, and he held her every chance he got, but he was terrified to make a move beyond that. What if doing so scared Viviana, or worse, pushed her away? He didn't want her to feel as if he was pressuring her, or like sex was all he needed.

Though Anton did need it, in some ways. The best way he could love his wife, the one way he always knew how to let her feel it, was to physically show her.

"Maybe it's me that's not ready," Anton confessed, letting the words slip out of the side of his mouth like they hadn't existed in the first place. Ivan stayed quiet and let him continue. "I mean I am. I always want Vine like that, of course I do. I don't have any indication she's okay or ready for that. There's no definite yes or no. I haven't pushed her for it, or even asked. Does that make sense?"

"It does," Ivan said. "Perhaps you should, Anton. You said it. You need her. She needs you. It works. Maybe the physical side of it is what's been missing because you haven't been looking for it, hmm?"

Damn it. Now, Anton really just wanted to go home.

"Go, man."

Anton turned on his heel. "What?"

"Go home. I'll make a couple of calls to get this shit fixed. Go see your wife."

Ivan didn't have to tell Anton a second time.

• • •

"Are you sad, Ma?" Anton heard Demyan ask in his tired, groggy voice.

"Hmm, no, I'm not sad, baby. Why would you think I'm sad?"

Anton rested his shoulder against the hallway wall and waited out the conversation, though he knew he should probably leave. He couldn't. He desperately wanted to hear what Viviana might tell their son, especially if it was something she hadn't told him.

"You cry," Demyan said.

Viviana breathed deeply. "Sometimes you have to."

"Boys don't cry. Uncle Erik said so. Only if you has a bad booboo."

"Have, Demyan. And Uncle Erik doesn't know what he's talking about," Viviana muttered. "Boys can cry."

"Papa doesn't cry."

The silence following Demyan's statement was heartbreaking. Was that was Viviana needed from Anton? Emotion, honesty? To know the anguish he felt but didn't understand what he was supposed to correlate it to? Anton wasn't sure he knew how to do that.

Finally, Viviana whispered, "Yeah, I know. Okay, it's nap time, little man. Papa will be home when you wake up, and you can ask him about boys and crying. All right?"

"Boys don't cry, Ma," Demyan repeated in all his two-and-a-half-year-old wisdom.

"Sure, sure. Sleep, baby."

Anton could have slipped down the hall in lots of time for his wife to not notice his eavesdropping, but he didn't. Viviana didn't seem all too surprised to find him standing with arms crossed and staring at the floor either. The tired sadness roaming in her gaze as she passed him in the hall, saying nothing, tugged deep down in Anton's soul. He followed her to their bedroom two doors down.

When the door shut behind him, Viviana sighed. "Boys don't cry, Anton."

Anton swallowed the immediate emotions that lodged in his throat like a stopper. "They do."

"Funny, your son doesn't seem to think so. I don't know how I feel about that right now."

"Boys cry," Anton insisted quietly. "Sometimes they just do it in a different way, over different things. Not everything is black and white. There are shades of grey, too."

Viviana tossed him a look over her shoulder as she began straightening the mess that had become the sheets on their bed. "Do you cry, then?"

Straight to the point, as always.

"More inside than out, I think."

"That's not the same," Viviana said, a little too hotly for Anton's liking.

"And you don't get to tell me how to grieve."

Viviana froze, the sheet in her hand falling to the bed. "I—"

"Let's be clear on one thing, baby. I cry. I hurt. I'm so concerned about you that I'm stuck in my own goddamn head, and I can't get out of it most days. Funny thing, though,

I'm okay with that. Because when I hurt, and when I cry, it's always for you."

"Anton ..." she said, taking a step forward.

Anton raised a hand to stop her. "I cry when the woman I love thinks that she's failed me. Or that her body is somehow wrong. I cried when she hurt for losing something because it wasn't just hers, but a part of me, too, even though she was so mad at me. I cried at night. I cried alone. You didn't want to be strong, and I didn't want you to see me weak. You needed to cry, to talk, to be angry, and to hurt. I let you. I don't think there is anything wrong with the way you grieve over this, so why is it wrong for me to do it the way I need, Vine?"

"I'm sorry," she whispered.

"Don't be. Just try to understand everything given at face isn't always the value."

Blowing out a harsh sound, Viviana shook her head. "I'm so fucking selfish."

Well, Anton certainly wasn't expecting that and he didn't necessarily agree, either. "I don't think you are."

"No, of course you don't. You love me."

"You love me, too," Anton shot back. "Are you saying the way you love me isn't worth the same as mine? That it's not as good?"

"No!" Viviana gasped. "God, you know how much I love you."

Anton hummed his agreement, stepping close enough that he could reach out to snag her wrist in his palm. "You're not a selfish woman. You never have been. I won't be the one to call you that, or allow you to do it."

"But I haven't even been paying attention to you. I asked you home, to be with me, and I don't even know what you're thinking about half of the time. I haven't bothered to ask."

"Yes you do," Anton insisted firmly, drawing Viviana closer into his embrace. With her face buried against his neck, and her soft lips pressing to his skin, he felt a million times better. "Maybe not with words, but in other ways. You let

Demyan call me throughout the day. Not once have you fought with me about the charges, or the shit storm we're facing with that. Even though I know you just want to lay in bed, you get up with me in the morning and talk. And when you talk, I don't have to, Vine. Sometimes that's just what I need."

Anton tilted Viviana's face up under his urging hands, swiping away the wetness on her cheeks with his thumbs. "You supported me, stood by me, even after you asked me to leave. With the feds, you didn't let them bully you, and you still acted as my wife. Our son is kept happy—spoiled, if anything. You allowed me back into our home, you let me close to you. Those are the things I need."

"And they helped, you know, with this," Viviana said with a wave at her midsection.

"In ways, yes. You can say it, baby. It happened, and you *can* say it."

"I don't like to."

"I know," Anton said gently.

Viviana shuddered when Anton leaned down to press a kiss on her forehead. "I just ... don't understand."

"Understand what, exactly?"

"Why it's so hard for me. It wasn't like I had weeks and weeks being pregnant. I was only a few weeks into it. If I wasn't paying attention to my cycles, I probably wouldn't even have noticed I was pregnant until I miscarried."

Anton felt a small sense of triumph at Viviana's utterance of the word she so viciously avoided. "Because you did know. You had already attached yourself to the idea of having the baby. You didn't consider this would happen, and really, why should you have? I don't think the length or severity of your hurt and grief should be measured by the duration of the pregnancy. If anything, this shows you're capable of feeling love. That you can, even so early and soon. The baby meant something to you—to me, too. There's nothing wrong with that."

Viviana cleared her throat, blinking away the tears still

shining in the corners of her eyes. All over again, Anton wished he knew if what he was saying was having an effect on his wife. If it meant anything at all to her. He only wanted to help.

"One of the nurses at the hospital, she was in my room when you left for a bit."

"And?" Anton pressed.

"I'm not sure if she was just trying to help, but she called the baby tissue."

Anton felt his spine crack as he stood a little straighter. "What?"

"You know, like cells and tissue. That's all the baby was, according to her. She said it didn't even have a heartbeat at the gestation it was and things like that. I don't think she meant any harm, just trying to—"

"Distinguish the difference between the soul of a baby and the worth of tissue to a woman who had just lost a pregnancy? For what, to dictate how she should feel? That's fucking ridiculous," Anton muttered angrily. "Why didn't you tell me?"

"Because in her own way, she was just trying to help, Anton. But it made me think, and it's been on my mind all month. Was that what you thought of the miscarriage, just … tissue? I wouldn't be hurt if you did," Viviana rushed to say when Anton stayed silent. "I might not understand, but I wouldn't persecute you for it, either."

"No, I didn't."

Viviana stared up at him, confused. "That's it?"

Yeah, it was, really. Anton correlated the pregnancy to his wife. It was something they, with love, had made together. Just like their son and their life. Maybe the form it was lost at was simply tissues and cells but it was much, much more than that, too.

"It was ours, Viviana," Anton said honestly. "That was all that mattered to me."

"Ours," she echoed.

For the first time in longer than Anton wanted to admit,

his wife smiled the tiniest smile.

Chapter Seven

Viviana used the tip of her finger to trace along Anton's cheekbone. The strong lines of his face always relaxed in his sleep, making his appearance more boyish than the intense stares he usually sported when awake. Wearing nothing but his boxer-briefs and covered with only a sheet, nearly all of his beautiful, masculine form was on display for her to enjoy while he slept.

She didn't feel so damned guilty, then. Viviana didn't even understand why it was that she felt guilty over looking at him, anyway. Maybe it was because she yearned and ached to be closer to him than what she allowed, but things were still holding her back.

The miscarriage would be an acceptable excuse, and certainly an understandable one, if that was the reason why. Viviana knew it wasn't. More than anything, she craved the comfort and intimacy Anton would give her physically, but she also didn't trust herself enough not to hurt when it was over.

Desperately, Viviana held onto the knowledge that Anton loved her. When she was fighting to be found, he wasn't far behind. When she was tattered in pieces, he was putting her back together. There was a strength in his love that had an almost suffocating quality, but she'd die happily wrapped in it. A certain devotion glimmered in his eyes that he reserved solely for her. He could be strong willed, possessive, jealous, and sometimes, just downright difficult, but he was *hers*. That love—all-encompassing and seemingly never-ending—was there. It was as true as it would ever be.

Viviana didn't deny that.

But, he'd hurt her, too. Even if a million parts of her heard Anton every time he promised it couldn't have happened the way it seemed, that he'd never touch another female willingly, something had happened with that woman. Anton allowed himself to be put in a position where his fidelity, both past and future, was in question. Viviana's trust was shaken. It rocked her foundation in a way she hadn't considered.

Viviana was finding it hard to move past that.

She wanted to, though. So badly.

Verbally and emotionally, the two were connecting. Maybe even in a way they hadn't been able to before because when they did need to connect, the first thing one reached for was the other, physically. To touch, to understand, and love—sex had been the link between them, and it worked. But, for the first time in their relationship, Viviana found both her and Anton were relying on different modes to make that familiar connection keeping them so close.

There were off days and some were worse than others. There were also hits and sometimes misses, like earlier in the day when Viviana assumed she understood the depth of her husband's pain, or lack thereof, over her miscarriage. If Anton was anything, he was good at wearing masks. He'd been doing it his whole life, after all. Some habits were hard to break. Viviana recognized his need to be a solid foundation when everything else around them seemed to be crumbling, but sometimes she needed to see his cracks, too.

Hell, they didn't even have time to deal with one thing before the next came in to wreck and destroy. Were they being tested? It certainly felt like it. Were they winning? That was harder to tell.

Viviana's fingers ghosted down over the faint stubble shadowing Anton's jaw before allowing her fingers to trail down further to his neck, where the pulse of his heart beat against her skin. For a moment, she reveled in that feeling.

I breathe for you. My heart beats, and breaks, and bleeds only for you.

God, she loved this man.

"Vine?"

Like an electric shock to her system, Viviana jerked at the sound of her name on Anton's mouth. She attempted to pull her hand away from his skin only to find him holding her fingers in place. Suddenly, his heart rate had picked up under her touch, beating much faster than before.

"What are you doing?" Anton asked a little groggily.

"Nothing." Viviana glanced up into the heated blue of his eyes. "Watching you, I guess."

"Sleep?"

"It's the best time to. I'm not so focused on you watching me, then."

"Ah," Anton murmured, his lips quirking up into a lazy grin. "I unsettle you, hmm?"

"Sometimes. Most times you just consume me."

"Consume. I like that better."

"Yeah," Viviana said, feeling unsure under his watchful gaze. "I always know when you are. It's like everything just fades away. You're not seeing anyone else when you look at me and I know it. All of me centers in on that. Like a camera with a million viewers just zoned in on only me. I can feel it, if that makes sense."

"Sure. Why do you think I just woke up, baby?"

Viviana sighed in the dark, feeling his hand encasing hers squeeze tighter.

"It *is* unsettling, though," Anton added quieter. "Knowing there's only one person in the whole world who has that kind of effect on you. It makes you vulnerable in some ways, and in others, you feel stronger. No one else is ever going to make every instinct you have react so completely. One heart brings you to your knees, makes you want to scream, fight, laugh, or cry. There's only one—you, I mean."

"Do you think we're different from other people?" Viviana asked.

Anton shrugged one shoulder, reaching out with his free arm to wrap around Viviana's waist. "I think we're us, Vine. I'm perfectly happy with loving one woman enough to give every part of me over to her—mind, body, and soul. It doesn't frighten me. Other people, they might not feel the same way, but they still love. You can't judge the worth of their love based on the amount of themselves they hand over. Some people need to keep something for themselves. It could be the part of their soul they gave to their first love, or maybe it's a broken piece they want to protect the person they love from it. Whatever it's for, protection, sanity, it doesn't matter. They need to keep it. No two people are alike."

"But we're—"

"Anton and Viviana," he interrupted. "That's all. When I fell in love with you all those years ago, every inch of your soul tattooed itself inside mine. There wasn't any way on earth I was getting rid of you. You were in my system, bleeding me out from the inside. People couldn't see it. They didn't know. I needed them to, so I tattooed you on the outside of me, too."

Viviana released a shaky breath of air at his admission. It was as heavy as the emotions filling up her heart, leaping into her throat. She'd always known his vine tattoo was for her, that it represented her in a personal way, but she never understood why he felt the need to permanently keep her on his skin. Viviana never felt the need to ask before, either. Or maybe she was scared to.

"Viviana, what's wrong?"

The tightening in her throat made it difficult to think. She'd cried so goddamned much over the last month, and even before that, when she'd asked Anton to leave their home. She was sick and fucking tired of crying, of feeling weak, and broken.

"If you love me like that," she whispered, still feeling his heart beat under her fingers, "...like you say you do, then why would you risk it for someone else? Why put yourself in a position where you could lose it, Anton?"

"I didn't," Anton said. "I didn't go to the club that night with someone else on my mind. I didn't let another woman touch me because I wanted her to. I might not remember a lot of the circumstances around the event or what came after, but I remember that. I didn't want that girl to be near me. The day you stepped into my life to be only mine was the last time I ever looked at another female. I can't keep telling you over and over again hoping you'll hear me. You need to hear yourself say it, Vine, because obviously it's not working coming from me."

"What do you remember, then?" Viviana asked sharply.

"Being confused. Hazy. Knowing something wasn't right, but I couldn't correlate it to anything. My first thought was that I was drunk and needed to lay down, so that's what I went to do in my office. That was all."

"That's not all."

Anton's jaw flexed in his aggravation. "That's what I remember feeling. Beyond that, I don't like what my memories bring up. I don't know if I gave her the wrong impression, or if she took it upon herself to approach me, but she was in my lap. She was on me, her hand was pulling at my shirt and then it was grabbing at my ..." His eyes closed, a grimace marring his mouth as he made a disgusted noise. "After that, it's a whole lot of nothing, but I know I didn't want her."

"If you can't remember most of what happened, how could you possibly know that, Anton?"

"Because she's not *you!*"

Viviana yanked her hand from his hold and moved to leave the bed, but she didn't have a chance. Anton's strong arms wrapped around her waist before she'd even gotten to her own side of the bed, forcing her back to the sheets. Looming over her frame, Anton's gaze had filled with tears. The heavy weight of his body pressing hers into the bed had awakened the simmering need still burning bright through her veins. The last thing Viviana felt was fear while staring up at him.

"She's not you, Vine," he repeated thickly. "She's not my wife, or the mother of my child. She doesn't share my bed, my life, or my heart. There isn't a single emotion that girl invokes in me but anger and disgust—mostly at myself. More than anything, the one thing I regret is not knowing. Not being able to give you answers or tell you why. All I can say is

I am sorry, so fucking sorry for letting you think for one goddamned minute that anyone could ever make me feel like you do. Nobody can. Never. I'm *sorry*."

Viviana swallowed the pain in her heart. "Have you had any contact with her since that night?"

"No," Anton said instantly. "Absolutely not."

"Why not?"

"Why would I?"

"To fill in the blanks, maybe," Viviana suggested. "That would be a valid excuse."

"I don't need a fucking *excuse*, Vine. I don't want a reason to talk with that girl. I don't need to be anywhere near her."

"Why, are you scared it'll happen again?"

Ouch. Even to Viviana, that sounded harsh and felt about the same.

"No, I'm scared I'll fucking kill her," Anton snarled.

Viviana blinked, surprised. "What, why?"

Finally, Anton released his hold on her sides, but he wouldn't answer the question. Rubbing a hand over his face, Anton shook his head and sighed, the fatigue in his actions ringing clear. Viviana took the moment he gave to try and pull something—anything—from what she already knew to figure out why her husband wouldn't want to answer that question.

Anton was Bratva. He just was. He was a husband, a father, a son, and a man, but above everything else, he was a Bratva boss. Whether Viviana liked it or not, her husband was involved in things she didn't like or approve of, but that was his life. She'd accepted it. If violence was something Anton felt he had to resort to in order to deal with someone, there was always a reason, and it usually led back to his brotherhood.

"Anton ..."

Wary eyes wouldn't meet her stare. "Don't, Vine, please."

"Anton, what aren't you telling me?"

"It's not an excuse, and I don't want it used as one for you to forgive me, Viviana. Just leave it alone."

More confusion filled Viviana. Desperately, she wracked her brain, searching for what she was missing.

"I can't," she finally said. "Please tell me."

Anton's hand came to rest on her hip, his thumb sweeping gently along the exposed patch of her skin. "I was arrested the afternoon after that night."

My first thought was that I was drunk ...

"Your drinks are always watered down," Viviana stated. Anton didn't like to be drunk when Bratva were around, she knew. He'd once said it muddled up his head too much so he couldn't pay attention. It wouldn't be like her husband to get hammered. It was irresponsible. "Who was mixing them that night?"

"Jen."

Jen was their friend—someone both Viviana and Anton trusted.

"And who was serving you?"

Anton's teeth clenched. "Natalie."

The tension in Viviana's body released as she sunk back into the pillows.

"Different drugs are meant to do different things to a person," Anton said above her. "Blow gets you up, makes you stay there. I used to love it once. Weed, it mellows you out, takes you to a calmer place, like bringing you down in a good way."

While Anton didn't partake in chemicals anymore, Viviana knew he still occasionally smoked a joint. She didn't care, really. Weed was the least harmful of the drugs he dabbled with on the Bratva side of things.

"Heroin takes everything away, pain, emotion, thoughts," Anton continued. "Pills are similar, depending on what you're mixing up. But ecstasy, Molly, things like that, they make you feel good. Physically, you want to be touched, it's like a drug in and of itself. It makes your head hazy, but in a good way. There's no inhibitions to hold you back, no cares ..."

"You used that a lot in high school, didn't you?" Viviana asked, her voice suddenly turning hoarse.

"Oh, yeah. There was nothing like it. I loved it. There was a point when I was using it every day, just because I could. My baseball dreams didn't end because I chose Bratva, it ended because I was caught giving X to my teammates in the locker-room after a game we won. They tried to say I was dealing in school, though I wasn't. I had a ready supply at hand, why would I need to deal to support it? My father could have easily paid my way out of it, but he didn't."

"If you enjoyed the sport so much, why not?"

"Responsibility, baby. I did wrong, so something I enjoyed was taken from me. For every cause, there is an effect. I needed to deal with that. At the time, I didn't see it that way, but I understand now."

Viviana mulled over her thoughts for a moment. "You weren't drunk that night."

"Not to a blackout point," Anton agreed. "I probably wouldn't have driven myself home, but I asked Jen, and she confirmed I only had maybe five orders brought for me."

Then, Viviana had another sobering thought. Sometimes with Anton you had to ask the right questions to get the right answers. It was likely she didn't ask the right one earlier to get what she needed to know from him.

"You haven't gone looking for answers from Natalie, but has anyone else?"

Tension thickened in the room. "Yes."

"And?" she pressed.

"No one could find her. Word was put out, but nothing has come back. Her uncle says the family hasn't heard from her, either."

That didn't bode well. Viviana had been made aware a little over a year ago that there was a serious investigation going on around her husband and his possible involvement in the death of her uncle, as well as the Belovs. When she asked Anton about it, he'd been honest about what he knew they had, and what he knew they didn't.

More evidence, that's what they need and don't have, he'd said.

"Do you remember talking to her?" Viviana dared to ask.

"I remember being confused," Anton replied, repeating his earlier words. "She touched me, my body liked it, wanted it, but my head and heart didn't. I wanted more, and I wanted her to stop. She didn't look like you, or feel like you, but I was still physically reacting, like I couldn't help it. There's a difference between knowing the reaction a certain drug will give you, recognizing that you're experiencing it because you took it, and having it surprise you because you didn't do it willingly. Mixed with alcohol, some things have a worse effect the morning after. Memories get mixed up or forgotten. The hangover is doubled, and so on."

Viviana forced herself to breathe. "I was under the impression the feds had yet to be able to infiltrate your family."

"They've tried. Once or twice, but we always got wind of who, or what, was happening. Women would have been useless for me, because they couldn't get close enough to gain my attention or respect. Certainly not enough to have me talk about Bratva business. I never would have suspected a woman in my club unless it was confirmed by someone else."

"You told me the feds needed more," Viviana said, fisting her hand and hitting her knuckles against his chest, frustrated. Tears welled in her eyes, the same tears that reflected in her husband's above. "You said we didn't have to worry!"

"The morning after that night, they had more, Vine."

"Would they really do that? Take it so far as to drug you to get what they needed for the investigation?"

"They need something," Anton said as if that explained it all. "Without some substance for their work, they're stuck paying for the protection of another person for the rest of their life, no matter if they got information or not. It's a lot of waste if they end up getting nothing. And she would need protection, because they know I will kill her if I find her, Vine."

Viviana sucked in air like it was a drug. She couldn't seem to take in oxygen fast enough to satisfy her lungs. She'd spent so long blaming Anton, when she didn't really understand or

95

know all of the circumstances. What had she done?

"Don't, Viviana," Anton whispered. "I know that look, so just don't."

"But—"

"Do not use that as the reason why you forgive me. Do you hear me? Don't use that. It's not an excuse. What happened was not acceptable. I put myself in a position— trusted someone I didn't know—when I was raised better. You were right, I allowed that woman to somehow get close to me. She touched me, she was on me—"

"Stop it," Viviana snapped, wiping away the tears on her cheeks. "Jesus, stop."

Anton's grip on her waist tightened, shutting Viviana up. "Look at me, baby. I need you to hear this and understand. My body reacted to that woman, but I didn't want her. I'm sorry I don't have more answers. Forgive me because you love me. Because you trust me. Not because she tricked or cornered me. I need to know when I walk out of this house, you're not worried I'm running around on you and that you know I love and want only you. You are the only woman who has *me*. Just you."

Viviana forced the tears to stop so she could look at her husband. She would only ask him one more time. "Did you have sex with her, Anton?"

"I don't know. I washed every bit of her off me that morning. I didn't want to believe that I did that to you. Is that your breaking point, Vine? Is this where you have to draw your line for us? Because if it is, if not knowing and understanding the possibility that you may never know is something you can't handle, I need for you to be honest with me."

Was it?

"And if it was?" she asked, trembling.

Anton finally let the tears he'd been holding at bay release. They weren't easy tears. Just watching him shaking from the force of his weighted sobs nearly broke her. His fingers dug into her sides, holding her tighter and closer to his own body.

Anton bowed his head and buried his face into Viviana's chest. Silently, she let him cry and held him all the while.

For the first time, Viviana finally heard him. All that guilt and regret he talked about, the things he didn't know but wished he did for her, and that love she felt radiating off him every moment of the day ... Viviana heard Anton.

She so needed to hear him.

"I would let you go, baby. I would give you everything of mine you wanted, let you take my son, and I would say nothing. I've hurt you, I know. It's the one thing I never wanted to do, so the least I could do for you is say goodbye and give you the promise I wouldn't hurt you more. If that's what you need from me, tell me now."

"No," Viviana said, strong and sure. "That's not what I want."

All of the sadness, hurt, and anger Viviana had felt washed through her again. Instead of fighting the feelings off, she allowed herself to experience them. She deserved to be angry with Anton if she wanted, to be hurt over his bad choices, and sad for what it cost them.

Above all else, she trusted her husband and forgiveness sometimes came in different forms than the obvious ones. She would continue to give him that faith, because she believed in the life they built for themselves surrounded in their devoted, smothering love that no one else could possibly ever understand.

Viviana dug her fists into Anton's shoulders. His hands at her sides slid underneath her back, slipping up under the camisole to lay flat to her skin. Anton still rested between her thighs and despite how studiously she'd been ignoring her body's response to his position and closeness before, she couldn't any longer.

Tender kisses dotted her chest, trailing up to her throat. Every so often Anton's tongue stuck out against her flesh, causing Viviana to shiver. The thin fabric of Viviana's sleep shorts and Anton's boxer-briefs did nothing to hide the hard length of his erection pressing to her sex. Just the feeling alone had her stomach clenching with need and every nerve in her body lighting up with sparks of want.

"Vine, Vine, Vine," Anton chanted, his mouth dancing dangerously close to hers. "I love you."

"Just me."

"Just you," he echoed.

Instinctively, Viviana legs tightened around Anton's waist as he moved up higher on her body. Leaning down, he caught her mouth with his own. The kisses that were shared between them since Viviana asked him home had been sweet, practiced, or gentle. They didn't speak of desire or wake up the raging flood of lust that currently electrified Viviana's insides. They were careful, and filled with hesitance. Nothing like the dominating, consuming battle Anton's kiss waged on her now.

The sensation of his cock grinding along her core as he grabbed her face, kissed her harder, deeper, had Viviana gasping into his mouth. Wide-eyed, she watched him pour everything he felt, wanted, and needed into his kiss.

I love you, it said.

I need you, it promised.

Forever.

"Only ever you," Anton said, nipping her bottom lip. "Let me show you, Vine. Let me love you like I do."

A whimper left Viviana's lungs before she could stop it. "*Please.*"

In quick movements, Anton had lifted Viviana up to the mountain of pillows behind them so quickly that she barely had time to register the change. The strength in the actions left her breathless and dizzy. With his hands on either side of her jaw, Anton rolled his thumbs along her cheeks, and Viviana sank into the affectionate touch with a sigh.

"Kiss me again," she demanded.

He did, bruising her lips with his own. The stubble on his jaw scratched against her smooth skin, surely leaving behind a redness she would see in the morning. The wetness still edging along his lashes from his earlier tears smeared to hers.

She could feel his body, from the strong muscles in his back, to the hands he used to yank her shorts down to her knees, trembling.

"Too long," Anton growled into Viviana's mouth. It had been so damned long, she knew. "I want you so fucking bad, baby. Tomorrow I'll love you slow, with my mouth and my fingers. Over and over. I'll taste you hot and heavy on my tongue, get me smelling like you all over, but tonight I just want *you.*"

"Take me, then."

Anton didn't waste time pulling the shorts away from her legs, or getting the camisole off, either. The boxer-briefs he wore were tugged down and kicked off, giving Viviana the best view of his thick cock, hard and ready for only her. Like it always had, her body responded to the rough and frantic nature of the lead up. Anton's two fingers sliding between her thighs to feel the warm wetness smearing along the seam of her pussy had her moaning.

Skillfully, he spread the arousal from her sex, sinking his digits in knuckle deep before pulling them out just as fast. "Soaked already, baby. Fucking *beautifully.*"

Under his urging, Viviana spread her thighs wider until her legs ached and her muscles were an inch away from protest. The pain only added to her excitement. She wanted more, so much more of that, and him. Abruptly, Viviana found her chin pinched between Anton's forefinger and thumb, forcing her to stare at him. She couldn't fucking think to look anywhere else.

Then, his hand between their bodies was grazing her pussy again, and so was his cock.

Viviana didn't have the time to react before he took her. Three hard, sharp thrusts found his cock seated inside her core to the hilt. The surprise of the sudden intrusion made Viviana cry out in a mixture of pleasure and pain. Breathing or thinking became impossible. Heat saturated her skin from the inside out, and it only seemed to get hotter.

She was so impossibly filled with Anton. The sensitive

tissues of her sex stretched, flexing around his length to accommodate what had been so long in the making. Viviana shifted her hips, tilting her neck back, and gasping in a lungful of air into burning lungs. Every nerve in her body that craved Anton had awakened with a vengeance.

There was a very thin precipice of sanity that Viviana was dancing on, and she couldn't quite bear it.

"I *can't* ... Oh, God ..."

"Shhh," Anton whispered, kissing at the corner of her mouth. "Just a moment, Viviana. Feel me. Relax and take me."

Slowly, the muscles clenching fist tight around his cock impaling her started to release. Pleasure licked through her blood like fire as Anton began to withdraw. When his fingers dug into the inside of her thighs, squeezing tight enough to leave marks, Viviana was lost. She found her own purchase against his back, her fingernails scoring lines along the tattoo of her he revered so privately.

Anton's restraint finally broke. The chain holding him back snapped. Their rhythm was punishing. The only sounds echoing in the darkened bedroom were the slaps of skin of skin, the drag of her teeth on his jaw, and the heady groans that built with every powerful stroke of Anton's body into hers.

Viviana would like to say their first intimate encounter after everything was slow and loving. She would like to say the touches were sweet and soft. That would be a lie. They never had been that way, not when they needed more than they wanted.

Instead, it was wild and unforgiving. His fingers fisted into her hair, exposing her neck for him to kiss and bite while she clawed lines along his arms and shoulders in her release— deep enough to draw blood. There'd be marks on both their bodies that would stay for days.

Dirty. Beautiful.

She fucking ached like this.

Anton made her so goddamned crazy.

THE SCORE

Viviana wouldn't have wanted it any other way.

Chapter Eight

"Has Ivan ever had an affair?"

Even with the large framed, dark sunglasses shielding her eyes from the brightness of the day, Viviana knew Eva was watching her like a hawk all of the sudden. Eva, Ivan's wife, was one of Viviana's few female friends. When she needed a day off, or just a woman's company, Eva was who Viviana usually called on. The woman was also the wife of a Bratva man, like Viviana was, so their conversations weren't as stilted or stunted as they were with women who sported husbands that weren't affiliated.

"Why?" Eva asked. "Do you think Anton is fucking around on you?"

"Beautifully asked," Viviana said with a quiet laugh. "The tact you have, I can only dream of."

"No need to beat around the bush, right?"

"No, I guess not."

"So, is he?" Eva questioned, lifting her glasses from her eyes.

"No," Viviana replied. Of that, she was most sure.

"Women who believe in the fidelity of their husbands don't usually question other women about the fidelity of theirs, Vine."

Viviana swallowed her pride and decided to tell Eva about the situation with Anton and Natalie. She didn't leave details out, even including the situation regarding Natalie's disappearance, the likelihood of Anton being drugged, and how it all possibly related to his recent arrest. Her friend stayed quiet as she spoke, watching their children play in the indoor play park.

"Did you know there was a time when Bratva men didn't believe in marriage?" Eva asked when Viviana finished.

"Sasha mentioned it once, but she didn't go into any depth

about it."

Eva hummed low, nodding. "Men like Anton's grandfather's father, the generation before him, and so on. They were strict on that. Women held the man back. She was his weakness, especially if he loved her. Children were another thing they didn't make an attempt to have, either. Whores, however, were something entirely different. They could have many women, but they couldn't attach themselves to them. If a child was a product of one of those relationships, it was the woman's responsibility to raise it. A man couldn't claim the child as his."

"What's your point?"

"My point, is that Anton's grandfather, or even Ivan's father, probably grew up watching their father's fuck around on their mothers, if their fathers were around to take care of them in any real way. It was commonplace for a man to have mistresses. Why wouldn't it be assumed the next generation of men who had been taught that was okay, think it was acceptable for them, too?"

Eva had a point. People were a product of their raising.

"You didn't answer my question," Viviana pointed out.

"I didn't." Eva leaned back in her chair with a frown, the tabletop suddenly gaining most of her attention. "If it had been a onetime thing, some girl he just met, screwed, and was done with, it might have been easier for me. Instead, it was a woman he'd known for years—one he loved. If she was a stronger woman, Ivan would have married her, but that was why they didn't work out in the first place. He didn't simply have sex with another woman, he had an entire relationship built with her. Around our marriage, of course."

Viviana stared at her friend, unsure of what to say. "I'm sorry."

Eva waved the apology off. "Don't be. We were young and stupid. Our first daughter was just a baby. The marriage we built wasn't a partnership, but a game of sorts. He hurt me, so I hurt him. Enemies sharing a bed. I hated him as much as I worshiped him. We fucked, we fought. That was it, really. It wasn't healthy."

The couple Eva spoke about wasn't the one Viviana knew. Ivan adored his wife and their three daughters. The respect he showed her, many men could learn from. At times, his devotion could rival Anton's, and that was saying something.

"I understood why it was her, though," Eva continued. "She was his past—the woman he had intended to marry long before he met me. Someone who had gotten under his skin in the best and worst way. Essentially, she was to him what Ivan was to me."

"That's not an excuse, Eva. He married you."

"I can assure you, as much as it tore Ivan apart, it is possible to love more than one person at a time in a romantic way." Eva shrugged, picking up her to-go cup of coffee and taking a sip. "Things that appear simple rarely are."

"You said she was a weak woman," Viviana said, wondering what that meant exactly.

"In her head, she was unhealthy. Mentally unstable and had been for years. From what I understood, she battled depression her entire life."

Viviana didn't like where this was going at all, but she stayed silent, anyway.

"That doesn't make a person weak," Eva added with a pointed look, "...don't get me wrong, that's not what I mean. What made her weak was that she used it to her benefit. Threatening to hurt herself, or worse, to bring him back, even when she knew he had a child, and a wife he loved. She wouldn't let him go, and Ivan felt responsible. I was just ... lost."

"What changed?" Viviana wondered.

"One day the threats weren't threats anymore, Vine."

Oh.

"And Ivan?"

Eva blinked away the shininess from her gaze, dropping the sunglasses back down in place. "He grieved. I let him. What else could I do?"

Viviana watched the four children make another round on

the rubber floor surrounding the play park. Ivan and Eva's oldest daughters towered over little Demyan and Gia. The two girls were only a year apart in age, which meant to Viviana that while Ivan and Eva had been struggling with the consequences of an affair, they somehow managed to have another child in the process.

"That must have been hard," Viviana murmured, staring at the second oldest girl.

"Hmm, what?"

"To have another child while struggling with the possibility of your marriage breaking down, and things. A different woman would have walked away and cut her losses. Hell, I would have walked away, Eva."

"Chrissy is not my biological daughter, Vine."

Shock poured over Viviana like a bucket of cold ice water. Frantically, she tried to catch up to speed without seeming like an idiot. "Ivan's and the other woman?"

Eva nodded once. "I didn't know until after, of course. It was the one thing Ivan kept from me the whole time. Ivan brought her home that day, Vine. He brought her home to where she belonged so that she could be loved and cared for, not used as a bartering chip between her parents. And I love her just the same as my other two because she needs and deserves a mother—a good mother. People know. Anton does, for example. It's not something you can hide, suddenly having a six month old daughter in your arms."

"Why didn't someone tell me?"

"Why would they?" Eva asked back, but she didn't sound harsh. "I adopted her the moment I was able. I share her last name. I love her and her father. She doesn't know, either, and I don't want her to."

"Why did you forgive him?"

"Because I love him, so I chose to trust him."

"Doesn't that make us weak, though?"

Eva smiled. "No, it makes us strong enough to see the truth and fight for it."

• • •

"Your music is garbage."

The Seether song whining through the speakers was turned down.

"It is not," Anton argued, flipping Ivan the bird behind his back.

Ivan snorted. "I hope you don't let Demyan listen to this."

"Actually, I do. It's not my fault my child has taste, Ivan."

Demyan could listen to whatever in the hell he wanted for music, as long as it was music and not The Wiggles, or some other vomit-worthy kid crap. Three Days Grace was a particular favorite of his son's, but the kid also shared Anton's love of Metallica. Demyan would crawl into a corner, play with his toys while his father worked out, and simply listen. The boy liked music. There was nothing wrong with that.

Like father, like son.

"Don't you worry he's going to repeat some of this?" Ivan asked.

"So? Does letting my child listen to his choice in music make for bad parenting?"

"I'm not saying it does, man. But his daycare might think differently."

Anton didn't give a shit about the opinions coming out of Demyan's daycare. Ever since Anton was arrested, the high-priced, hand-me-down-riches daycare wouldn't even allow his child to return. It didn't look good on them, they said. Other parents were concerned about how Demyan might affect their children.

Right. The toddler with a mobster father was sure to be a bad influence, what with his preference for loud music, the occasional shot of apple juice, and matchbox cars. Whatever. Give Demyan a decade of growing up in the Bratva way, and Anton knew they'd know what a bad influence really was. Then, he might actually accept their bullshit. Right now, he was just a baby practically.

Anton refused to play into their high society games. He swallowed the tuition lost, having his son blacklisted from all the other daycares of the same standard, and said screw it. Everything Demyan learned was taught from his mother and father, anyway. That daycare had done little but introduce his son to some of the children of New York's richest. That was it, really.

Eventually, Demyan would rub elbows with those same kids all on his own.

"The daycare kicked him out for being my son," Anton finally said.

"Why didn't you tell me? They'd have had a lawsuit shoved down their throats so fast they wouldn't have known what was choking them."

"It's not important. Vine was pissed off, but she knows it's better to leave it alone."

Anton shrugged, stepping away from the punching bag. After un-taping his knuckles, he pulled off the T-shirt he wore and reached for the towel to wipe the sweat off his face and neck.

"Jesus, Anton," Ivan exclaimed.

Anton looked over his shoulder at his friend with a furrowed brow. "What?"

"Did you fall on a cat, or what?"

A devilish smirk formed on Anton's lips before he tossed the towel back to the bench. Seven Lights was still a no-go for Bratva business, and they hadn't been able to open the place back up for regular business quite yet, so meetings were required to be held elsewhere. Anton decided to take a week and chill in an attempt to get some of the media and stress off his back, so his home seemed like the best place to do that.

"No, not a cat. Call her kitten, though, and the claws really come out."

Fuck, there were a particular set of scratches along his neck that stung like nothing else every time he turned his head, but Anton loved it.

"Are you two …?" Ivan trailed off with a lift of his brow.

"Getting there."

"Well, that's good."

"Yep."

That was a bit of an understatement, but Anton wasn't in the mood to discuss his sex life with his friend. Over the last week, things with his wife were great. More than, even. They could talk, or be quiet if they needed. Neither held back if something was bothering them. Sexually, well …

Anton was exhausted from keeping his wife up at night the way he liked best or being woken up by her early in the morning, he was sore as hell in the best ways, and he was fucking *satisfied* with it all. It'd been far too long since he could say that and mean it. Yes, they were rough, like they were fighting to find the softness in sex again, but that was just fine, too.

Reviving the physical intimacy with Viviana seemed to help her, as well. The depression was starting to wane, Anton noticed. She wasn't as quiet and she was actually starting to discuss the possibility of going back to the bookstore.

Anton sympathized with Viviana on that one, though. While the small amount of blood she had lost there was cleaned, and everything was back the way it was, it was the memory of knowing their baby was gone in that place she couldn't get rid of. Anton wasn't about to push his wife to go back to work if she wasn't emotionally ready to do so.

"Do we have a trial date?" Anton asked.

"Not a definite one, but it'll be within two or three months. That's the best approximation I can give."

Anton was starting to get nervous over his upcoming legal issues. This wasn't some little case about him being involved with dealing drugs or guns. It wasn't about him being suspect in something worthy of a few years' probation. No, this was his life on the line.

"There is no way in hell I am looking at a ten by eight cell for the rest of my life, Ivan."

"You're panicking."

"Wouldn't you?" Anton snapped back.

Ivan shrugged and took a seat on the weight bench. "Sure, but we have a while to get our plan perfected. Besides that, you've been staying out of trouble and whatnot."

"They did a fucking press conference yesterday. Talking about taking a stand on crime in New York and cleaning up the dirt in the city. All the while, we both know the mayor is sitting in his office having his cock sucked by a ten-thousand dollar a night whore and getting the blow I import delivered to him on the city's key. This city is so damned corrupt, the last thing they have to worry about is *me*."

"Yeah, I saw that," Ivan said, grimacing. "It's tough, but turn cheek. It's better on you to keep your mouth out of it."

"They're slandering the hell out of me, Ivan. A fair trial is liable to be a joke the way this is playing out. And really, I don't care, but I have to think of Viviana and Demyan, too."

"Anton—"

"Viviana brought home one of those socialite magazines—fucking rags. I took her to dinner the night before, and we're on the cover the next day. Instead of gossiping about us like they usually do, they're talking about my wife standing beside her criminal husband even with the possibility of me spending life behind bars. It's no wonder why Demyan isn't allowed back to daycare."

Ivan clamped his mouth shut and let Anton rant. It was exactly what he needed to do, after all. The last thing he wanted was to worry Viviana over his thoughts and concerns, never mind his frustrations. She had more than enough going on in her own head without him adding to it.

"And Oceana is a *gated fucking community*," Anton added. "I know what Nicoli paid for this property. There should be absolutely no way reporters are getting inside, let alone sitting on my doorstep when I go out to run."

"It's winter. What in the fuck are you doing jogging in the snow?" Ivan asked.

"Because your wife called here at six-thirty this morning and woke up Demyan while I was busy with my wife.

Meaning, Viviana didn't get to finish what she woke me up to do because Demyan doesn't understand closed doors are meant to stay that way. I haven't had blue balls that bad since my kid was a newborn, okay? I needed a cold run."

Ivan chuckled, avoiding his friend's glare. "I didn't need to know that."

"Eva shouldn't be calling here that early."

"You're not really pissed off at Eva, though, are you?"

"No," Anton mumbled into the palm of his hand. "I'm just ... frustrated."

"Some of these things are easily fixable if you want them to be, man."

Anton sighed, feeling useless. "I'm not usually so distracted."

"You've got a lot on your plate. I think we can excuse it," Ivan replied. "But like I said, some of this stuff can be fixed, you just have to ask for help."

"I shouldn't have to do anything," Anton said, frowning up at the ceiling. "I'm more than capable of handling my own business. I always have."

"Your father and Nicoli needed help, too, Anton. They didn't do everything by themselves. You can't possibly expect to run your guys, keep an eye on your businesses, deal with the public, this trial, and handle the family side of it all alone. It's a lot, considering you're needing to do most dealings under the table. It's no wonder you're frustrated and snapping out at people. Just ask."

"I feel fucking shady. Like a drug dealer on the corner. Having to hide or dance around because all eyes are on me, knowing exactly what I'm doing."

"Sucks, I know," Ivan murmured. "But even when I get you off of this, the eyes are still going to be watching, man. The public, especially."

That just disgusted Anton in a way he couldn't explain.

"You're so sure you can win, Ivan."

Ivan smiled his cocky grin. The one he'd learned from Anton. "Of course I am. I wasn't chosen to be your lawyer

110

for nothing. There are so many guys out there looking for Natalie it's fucking ridiculous. She won't make it to the courtroom to tell her lies, I promise you that. And if all else fails, we're just going to feed the mouths cash or threaten our way out of it. The Bratva is nothing if not full of money and bullies. We're not the first to do it, Anton. You will not spend time in prison for murder. Trust me."

Oddly, Anton did. A slight bit of his stress eased away at Ivan's declaration.

"I need a backup plan, though," Anton said quietly, avoiding his friend's gaze.

"What kind?"

"For me, Vine, and Demyan. If all goes to hell in the trial, we don't find that bitch—"

"We *will*."

"But if we don't," Anton insisted. "I need a guarantee. Something, I don't care."

Ivan drummed his fingers to his knee, resting back to the wall as he contemplated Anton's words. "Like getting out of this country's extradition reach, you mean."

"Could be one way."

"It'd be the only way," Ivan said. "And you would have to make sure you kept your ass out of trouble because if you lost your bail, you're back in until the verdict. There's no chance of getting away, then."

Anton swallowed the sinking feeling in his gut. "I've done okay so far."

"You have, but all they have to do is get wind of the possibility you're planning to leave the country and you'd be back at Rikers so fast ..."

A shudder crept up Anton's spine. "I hate that fucking place."

Ivan pursed his lips, studying his fingers with interest. "There are men in the Bratva who would consider this a betrayal on your part, also. That's something you need to consider. You wouldn't just be running from the law, you'd be running from your family."

"I was raised with the same rules and values as those men," Anton said, knowing it was true. "The only difference from me and them was that Nicoli made it seem like he was repeating Bratva code all the damned time, but I knew what he wasn't saying, too. He had one child by blood—Vine. He made damned sure when he was gone, I could and would take care of her first no matter what. Family comes first. Love and honor my family above all else. Protect what is mine at all costs. I'm the only one who gets to choose which family I do that for."

"So far," Ivan mused, cocking a brow, "... it's been the Bratva."

"I've done everything asked of me for my family."

Ivan cleared his throat, looking uncomfortable. Anton wasn't accustomed to seeing that from his friend. He wondered, momentarily, if he had made a mistake in telling Ivan his true feelings about the Bratva and where Anton would draw his line. After all, Ivan was a vor, too.

"Did Nicoli ever tell you what happened the night he made me?" Ivan asked, his voice a whisper.

"No. I was seventeen and unmade. I wasn't allowed to be inside to watch."

"I accepted the *Vor v Zakone,* but I refused to swear allegiance to him, or any other man in that room."

Anton's gaze snapped up like a lightning bolt had swept his insides. Ivan never should have been made if he refused. In fact, he should have been killed for knowing what he did and making it as far as he had, but being unable to finish it. To the Bratva, that was weakness.

"What?"

Ivan gave a single nod. "He was looking me right in the eye, and I couldn't say it. No one else was close enough to hear Nicoli pleading with me to just say it, telling me what he'd have to do if I didn't. *Give me something, Ivan,* he'd said. *Anything for me to trust you.*

"So I swore to you," Ivan finished, shocking Anton a little more. "And only you. You were the reason I was still alive as it was. Just this crazy kid I respected in my own way, so confident and cocky. I knew, even with your ridiculousness at the time, you were going to be great one day. You only needed the chance to be. Nicoli knew he was going to have to surround you with people like me so you could make it, Anton."

"I know."

Anton owed everything he had to the men he was closest to. He never denied that.

"I know you think he was preparing you for his daughter, but man, he was organizing everybody else for you, too. So whatever you need, I'll do it. Always."

Sometimes, with men, it was better not to acknowledge emotional shit. Other times, it was needed. Anton wasn't sure which one this fell under. Ivan didn't give him the chance to figure it out, either.

"As far as those goddamn reporters you talked about, that's a pretty simple fix."

"How so?"

"I know Vine doesn't want bulls at the house anymore, but at least one outside would keep the bastards away and out of eyesight, Anton. She likes Rory, and since he hasn't had much work to do with keeping an eye on Demyan lately, apparently—you still should have told me about that fucking daycare—there's no reason why he can't be here watching after your wife and son. He'll be happy to, and you know it."

"True," Anton admitted begrudgingly. "I could just scare them off myself."

"I'd rather you didn't. It would only make my job harder."

Anton rolled his eyes. "Fine, whatever."

"I'll get Erik to put a couple of calls in for some city people," Ivan continued, not missing a beat. "Fill up their pockets so they'll shut their mouths for a while and get off your back with the press conferences and slandering. We can't control everyone, but we can sure as fuck blackmail a few into keeping their opinions to themselves. After all, there's a reason we have their home numbers."

Anton smirked. His lawyer could be a downright bastard when he wanted.

"I was trying to be clean about it, Ivan."

"Sometimes clean doesn't work. Let's dirty it up a bit and throw some mud back."

A great deal of the frustration and stress Anton had felt earlier was waning. The tension in his body that he'd been attempting to work out with the punching bag seemingly gone with one simple discussion. Damn, he should have done this sooner.

"Tell Viviana to leave those rags at the store where they belong," Ivan added with a pointed look.

"Already did."

"And keep going out with your wife, even if they do put you on the cover of every magazine in town. Anton, whether you like it or not, people want to see your face right now. They need to see you doing normal things, not the bullshit they're hearing about. Take Demyan to the park with Rocco, or Vine to dinner. Don't let those idiots stop you from living. You can't stay in this house forever. It makes you look guilty."

"I am," Anton said.

"But they don't know that for sure," Ivan replied just as fast. "What's left?"

"Nothing, really."

Ivan cocked a brow. "The daycare."

Anton's scowl didn't affect his friend in the least. "I don't care about that place. They can take their high society attitudes and their hand-me-down trust fund kids and shove it up their asses."

"You don't care, but your wife does," Ivan interrupted. "And it has nothing to do with how she looks to the public, or your son. You know why it pisses Viviana off, Anton."

"The private high school she attended expelled her in freshman year because of other girls starting crap revolving around her father," Anton said, hating to even hear it himself. "The school thought she was a bad influence and a distraction to the other students. Yeah, I know. She loved that school, and they made it hell for a long while until Nicoli and Roman stepped in to stop it all."

"This isn't any different, man, simply a younger version of it. It's no wonder she doesn't want to take it again for her own son." Ivan shrugged, sighing. "Demyan is intelligent. Like crazy smart. Sometimes it freaks people out how well he converses and what he already knows at his age. That kid needs to be challenged. He needs his schedule, his daycare, and he needs to be mentally fulfilled when he gets home at the end of the day so he can shut his brain off."

"My kid does not freak people out," Anton muttered under his breath, offended at the idea. Fuck those people if an intellectually bright child scared them.

"For some he does. They're wondering how much he really understands, especially when he's quiet. Like it or not, that kid is you all over again. Don't let him be bored and restricted at home because you have a superiority complex. There's a reason why we need to put our kids in those schools and it has little to do with keeping up with the rich appearance and more because of who we are. Public schools are dangerous for our children. It's too easy for people to get to them there. Demyan has to be in a private establishment where he can be watched and protected. Swallow your pride and play their games.

"What is it they want exactly?" Ivan asked.

"What else? Money, likely."

"I'll get Erik on it Monday." Ivan stood up, brushing off his pant legs before tossing his hands into his pockets. "We both know you could have handled most of this on your own, so let's be honest. It's not that you were worried about how it was affecting you, you're concerned about it bothering your wife. Vine gets up in arms and you get stressed out. Am I right?"

Anton made a disgruntled noise. Ivan knew him too well. "Don't feel too smug, asshole. You've had nearly two decades of learning my habits and moods."

"And I've only seen you with your wife for three of those years," Ivan quipped. "Regardless, this isn't what I came over for today. Eva called earlier. They were just stopping for something to eat and then they were going home. Anyway, Gia asked if Demyan could come to our house for the night. Vine didn't mind, but told Eva to call me to make sure it was cool with you, and I figured it'd be a good time for him to."

Anton snorted. "Man, when he's sixteen instead of nearly three, you'll be running him out of your house with a gun when your daughter calls on him."

"They're just kids, Anton."

"Not for long. You said it, he's my son through and through, and if Demyan really likes Gia now, how do you think he'll feel when he's older?"

Actually, Demyan's fondness of the girl was kind of cute, in a kid way. Whenever they were together, he followed Ivan's youngest daughter around with little interest for anything else. For a toddler, that was quite a feat.

Ivan's gaze narrowed. "Quit it. Stop distracting me with future nonsense about my daughters. I don't have to deal with that for at least another ten years."

"Your oldest is twelve. What do you mean ten years? Get a fucking clue."

"I hope you have a daughter someday, Anton. Just for that."

Deciding he'd antagonized his friend enough, Anton asked, "So why is tonight a good night for you to take my son?"

Ivan scratched the back of his neck. "Yeah, about that … Adrik—"

"Fuck no," Anton interjected, throwing his hand up. "No way. I am not messing around with Jersey again. The Belovs are gone, so any and all contacts between our families is done. Leave it that way."

"Adrik isn't a Belov and you know it, man. And, he's the new boss for Jersey. You haven't made any effort to—"

"Why would I?"

116

"Stop interrupting me for a goddamn minute, Anton. Listen, he's only a year younger than you. From the Jersey side of things, he's garnered a lot of respect for the way he cleaned house in that family."

Anton forced himself to hold back his irritation. "Our Bratva doesn't need to be mixing with Jersey Bratva after everything. Hell, I'm being charged with their old boss's murder for Christ's sake. It's that simple. Leave it alone."

"I'm not suggesting you should mix business," Ivan replied carefully. "However, there very well might be some deals Adrik has that could be of use to us for. Like I said earlier, once this trial is done, you're going to have to take some steps back into the shadows."

Anton's mind went silent for an entire thirty seconds. "I hope you're not suggesting I give any fucking control of my brotherhood to someone who is not an Avdonin."

"Absolutely not. But, Adrik is looking for something particular, and you will be, too. I think you should have a sit-down with him."

"And what does my son staying with you have to do with a sit-down with Jersey?" Anton wondered.

"Well, he wants to have dinner … with you, your wife, and your son."

Anton groaned, finally getting the point. "Viviana is in no mood to play the Bratva wife, Ivan. Beyond that, my son has no reason to be a part of it, either."

"Trust me on this, man. Good thing you have a child-free night to convince Vine, huh? Thank me later."

Chapter Nine

"Something smells amazing," Viviana said, dropping her purse to the counter.

Clarissa beamed from the other side. "Dressed herring and kissel for dessert."

Viviana's stomach growled at the thought. Kissel was a particular Russian dessert soup both her husband and her son loved. Viviana enjoyed it, too. Despite her skills in the kitchen, she couldn't seem to get the kissel right, though.

"Are you making those puffy pancake things, too?" Viviana asked.

"*Syrniki*, Vine. Yes, once this is all just about finished, I'll drop them in the fryer and get the garnish ready. What do you want to top them with, jam, honey, or apple sauce?"

Yeah, the drool was starting to build up in her mouth. Viviana had a certain appreciation for Russian food and if she was asked what she would want for supper, these probably would have been her choices.

"Demyan loves honey on them," Viviana said, even though her son was spending the rest of the day and night away from home.

Clarissa smiled. "So does his father."

"Let's do that, then. You could have called me. I would have come home to help."

Clarissa waved the comments off. "I think you needed the day out of this house. You look better, not so tired. Anton will like to see that, I'm sure."

"Really? Because I'm exhausted."

After a couple of hours at the play park, Eva and Viviana took the kids to a pizza place to eat. After handing Demyan over, Viviana ran a couple of errands that lasted until one in the afternoon. Then, she found herself standing in front of her bookstore. It still made her heart ache.

"Sometimes being exhausted is a good thing," Clarissa murmured, studiously watching her hands in the dough. "It shows you've allowed your mind and body to feel, which means you're healing."

Viviana felt like they were talking about something else, now. Nearly a month and a half after her miscarriage, she figured her mind and body had felt enough. She decided to change the subject. "How old were you when you began working for Nicoli?"

Clarissa's kneading of the dough stopped long enough for her to look up. "I didn't begin working for him, exactly. I simply changed hands—from one man, to another. It was after, when I knew he didn't want to hurt or use me, that I began working for him of my own free will."

"Oh," Viviana said quietly. "But, how old?"

"Thirty-eight."

Nicoli died in when he was only sixty-one. "Anton says you two were close."

Something unknown flashed in the maid's eyes. "What else does he say?"

"Nothing."

Viviana's husband left Nicoli's private life, especially where women were concerned, locked up tight. What Viviana knew for sure was that her biological father had only one woman he married, to help her and her son leave an abusive marriage and because he grew to care for her, but she died while Anton's mother was still pregnant for him. A year or so later, Nicoli met Viviana's mother, Christina. Their relationship was a onetime thing, leading Viviana to believe he probably had more of those.

As far as Clarissa and Nicoli were concerned, that was somewhat of a mystery. Clarissa had not been a free woman, of that Viviana knew for sure. She was also aware her friend and confidant had been treated badly, hurt, and abused before she came to Nicoli's home. Clarissa didn't talk about it, and Viviana didn't push her to.

"I have his journals and things, but they felt clinical ..."

Viviana trailed off with a shrug.

"And you've never really gotten a glimpse inside his head or heart," Clarissa finished for her.

"No, I suppose not. Was he a nice man?"

"Very. I would say tender, actually, but Nicoli is probably cursing me from the heavens. But, he was also tough. He watched a great deal more than he talked, and some found that unsettling."

Viviana found herself leaning on the counter, attention captured. "Really?"

Clarissa nodded, a small smile forming. "He wasn't a loud man, despite his size. Nicoli liked to command, to be in control. He was very regal even at his dirtiest times. Sometimes it was all too easy to forget he was a Russian mob boss and not just a charming, dangerous man."

"Reminds me of someone else."

"Doesn't it?" Clarissa asked, her smile turning into a conspiratorial grin. "I began living with Nicoli when Anton was about ten. Already he was a handful, looking for trouble in corners. The home they lived in was sectioned off into two homes. Nicoli had the smaller bottom section of the house, and they had the top. That boy spent more time downstairs than he did upstairs."

"Were they always close?"

"Always, from what I remember. Even when Anton was going through his phases as a teen and scaring the life out of his mother. When he would come home late and find the stairwell locked to get up to his home, Nicoli would leave his own door open. I'd wake up in the early morning to find them in the living room talking quietly like they did. While Anton was trying to fly too high, Nicoli helped to keep him grounded."

Feeling as if she'd gotten a small look inside a man she barely knew, Viviana pushed away from the counter to stand up straight. "Thank you, Clarissa."

The maid shrugged. "No problem. And Vine ..."

"Yes?"

"Nicoli's home only had two bedrooms. One of which was his office, the other was his room."

Oh.

Finally, Viviana had an answer to her question.

"Did you love him?"

Clarissa smiled down into her dough, but tears wet her bottom lashes. "Very much. I was able to give him what was left of me, and he gave me the pieces of him he hadn't left behind with the others. We were older, had lived, and lost. Certainly not the kind of people who were whole in our hearts. For us, it worked."

"Others?" Viviana asked, curious.

"His wife. Your mother."

"He didn't really know my mother, though."

Clarissa's grey eyes held a conviction Viviana couldn't deny when she said, "That doesn't mean he didn't fall in love with her. Now, go get ready for supper. It'll be done in about an hour."

"Where's Anton?"

A floury hand waved towards the upstairs. "Napping, I think."

Despite Clarissa believing Anton was sleeping, he wasn't. Viviana entered their master bedroom in just enough time to hear the shower start in the connecting bath. The sound system in the bathroom began as well, a sweet melody echoing out from the space. A song that was nothing like the harsh loudness her husband usually listened to.

Padding quietly across the room, Viviana leaned in the doorway of the bathroom. Anton, inside the shower under the spray of steaming water with his back turned, didn't seem to notice his wife watching him.

Water wet his dark hair, rolling off his shoulders and down the line of his strong back. The black licks of his tattoo seemed to turn even darker under the wetness. The stars on both his shoulders moved with the flow of his body.

Like this, Viviana loved to watch her husband. Natural, quiet, and free. Every line and curve of his body available for her to see under the glow of the shower spotlights. Anton rolled his neck, placing both hands to the tiled wall and allowed the hot spray to fall on the back of his shoulders.

Visibly, Viviana could see the stiffness leave his tense muscles. Relaxed, his stance took on a more sensual tone. The sexy confidence he usually sported was back in place. But for a brief moment, she had seen his stress.

"You could join me instead of only staring at me," Anton said so low Viviana strained to hear over the gentle music.

"How long did you know I was standing here?"

"I heard the bedroom door open," he answered.

Viviana licked her lips, taking a step further into the bathroom. "Did you know Nicoli loved my mother?"

Anton's shoulders jumped at the question. "I assumed he did, but I never outright asked. It wasn't my business to, but I knew him. Nicoli didn't use women. Was he a saint? No, but he was the kind of man who needed a connection with a woman to be with her."

"Huh. Why didn't you think to tell me that before?"

"Because your mother loved Roman, even in her anger and hurt. The feelings he had weren't shared and Nicoli was aware of that, probably. You're still staring, Vine."

"I like to stare at you."

A simple glance over his shoulder, staring through the spray of water, heated Viviana's insides up to a fever pitch. The blue of his gaze was burning, knowing. "Missed you today, baby."

"Did you?"

Anton nodded. "I always do, but I'm glad you did something other than clean the house and look at the walls."

Viviana flinched, ignoring the sadness rushing her veins. "It's getting better."

"I noticed. I'm relieved."

Anton turned around, leaning back into the wall. While the water rushed down in front of him, Viviana's vision of him wasn't blurred in the least. The dark trail of hair that led from his navel down to his groin caught her gaze. Between his thighs, his cock hung semi-hard and heavy. Their morning had been interrupted by a phone call and an overzealous Demyan, but she'd had him the night before—twice over, actually. He'd woken her up around three with his teeth scraping along her neck and his fingers working a rough beat between her legs, too.

Still, Viviana's heart picked up and her lungs stuttered on the intake. Anton was a man, so words like handsome and distinguished should be the first that came to her mind. Instead, Viviana got stuck on words like beautiful and aching. That's how he made her feel.

"Come join me," Anton repeated.

"I shouldn't. Supper is almost ready," she offered in explanation.

"Not for a while, though. I know what she's cooking. I didn't say we were going to fuck."

Viviana laughed at his brazenness, but she couldn't hide the shiver of want rolling up her spine, either. They would fuck if she got in the shower with him. Of course they would. Already, desire was pooling in her gut, heating her core. The lace panties she wore were likely damp with arousal.

"We both know it'll lead to that eventually."

"And that's a bad thing?" Anton asked, cocking his eyebrow.

"No, I didn't say that."

"If I promise to be good, will you come in here and help me wash the sweat I worked up beating the hell out of the punching bag off me, please?"

Viviana couldn't deny Anton a thing when he asked so nicely. "Fine."

There was no time wasted on getting undressed. Viviana pulled the elastic holding her hair back in a ponytail free, tossing it to the counter before she stepped into the large stand up shower to join her husband. Without warning, Anton's fingers were tangled in her hair, bunching the strands up to the back of her neck with a tender touch that took Viviana by surprise. Then, she found her back to the cold wall as Anton stepped between her legs.

"You promised to be good," Viviana warned breathlessly.

Kisses from his mouth pressed down to her collarbones, up under her neck, and back to her ear. A burning heat began to spread from Viviana's middle outwards. Anton's free hand drove down her side, stopping at her hip to grab tight.

"Tell me it's ever not good with us. You get me so fucking hot. It's ridiculous."

"It is always good," she said in a hum. "But you wanted me to help wash you."

"I'm a big boy. I've been showering alone for years. It's not my fault you're gullible, Vine."

"I am not! I told you what would happen if I got in this shower with you."

Viviana let her fingers dance down Anton's chest, feeling his muscles jump under her touch. At his cock, she palmed his length gently, getting him harder, working him up further.

"I was dying up here this morning." Anton's tone turned gruffer, his tongue peeking out to wet his lips. "I think you enjoyed knowing I had to finish myself off, thinking about that sweet mouth of yours. Fucking candy mouth, Vine. Sweet like sugar and it kills you like a poison."

Viviana laughed breezily. "I could make it up to you and finish that now, if that's what you were looking for."

"No," Anton said with a shake of his head. "Not below me. You know I don't like seeing you like that."

Three years of marriage and never once had she sucked his cock on her knees while he stood above her. Anton was a controlling, possessive man, especially in the bedroom. Viviana might not have understood his aversion to seeing her like that, but she respected him and didn't push his boundaries on it.

"What's got you so stressed out, huh?" Viviana asked, deciding to distract him from his sexual appetite for a moment. All the while, she kept her hand working a soft beat to his cock, tightening her grip every time she reached the tip of his shaft. Anton shuddered under her motions, but he talked.

"What makes you think I'm stressed out?"

"I'm your wife, I notice things, Anton. Was it that reporter trying to question you this morning?"

"Partly," he admitted quietly. "It's a lot of other things, too. I let it pile up instead of handling it."

"The trial?"

"Again, kind of."

Viviana was terrified of the trial. "You keep telling me everything is going to be okay. Do you actually mean it, or are you saying it to make me compliant?"

"I say it because I trust the people around me. That's all," he replied. "As far as the other things that were bothering me, well, it's worked out. Demyan will be back in daycare within a couple of weeks. Rory is going to be around more to keep the media away from our home. I'm going to get back to work as soon as I can get the go ahead for Seven Lights. It's handled. I'm good, now."

"Ivan?"

Anton grinned, rolling his eyes. "He's a cocky fucker when he wants to be."

"I wonder who he picked that up from."

"At least he learned something good from me."

Viviana sighed, glancing down between their bodies. "Eva told me about Chrissy today."

"You didn't know?"

"No."

Anton frowned. "She's the only one of the three girls with brown eyes and an English name, Vine. She got them from her mother. Besides that, she doesn't even look like the other two, and she really doesn't take much after Ivan, either."

"I never thought to question her eye color or features, Anton. And if I had, I certainly wouldn't have thought Ivan was the one who stepped out on his wife. He adores her."

"And she adores him. Eva is a good woman," Anton stated firmly. "Always was."

"Seems complicated."

"I imagine it was, but they've worked it out privately."

"I love you," Viviana whispered.

Anton smiled a genuine sight. "I love you, too, baby. Now, one more thing ..."

"One more—*oh*!"

Viviana let go of Anton's cock at the same time her head fell back to the wall. He'd released her hip only long enough to get his hand between her thighs, spreading her sex with two fingers while his thumb pressed to her heated clit. Then, Anton was lowering down to his knees. Viviana blindly hit out at the shower head to move the direction of the spray. Instead of drowning Anton in water, it rolled off his back as he looked up at her with a sexy smirk that had her insides quivering.

In a swift movement, he was grabbing her ankle in his palm and hooking her leg over his shoulder. Heated kisses landed on the inside of her thigh. Anton's breath washed along the seam of her exposed sex, close enough to make her ache, as he stared up at her. Already, Viviana could feel her limbs beginning to shake and he hadn't even started, yet.

"I said I'd be good," he muttered darkly. "I didn't say good at what, Vine."

"Jesus—"

"I'll accept God or Anton only. Thank you very fucking much."

No, her husband would never let her get on her knees for him, but she couldn't count the amount of times he did it for her. Instead of the dominant, commanding man he could be, demanding from her body, working it to a sweat, to tremble, and to release, like this, he became the submissive one of the two, giving her what she needed and wanted.

Anton never fucked her with his mouth; he loved her with it. Worshiping every part of her sex slow, soft, and gentle. Tender kisses along her folds, flicks of his tongue that tantalized, and nibbles of his teeth that teased. Taking his time to explore, to make her nerves snap with need, and her mouth beg with want. She became the feast and he was a starved man.

Viviana loved it.

Anton kissed Viviana's waxed sex, keeping his gaze locked on hers. Then, his mouth was encasing her swollen clit, his tongue striking out to sweep through her folds. The deep, dark hum building in the back of his throat confirmed what Viviana already knew—Anton loved the taste of her in his mouth. Suddenly, blinding fast flicks of his tongue licked along her entrance, teasing her further, breaking whatever resolve and sanity she had left.

"Oh, God," Viviana breathed.

Anton released his mouth's hold on her pussy just long enough to grin his smug smirk up at her. "That's acceptable. A little louder, though. Let's see if I can get you screaming it, baby."

"Anton—"

Viviana was going to tell him their house wasn't fucking soundproofed, but she didn't have the damned chance. Before she could even think to breathe another word down at him, Anton's attention was back on her sensitive sex. Every nerve in her body seemed to wake up, jumping alive when his tongue struck her clit with repeated strokes.

The quiet cries escaping her quickly turned to gasping octave. Over and over, his name fell from her lips. Viviana felt her hips rolling into the rhythm of his tongue without her even realizing it. Anton slid his palm along her raised thigh up under her ass, holding firm to keep her still while his other pressed to her hip, pinning her to the cold wall.

Viviana felt trapped under his want in the best way.

"Fuck, fuck, fuck," she chanted, the burning coil in her womb tightening with pleasure.

God, he did that so damned well.

Something hot and heady swept through her blood, making her feel dizzy and drunk. Wanting to move or have some control, Viviana reached down and weaved her fingers into the damp strands of Anton's hair. Chuckles rocked against her sex. The buzzing hum of ecstasy rolled over every inch of her body.

As close as she was to her orgasm under the speed and skill of his tongue, Anton slowed his tempo down. Like she knew he would, he took his time to explore her pussy, licking along her fleshy folds, kissing her inner thighs, and whispering her name so sweet and loving while he did so.

Finally ... *finally* ... he gave her what she needed.

The hand holding firm to her backside let go and two of his fingers slipped through her folds, entering her sex with one thrust as his tongue went back to her clit. Scissoring his digits on the withdrawal, Anton stretched her sensitive tissues, making her feel so full all the while, urging the rest of her to orgasm with spearing strikes of his tongue to her quivering nub. Viviana's fingers tightened in his hair as she came, crying out so loudly the sound of her voice bounced back several times over. Pleasure fell over her in crushing waves.

While the tremors of the orgasm subsided, Viviana met her husband's blazing gaze.

"I have a favor to ask," Anton murmured before laying a kiss to her mound.

With an arched brow, Viviana managed to ask, "Hmm?"

"How do you feel about a dinner, with the Jersey boss?"

Viviana's grasp in his hair gripped harder and she might have enjoyed his flinch just a little. "Anton Daniil ... I swear to God, if you did this to convince me—"

"No, I did this because I've been thinking of tasting you all fucking day, Vine."

She chose not to push him on that end. "We can't afford for us to be seen mingling with people affiliated with the Bratva right now, Anton. It won't look good. That'd be all we need is for some goddamn photographer catching us having a sit-down."

"We'll be careful. Ivan thinks I should do it."

Anton was still on his knees with Viviana's leg slung over his shoulder. She might have been extremely pissed off at the idea, but she was highly aware of her husband's weakened position before her, too. Instead of standing up as her equal to discuss it, he was giving her the power to decide while he was on the ground.

Viviana took a breath, willing away some of her frustration. "I'm not playing games at this dinner, Anton."

"I'm not asking you to, and I don't expect you to be anything more than my beautiful, respectful wife," he assured quietly. "Also, he requested our family, not just you."

It took her an entire minute to figure out what Anton meant. "Demyan, too?"

Oh, no way.

"I don't think so," Viviana stated fiercely. "He's a baby, Anton. He has no reason—"

"Adrik will be coming alone. No bulls. No men. Nothing. It will be a dinner, Vine, with our son. I would say that's a trustworthy show on his part, no?"

Viviana clenched her teeth and stared at anything but the man below her. "Do you trust him as a boss?"

"I don't know him well enough to give you an honest opinion."

"Well, that's a fucking problem, isn't it?"

"Viviana," Anton said, warningly.

"Is his wife and child coming, too?" she bit out.

"As far as I know, he's unmarried. I don't know about any children, either."

Yeah, now Viviana was even less impressed. "Move, Anton."

"No, you listen. I know it's not the best time. I'm not real pleased about including our son in on it. Believe me, I'm not," he insisted at her snort. "But, I have to think about my business and Bratva, too. Like it or not, you're my wife and sometimes you have to show face. Adrik may have an offer for me, something I need. I'm going to give him the chance to offer it. I would like if you were there, also."

Viviana sighed. "Fine, but can he at least wait until spring to make the trip?"

"Vine, that's a month or more away and a lot closer to the

trial than I'm comfortable with."

"Spring, or no me."

This time, it was Anton who sighed. "Fuck it. Spring it is."

Chapter Ten

"Ready?" Anton asked, holding out his hand to his wife. Viviana met his palm with a cold stare and allowed him to help her step out of their SUV. "Smile, baby, please."

Viviana did, but she didn't look all too happy about it.

Winter had melted into spring with its usual slowness and storms. Before they knew what happened, March turned into May. Viviana was still sour about the dinner with the Jersey boss Adrik. In fact, she was so aggravated about it, she barely spoke to Anton all damned day leading up to the event. He was dying.

The valet at the restaurant waited patiently to take the keys for the Mercedes while Anton spoke to his wife. "Vine, you know how much I appreciate you, right?" he asked, leaning down to kiss her cheek.

Viviana flicked a look in his direction, one that stung. "Did I dress appropriately for this?"

The grey dress, knee-length, V-neck, with sleeves reaching to her elbows, was perfectly fine for the dinner. The silver studded heels she wore gave that usual spice and hint of sexiness while keeping it appropriate. Silver bangles hung from her right wrist and a dainty chain with a small diamond rested below the hollow of her throat. Even the little bit of makeup she wore was flawless and not overdone.

"You look beautiful, Viviana. Like always."

"Good. Let's hope your toddler son can make it through this dinner without messing up his suit."

Demyan, still sitting in his safety seat with his matchbox car in hand, was dressed similarly to his father in a black suit with a white shirt underneath, and a tiny black tie to match. He was terribly sharp looking for a nearly three-year-old boy. It helped that he didn't fight too much to get dressed up, given his father pointed out he looked just like him.

Anton thought he was cute as hell.

"I don't think anyone cares if he stays clean, Vine. He's a kid."

Viviana waved at the restaurant. "You do realize this place is not kid friendly, right? It's four-hundred dollars a plate, Anton."

"I know. I also know the upstairs, reserved for VIPs, is whatever the hell we want it to be tonight."

That caught her attention. Anton barely held back his smirk at her surprise. "Really?"

"Really," he confirmed. "Actually, Ivan let me know Adrik suggested it for the private conference dining space upstairs. He arrived about an hour ago. My guys are already downstairs."

"They won't be up there with us?" Viviana asked.

"No. I don't think they need to be, given this is more an introduction and not a business meeting where opinions need to be involved. Smile, let Demyan run around, and enjoy the food, baby. That's all you need to worry about."

Viviana sighed. "I hope so."

Anton stopped to speak with one of the bulls who met with Adrik and the man assured him that as promised, the Jersey boss arrived alone without his people. Well, Anton begged to differ, considering the small girl dressed in a pink chiffon dress with her hair in ringlet curls and a bow holding tight to the man's hand as they entered the upstairs dining room. She looked to be at least Demyan's age, if not a little younger. She was blue-eyed and blonde, much like Adrik.

Adrik Vasin, like Anton, was a commanding man without having to do or say much. It was the first thing Anton noticed about the man. He exuded confidence, and sported an easy smile, though his eyes constantly swept the room, looking for oncoming trouble. That was something Anton knew all too well, also.

"Anton Avdonin, it's a pleasure to finally meet the man who paved the way for my position."

Anton glanced down at the little girl, keeping his son

balanced on his waist while holding his wife's hand. "Who's this?"

Adrik bent down to one knee, tipping the girl's chin up under two fingers. "Sofia, say hello, baby."

Bright blue eyes blinked up at Anton, shocking him at how clear and sweet she looked. In her features, Sofia was the feminine, child-like version of Adrik, telling Anton the man was obviously her father, or very closely related. Anton was positive he was told Adrik had no wife, and there wasn't a woman in the room other than Viviana, so little Sofia's mother clearly wasn't invited to the dinner. Why hadn't he been told about this child?

"Hello," Sofia whispered.

Demyan grinned and wiggled at his father's side. "Hi. My name is Demyan."

"She just turned three last week," Adrik informed. "So these two should get along just fine."

Anton allowed his son to climb down his side to the floor. Once the two children acquainted themselves, they disappeared under one of the many tables, childish giggles following.

"She's beautiful," Viviana said with a smile.

"Thank you. Sofia is the one thing that keeps me sane most days."

"She's your daughter," Anton assumed.

"Yes," Adrik replied.

Anton crossed his arms, taking on a more defensive stance. "Funny, I was told you weren't married and you'd be coming alone. Somehow, I feel duped or lied to."

Viviana used her hand, tucked inside Anton's elbow, to pinch him through the jacket of his suit. "That's enough."

Adrik waved it all off. "My apologies. My daughter's safety is my first concern. After I started making the move to take over Sergei's spot once he was gone, my life was in constant danger, as was hers. Let's be honest, it still is. She was only a baby. I keep as much about her to myself as I possibly can."

"And her mother?" Anton asked.

"She didn't want Sofia. I did. We had an arrangement of sorts, now we don't."

The answer was so frank, it took Anton by surprise. He struggled for an appropriate response. "That's ..."

"Unfortunate, and her loss," Viviana finished for him. "Sofia seems like a sweet child."

Anton could hear the sadness in his wife's voice for the motherless girl.

"She is," Adrik agreed. "Can we allow the servers up and order?"

"Yes, let's do that."

A little under a half an hour later, Anton was pouring a round of vodka into a shot glass. Quickly, he slammed the liquor back, dropped the glass to the table, and slid it towards Adrik who grinned as he plucked it up to take his own. Usually Anton wouldn't drink while out with his family, but this was more of a traditional thing than to get drunk.

To the start of a friendship, and that sort of thing.

He had to admit, in just the small amount of time he knew Adrik, he liked the man. Frank and honest, Adrik said it how he witnessed it. It was clear he also had a magnetic personality, so it was no wonder why the men in Jersey took to him like they did for a boss.

After Adrik dropped the shot glass to the counter, he said, "You have a beautiful wife, Anton."

Anton coughed away his shock at the blunt comment. "I'm aware."

Adrik chuckled. "Don't be offended or worried. I'm not interested, simply stating a fact. She's ..." Trailing off, he turned to nod at Viviana as if in explanation. Currently, she was chasing both Demyan and Sofia around and around the tables, smiling brightly. As if she didn't care about her eight-hundred dollar dress or the shoes she'd kicked off earlier. "Fascinating," Adrik finished quieter. "I never intended to have a wife. I wasn't in the business for one."

"And yet you have a child."

"Ah, well, I didn't plan her, either."

Anton smirked. "That's how they usually come along. I was a bit more careful about my ... activities ... before my wife, however."

"If you don't mind me asking, why was that?" Adrik asked.

"It would have disappointed my family," Anton answered honestly. "I wasn't in agreement about the arrangement they made for me and Vine, but I also knew there was only so much rebellion they would accept from me, too. At eighteen, I had pretty well decided on Viviana all on my own. The rest is history."

"Seems as though an arranged marriage worked for you two," Adrik said, not hiding his surprise in the least.

"If you want to call it that. The agreeing parties were long dead, so I could have just as easily let it go and continued with the way I was. Viviana and I chose this after, not them. We did so because we wanted each other. She's mine, that's all there is to it."

Anton realized how easily Adrik seemed to get the most personal information from him without even trying. It was unsettling and interesting at the same time.

"People must find it's easy to allow you close, Adrik. I can't help but wonder how they felt when you killed them for it."

Adrik cleared his throat and rested back to the bar's top. "I'm not interested in killing you, Anton. Unlike the old boss, I don't want Brighton Beach. I wasn't raised there, it's not my home like it is yours. I'm a Jersey boy through and through."

"I should hope your interest in being here isn't to scope me out. I can assure you if you tried to come after me, at any point, my Bratva would not be an easy target."

"Point taken. I'll remember that. However, I did what I had to. I refused to work under men who were no different than Sergei. No one suspected me, Anton. That's why it was so easy to do it. I was the young brigadier, just a captain. Not at all important and they certainly didn't fear me to make a move to take the boss position."

"I was told you were ruthless about it," Anton murmured.

"I was," Adrik confirmed, nodding. "I needed to make a point. They were either with me, or they weren't. If they weren't ..." He made the sign of a gun with his forefinger and thumb, pulling the trigger. "There was no reason or need to talk about it. Simply finishing it."

Anton said nothing for a short while, instead turning to stare at the young girl who had climbed up on his wife's lap, chatting animatedly with Demyan still on the floor. "If you can ask me personal questions, surely I can ask you one? We're becoming friends, after all."

"Go on."

"Your daughter ... the same question goes for you that you asked me. Why? You said it yourself, you didn't want to be married, and her mother didn't want her. It would have been easy to let her mother get rid of her and move on."

Adrik sucked in a harsh breath, sending Anton a look he couldn't decipher. "You have a son, so surely you must understand what it's like to have a child."

"I always wanted children eventually, just not when I was younger. I think it's a different situation we're talking about here, Adrik."

"Fine, that's true enough," Adrik said a little begrudgingly. "I always knew I was going to make the move someday to take what I wanted. Being boss, I mean. I also knew in doing that, I didn't want to have someone I loved in danger because of my position. That was why the idea of marriage and children turned me off. But, when I found out about her, it was different. I knew that child might very well be my only one. That was why I wanted her so fiercely, why I did everything I could to force her mother to keep her and give her to me."

"And she did, just like that?" Anton asked.

"Nothing is ever simple," Adrik replied. "But yes, just like that, in a way."

"The arrangement you said you had with her mother— what was it?"

Adrik smirked, cocking a brow. "I don't imagine it's any different from the one you have with your wife in bed, except for the fact that I didn't need to share any part of me with her. That's not what she was looking for, either. We fucked, that was all. There were times we weren't as careful as we should have been, but I can't find it in me to regret Sofia."

"Someone should have told me about your daughter, Adrik. I'm extremely offended they didn't. I would have appreciated you bringing her as another show of your trust for me."

"Don't be too angry with them, Anton. Most of them don't know."

Anton barely held back his scoff. "She's three!"

Viviana's head popped up to look in their direction at her husband's raised voice. A simple glance asked a million questions, but Anton dismissed her concerns with a shake of his head. With a frown, she went back to conversing with the kids.

"Fascinating," Adrik said again, watching Viviana. "Most women would get up and insert themselves into a conversation they're aware isn't for them to be included in. She looks to you first."

"Of course she does," Anton snapped. "She's my wife. She trusts me, and besides that, she was raised with Cosa Nostra values by a Don for a father. Viviana takes her concerns about my business to me, and me alone. She doesn't feel a need to voice them publicly."

Once more, Anton realized he'd blurted out personal information about his family to a man he barely knew.

"About my daughter—"

"She's three-years-old," Anton repeated lower, turning to face Adrik. "Please don't insult my fucking intelligence by saying people don't know about her. That's ridiculous and you know it."

Adrik shrugged, waving at Viviana. "What are your biggest weaknesses, Anton? The first people someone would go after to hurt you, to get to you? I think we both know the answer to that question. You don't hide your affections well, not that I blame you. In fact, you've kept your eyes on your family all night. It might seem like I'm slighting you, but really, I respect you for it. You're confident in your position and in the trust you have for your men. I am not.

"Some men, many more than I am comfortable with, would hurt my daughter if they were aware of how much I love her," Adrik continued, meeting Anton's gaze head-on. "If they thought it would ruin me—and it would—they would do it. Sofia has lived apart from me, and while I visited with her every day, I did so in secret. I needed to keep her safe. I couldn't risk someone getting idiotic ideas when she's just an innocent child. So yes, the people I trust have access to my daughter, and only them. And even those people do not get to see my affection for her, they only know of her existence and relation to me."

Adrik had given Anton access to his daughter and he'd been very open about his feelings towards the little girl. He wasn't entirely sure what Adrik expected to gain from doing it, but Anton understood the point of what he was saying. "You trust me."

"I'm trying to," Adrik said, offering a smile. "But I can understand why I made you uncomfortable, keeping her presence quiet like I did. Your men, don't be angry with them. They likely assumed a tiny girl wouldn't be of much danger to you or your family."

"Be honest, Adrik, what did you come here for?"

"To meet you. I have a lot of respect for you, Anton. I owe you a great deal, if we consider all that you've done."

"There has to be more than that," Anton muttered.

"You're right." Adrik took the time to pour another shot, offering it to the Pakhan across from him. Anton tossed back the shot and waited. "For the last two years, I have been cleaning house. Fixing problems. Getting rid of the issues. Smoking out the rats. Money, or making it, has been the last thing on my mind."

Now, Anton's interest was piqued. "Outside of the normal

dealings, Sergei was dabbling in importing substance and diamonds. He tried to get me in on it the latter. I'll tell you the same thing I told him. I don't do diamonds. I don't see the point. I also won't touch human trafficking."

Adrik agreed with a nod. "My issue isn't what to import. I'm fine with drugs, and we have more than a big enough territory and market to get it on the streets and sold. That's not the problem."

"Then what is?"

"Getting the product," Adrik explained simply.

Ah, Anton thought. There it was. "You don't have the contacts."

"Or the reputation," Adrik added. "Coming out of the woodwork like I did, so unexpectedly, had its downfalls. No one knows my name. Shippers aren't willing to work with someone who hasn't built up any work relationships to reflect on. Runners don't trust a man they don't know. I'm in a difficult spot."

"I can see that," Anton said. "Did you think I would hand over my contacts?"

Adrik laughed loudly, shaking his head. "Of course not. I expected you to tell me to go fuck myself if I asked like that."

"I'm pretty close to it," Anton admitted. "We've worked with our shippers and runners for years. My grandfather and his men built up those relationships. It wasn't easy. They trust me for a reason. I can't simply hand their names over to you, Adrik. Besides that, it'd be a competition. Who is paying more ... things of that nature. Money makes people greedy and messy. It just wouldn't work."

"But you can vouch for me. And the fact of the matter is simple, Anton, you need a little less spotlight right now. Everyone is looking at you. The officials are chasing your people like dogs. Whether you like it or not, your contacts are going to start seeing you as a risk—their liability. Even if you can get off on these charges—"

"I will," Anton interrupted sharply.

"Even if you do, you'll still be the face of organized crime in New York. The one boss the officials look to every time something happens. Your contacts will start turning your men away, refusing your jobs. You know it, and so do I. You need a backup, and you need it now."

Anton tossed his clenched fists in his pockets, attempting to hide his frustrations. Adrik was right in all he said, and that pissed Anton off something fierce. He'd been so caught up in the drama of his upcoming trial and the difficulties he and Viviana had faced over the last few months that his Bratva business had been pushed to the side.

No wonder Ivan wanted him to do this dinner.

Fuck.

"Are you offering to work with me?" Anton asked, not bothering to hide the sarcasm in his tone. "Because again, I don't think that'd work out too well on the competition side of things, Adrik."

"No," the Jersey boss replied instantly. "I'm offering to work *for* you."

Anton's thought process cut off. Bosses didn't work for other bosses. That wasn't how it worked in their world. That would, essentially, make him Adrik's boss.

"Forgive me, but that makes even less sense. If you're wanting to make your own way, make your mark and reputation, working for me surely won't do it."

"I'm aware of that," Adrik said dryly. "The arrangement would be a little ... unconventional, sure."

"That's saying it lightly."

"But it would also require a great deal of trust. Have I not shown you that? And respect, that too?"

Anton chewed on his thoughts. "You have. I'm listening, Adrik."

"That's all I want, Anton. Just listen. If you think it can be done to your satisfaction, I'm more than happy to work with you for the deal to be more to your benefit than mine, because eventually, it'll come back to me tenfold, anyway."

Anton watched his son climb up on a chair, kicking his little legs out and sitting straight and proud. He knew, without a doubt, he needed to set things up for his boy. Already, Demyan was so much like his father that it was hard to deny the likelihood of him not being involved in the Bratva when he was older.

"So," Anton mused, drumming his fingers to the bar, "… work for me, hmm?"

Adrik grinned. "You're as arrogant as they say, aren't you?"

"Oh, yes. More so. Talk, I'm listening."

Before the conversation could continue, three servers began bringing the dinner order up. Anton helped his wife get their son settled into a chair, though Viviana tried to convince Demyan to let her feed him.

"I's a big boy, Ma," Demyan said. "I's can do it."

Anton snorted under his breath. "*I'm a big boy*, little man. *I can do it.* Try not to make a mess."

Demyan didn't even bother to respond, instead focusing on the fork that was much too big for his tiny hand. Adrik's daughter, however, jumped up into her father's lap, happily allowing him to feed her bites from his plate and hers. All of Adrik's attention was back on Sofia, as if she was his little princess.

Anton was reminded of how much he desired another child.

"That looks good," Viviana said, pointing her fork towards the steak on Anton's plate.

Raising his brow at his wife, Anton asked, "You're interested in my steak, Vine, really?"

"I said it looked good. It does. What?"

Since when was his wife big on steak?

"Nothing, here …" Anton cut off a bite and held his fork out to Viviana. Grinning, she took the bite with a wink. "Good?"

"Very."

"I can order another, if you want."

"No," she said. "I'll just take bites of yours."

"Fantastic," Anton muttered. "So, I go home hungry. I see

how this works, baby."

Adrik watched the exchange with amusement. "You've been married three years, right?"

"A little more, yes," Viviana replied. "Are you interested in being married? Maybe finding a mother for Sofia, Adrik?"

Anton nearly choked on the vegetable in his mouth. "Jesus, Vine! Not our business."

"No, it's okay." Adrik smiled down at his daughter, offering her another small bite. "Eventually, maybe. Right now, though, my only concern for her is that she's happy."

"She's a little girl," Viviana said softly. "Right now it's toys, dresses, and daddy. There's going to come a time when she grows up into a little woman. Dances, dates, sex, periods—"

"Viviana, I am eating," Anton managed to say, not remembering a time when his wife had embarrassed him so thoroughly before. "Not appropriate conversation for dinner."

"Stop it," she told him, rolling her brown eyes. "You're being ridiculous. I'm only asking for Sofia, not to mortify you, Anton. Give it up and stop acting like a teenage boy. You know what a period is."

"She has a point," Adrik said, shrugging. "I'm aware of what my daughter needs, Vine. As she needs those things, I'll provide them."

"So you are looking for a mother for her."

"Not actively, but I know she needs one."

"But what about you? Don't you want to have a woman you love and trust?" Viviana asked.

Anton desperately wanted to change the subject. "Adrik, our earlier conversation. What were you thinking of suggesting?"

Viviana took the hint and went back to eating, occasionally picking off Anton's plate.

Adrik shot Anton a thankful glance before he said, "With your contacts and your assurance of my reputation to them, I could easily slip into the spot you hold now. I could ship and import, just the same as you do. However, they'd be working under the assumption they were dealing with only me."

Anton waved for him to continue, chewing his steak.

"Like I said, you need the spotlight gone. You want to keep doing business. I can help with that. Your money, your product, and I can keep up the shipping end of it under my watch and name."

Anton swallowed his food. "I can see what you mean about trust. You do realize I ship in the millions worth of product monthly, right?"

"I'm aware."

"I won't give you a percentage or product, Adrik."

"I don't want it. Just having the ability to get my own product in and a way to get it here gives me exactly what I need. But, I needed your contacts and your word to do it. It's a good arrangement, for both of us. You get what you need, without doing much, and I get what I need."

Anton picked up the napkin and wiped his mouth, leaning back in the chair. "If you stole from me—money, drugs, whatever—I would kill you."

Beside him, Viviana didn't react a bit to the declaration. While she had embarrassed him earlier, she was making it up to him tenfold now.

Adrik kissed the top of his daughter's head. "I like my life, thank you."

"I should hope so. You might be known for being ruthless, but do you know what they've come to call me, Adrik?"

"Brutal when crossed." Adrik cocked his head to the side, amused. "Unstoppable. You have hordes of men loyal to you for the way you work and handle issues. I aspire to that. Who wouldn't?"

Yes, Anton had to admit, he liked Adrik.

"To friendship, then?" Anton asked, feeling his wife's hand squeeze his knee supportively under the table.

Adrik dipped his head. "To a friendship."

With the dinner finished and the plates cleaned,

conversation flowed to easier topics. Despite Demyan being a big boy like he professed earlier, he was curled up on his mother, his head resting against her chest and snoring while she rocked him like a baby. Even big boys got tired, apparently, and only then was it okay for them to act like infants. Sofia, too, had fallen asleep over her father's shoulder.

"There's one more thing I wanted to ask you, Anton," Adrik began, still rubbing his daughter's back.

Anton traced his fingers along his wife's arm, content and quiet. "What's that?"

"I've made it clear my first priorities are with my daughter …"

"You have," Anton replied, confused. "I can relate. Why?"

"I want to insure her future, her safety. Things of that nature. I want to know that if something happened, and I was taken from her, she'll be taken care of, loved, and protected."

"Don't we all," Viviana put in from Anton's side.

Anton agreed with a hum.

Adrik gave Viviana a pointed look that she missed, though Anton didn't. "You did that quite well, didn't you?"

"I tried," Anton replied. "But I love Vine. I couldn't imagine not being with her."

Viviana's head popped up, a bright smile coloring her beautiful features. "He did just fine."

Anton wasn't focusing on the words that were being said, he was focusing on the ones that weren't. "What are you dancing around, Adrik? You've been frank with me all night. Suddenly you're clamming up. It's making me fucking nervous."

"You risked a hell of a lot for your wife. You're still facing the consequences, too."

Viviana cleared her throat and stopped rocking Demyan. Clearly, by the frown she sported, Adrik's comment had put her on edge. But, like the lady she was, she chose to take herself out of the equation.

"Anton, I need to use the ladies' room, so if you wouldn't

mind taking him, please."

"Sure, baby."

Demyan switched arms, seemingly not noticing his new bed was his father's much larger form. Anton reveled in the heat and quietness of his son as Viviana made her way through the dining area. Once out of view, Anton turned back to his new friend and ally.

"I think you offended my wife," he said quietly. "Though I'm not sure why, so I'm not too angry about it."

Adrik chuckled lowly. "Maybe she heard something you didn't."

"Like what?"

"Would your son do for a woman what you've done, Anton?"

"Excuse me?" Anton asked, confusion muddling up his mind.

"They're close in age. They seem to get along just fine. Over the years, with the understanding of what was expected of them, they could very well find affections have grown between them. You and your wife a perfect example of this."

Anton's mind finally caught up to speed. Fuck, he was usually a lot quicker at shit like this. "You're suggesting an arranged marriage between Demyan and Sofia."

"It's an interesting idea, you have to admit. Not only would it guarantee my daughter a future, you will have cemented your son with part of his."

"Adrik, I think you have some things confused. My wife and I had but two meetings growing up. I resented my family for the choices they took away from me. Actually, I gave them hell for it."

"Yet, it's obvious you love her, now," Adrik pointed out quietly.

"Because I fell in love with her. In the end, I made the choice myself. Not because my family wanted me to. Viviana and I are a special case. Had she been a different woman, we wouldn't be like we are. I'd likely have a mistress, or more. Maybe I'd have had a woman I loved on the side, and a family with her. I'm aware what I could have been like. I see it in men around me every day."

Adrik looked off to the side, sighing. "I want to know my daughter will be more than just okay in the future. Especially where a husband is concerned."

Anton nodded, understanding that more than anything. "Then let her. I don't know how my son will grow, or who he's going to be, but I know he's going to do it on his own. By his own will and his own choices. Not because I made them for him. If he falls in love with a woman, it will be because he picked her, not because I did.

"And," Anton continued with a conspiratorial grin, "… if this partnership of ours continues to be good, then our children will cross paths more than once, I imagine. Let them grow, Adrik. If they find affection, as you said, they find it. I don't think you have to worry about cementing your daughter's future. She has you for a father, after all. Look at all you've done for her so far."

"Considering everything I've done so far has been for her, that," Adrik said, staring down at Sofia, "… is what scares me the most."

Chapter Eleven

"Mmm, fuck you taste good right here," Anton murmured, his teeth scraping along Viviana's pulse point in her neck. "And here ..."

"Sure," Viviana replied, her voice muffled by a pillow. "I probably taste awful right now. I need a shower."

"No, no. More like sunlight and sex. I had to get up early anyway for a meeting at Seven Lights, so I figured you might want to get up with me before I go."

Seven Lights was finally opened back up for regular business, but Anton made it clear to her the Bratva side of things were being taken care of elsewhere. Whatever business meeting he put together was probably for his employees.

"Are you going to drop Demyan off at daycare?" Viviana asked.

"I can if you want me to. You're going in to open the bookstore, right?"

"Yeah, around noon, but I need to go into the clinic for my appointment."

Anton didn't question her on what the appointment was for, and Viviana was grateful. It was bad enough he'd began asking her when, or if, she wanted to think about trying for another child. She did, and she told him that, but she also wanted to wait until after the trial, for obvious reasons. Beyond that issue, Viviana's cycle hadn't returned since her miscarriage in February. It was now May. Why hadn't her cycle returned? She couldn't actually get pregnant if she didn't have a period, for Christ's sake, but she didn't want to tell Anton there might be something wrong with her body and worry him. Hence, the appointment.

While Anton kept up his kisses and bites along Viviana's neck, waking her body up to the morning light filtering into their bedroom, she turned to look at the clock on the nightstand. It was way too early for Anton to be waking her up like he was.

"I could use the extra thirty minutes of sleep I might have left, you know," Viviana muttered, tilting her head away from another one of his tantalizing kisses. The heat between her thighs was starting to spread, never mind the juices she could already feel leaking from her pussy. Another gentle bite landed to her shoulder, Anton's hand slid between her legs to cup her heated sex, and Viviana gasped. "Jesus, come on, Anton."

"I'm going to use those thirty minutes to do something terribly naughty to my sexy wife. Like fucking her soft and slow from behind while she plays with that sweet pussy of hers. Wake up, Vine, and I promise you'll be coming really fucking soon."

That dirty mouth of his was something she found impossible to resist.

"You're awful," she told him, looking back over her shoulder. "Just terr—*oh fuck, yeah.*"

His fingers between her legs spread her fleshy folds. Using only two fingers, he circled the sensitive entrance of her pussy, gathering the slick arousal on his digits, before running his touch back up to her clit. Over and over he provoked her body like that, slow and gentle, making her jerk every time he came in contact with her swollen, needing bundle of nerves. Anton never penetrated her with his fingers, though, simply teased her entrance until she was backing into his hand, begging him for more.

"Mmhmm, that's what I want to hear from you, baby."

Reaching out, Viviana caught his free hand with her own, intertwining their fingers together. The weight of Anton's body behind her, his cock hard, driving into the small of her back, pushed Viviana deeper into the bedding. God, she loved the weight of him—all of him. Tighter she squeezed his fingers as he circled her clit once more with a little more pressure than before. Enough to make her legs tremble and the muscles in her stomach clench. More wetness seeped from her sex.

"You smell so fucking good. Get those fingers of yours down here. Come on, Vine," Anton breathed, dark and sinful into her ear. "Give me what I want, and I'll give it back just how you like."

"Fuck, *please*! Just … God, *Anton*, don't stop, just don't fucking stop."

"Never, baby. Now …"

Anton drove their connected hands under Viviana's body, stopping only when he'd come to the needing junction between her thighs. Spreading her fingers wide, Viviana could feel how wet he'd made her with his simple teasing and light touches. Slick from arousal and tender from being coaxed into near bliss, her clit was hot under her touch. Slowly, she began a gentle circling rhythm of her own, feeling her husband's fingers finally slip into her tightening core.

Viviana moaned at the intrusion. "You don't even know …"

"Know what?" Anton asked, surprising Viviana at how close to her face he was. "How high you are already? That you're burning up just how I like? Oh, I know. I always fucking *know*."

Then, his fingers were leaving her soaked sex, trailing up higher with an enticing leisureliness. It was only when he came to the entrance of her ass, spreading the wetness from her pussy that he finally stopped. With each circle he drew over the tight, puckered hole, Anton pressed with a little more pressure until his digits were sinking in past the clenching ring.

"Love your ass," Anton told her, his tone thick like rolling molasses. "So tight, baby. Breathe and feel, Viviana."

Viviana's back arched at the delicious sting his fingers created when they thrust harder, and deeper. It wasn't that she put anal on the table often, because she didn't, but she loved when Anton played with his fingers, working her ass while he fucked her, or even when he was on his knees and his mouth was tasting her pussy.

Melting into the ravenous hunger building inside her body, twisting deep in her womb, Viviana barely recognized Anton's hand leaving her own between her thighs. His arm wrapped around her waist, pulling her up to her knees so her ass was higher in the air. The cool air of the room whispered along her exposed sex and Viviana knew without a doubt, Anton had the best view of her pussy and ass on display for him.

She couldn't even bring herself to care.

The keening cries in the back of her throat built in intensity, moving higher like the wave of pleasure washing over her skin and nerves. Every thrust of his fingers inside her ass took her closer to the cliff. Every swipe of hers along her clit threatened to break her further.

Viviana was so fucking close to coming it was ridiculous.

She couldn't even speak to tell Anton.

She didn't have to. In the next second, the arm he held snug around her waist released its grip only long enough for Viviana to feel the crest of his cock sliding up and down her slit, spreading more of her juices. All the while, his fingers in her ass kept up that punishing, deep rhythm while hers rolled faster over her pulsing clit.

Anton took her slow, working his cock through the clenching muscles of her pussy. Every inch he gave, he took it right back until Viviana was backing into his shaft on her own, needing to feel him fill her, fuck her, and own her like only he could. It was only when he'd filled her totally that Anton let go of the base of his cock.

For a moment, Viviana stayed still, reveling in the way he'd filled her sex, her ass, and how her body quivered from the attention she was giving to her clit, too. Wet and hot was a fucking understatement. From the wetness between her thighs to the perspiration beading on her skin, she felt soaked and burned.

"Oh, God," she choked out.

"How's that for what you wanted, baby?" Anton asked, breathless and chuckling at the same time.

Clenching her free hand into the pillow, and forcing the cries wanting out in the back of her throat to be swallowed, Viviana squeezed her eyes shut and just felt. Anton's free hand rubbed from the base of her spine upwards, coming to rest at the junction between her neck and her shoulder. When his fingers gripped tight at that spot, she felt her pulse began to race.

Viviana knew what was coming and she still couldn't have prepared for it.

The sensation of his entire body thrusting into hers, bottoming out and hitting every beautiful, unaware spot inside her pussy at the same time took her breath away. The next one had her whimpering. Before long, the thrusts didn't have a pause between them, each one a little rougher than the one before. His fingers at her shoulder pressed harder, his nails digging in and making her eyes fly open wide.

The orgasm that ravaged her started from her womb and radiated outwards. Like a bucket of ice cold water was dropped over her spine, turning every nerve in her body numb. Viviana heard nothing but the quiet reassurance of her husband's dark tenor behind her and the cattish cry that ripped from her throat.

"*Shhh* … Fuck, that was beautiful. Let's do it again," he said with a quiet laugh.

Anton's fingers slowed in her ass while her hand at her sex moved away as if it'd been burned. She was far too sensitive to keep touching. In a blur of movement, Viviana was turned with Anton's body until his back was resting against the bed and she was the one on top with her back facing him.

"What—"

Suddenly, the new position had his cock hitting a particular spot that made Viviana gasp.

"Jesus, yeah, okay," she mumbled, still dizzy and overwhelmed from the force of her orgasm. "Let's do it again."

• • •

"Pregnant?" Viviana asked, her throat feeling tight.

The doctor sat on the edge of his desk, tapping the little square pregnancy test in his palm. The tests at the hospital didn't look like the ones available at a store. Instead of a long, thin plastic device, the hospital grade urine tests were square with only two circle windows. If a line showed up in only the first window, the patient wasn't pregnant. If a line showed up in both windows, the pregnancy hormone had been detected.

Viviana's test showed bright blue, thick lines in both windows.

"I can't be pregnant," she said quietly, still staring at the test.

"I can assure you that you are," the doctor replied just as softly. "I understand from your charts that you recently miscarried, right?"

"In February," Viviana confirmed, swallowing her rising sickness. "I was only a few weeks along."

The doctor nodded, his face expressionless. "I can see why this would be a shock, then."

"A shock?" Viviana coughed out a laugh. "Jesus, I haven't even had a period since I lost that pregnancy. That's what I was here for, not … *this*."

"Yes, well, a pregnancy test is a standard procedure when a woman says she has had no menses for more than forty days."

Viviana clenched her teeth, staring away from the man. "Please don't patronize me. I'm twenty-eight, not sixteen. I just lost a pregnancy and was told it could take up to three months for my cycles to return. That's why I'm here. Not to be scolded like a child."

"My apologies, Mrs. Avdon—" The doctor stopped abruptly, staring down at the chart on his desk. "*Avdonin*. Viviana Avdonin."

Viviana still refused to look at the man. "Great, so you know my name. That's good."

"No, I recognized your name. That was all. You're the

wife of—"

"Anton Avdonin, yes," she interrupted sharply.

The doctor's shoulders relaxed, his posture softening. "It's no wonder this is a shock. Given what I've seen in the press lately, you've been dealing with a lot. His trial is in two months, yes?"

Thanks to Ivan's trickery, Anton's trial date had been repeatedly pushed back due to delays and things Viviana didn't understand. "Yes."

"I'm sure you know your husband uses this clinic for ... things," the doctor said, shrugging. "I am sorry for seeming rude, it wasn't how I meant to come off."

Viviana took a breath, blowing out her frustration in a huff of air. "I haven't had a cycle, so no, I wasn't expecting to be pregnant."

"That's a common mistake women make. Fact of the matter is, you were probably actually having a cycle, and you would have had a period, but in the process, you needed to ovulate first, and obviously did. During that time, you conceived, so as would be expected, you didn't have that period. I would normally ask about birth control and things of that nature, but if you would rather not ..."

"They didn't want me to take the shot again until after my cycles had resumed to a regular thing."

"That's not unusual," he replied.

Viviana didn't feel the need to point out that condoms weren't exactly a favorite of hers, or her husband. That was, if they even managed to remember to get one. Like they always had been, Viviana and Anton were fast, dirty, and usually in the zone when it came to sex. They were stupid about it, really. But given their age and the fact they were married, no one had a right to judge them on their contraceptive choices, or lack thereof.

Even so, what an idiotic, ridiculous fucking mistake to make.

"Not really," the doctor interjected gently.

Had Viviana said that out loud? Great.

"Listen," the doctor said, moving off his desk. "Your miscarriage was an early termination. Your body was likely healed within a month after. How long did the bleeding last?"

"Two weeks or so."

"Sounds about right. Chances are, you're in the normal range for women who miscarry. About two months, or even three, before your periods resume. I don't think you're very far along in this pregnancy, but I'll order a blood work up to be done before you leave. I'll even put a rush in on it at the lab so you can have the results by supper time today. By the hormone levels in your blood, we'll have a near exact approximation of how far along you are and your due date."

Viviana forced herself to thank the man, but tears still prickled at her eyes. Panic waged a war through her insides, the anxiety making her sick to her stomach. The doctor didn't miss her show of emotions.

"Viviana?"

"It's Vine. Just call me Vine."

"Okay, Vine it is. I know I work for your husband in a way, but if you don't want to have this pregnancy, I can set you up with an abor—"

"No, no I do want this baby. It's not that," she rushed to say, wiping away the wetness streaking down her cheeks. "Of course I want this baby."

It wasn't just hers, it was Anton's, too. There was no way in hell she would get rid of it.

"Then what is it?"

"I don't want to lose it," she answered in a breath. "I just lost a baby. I'm pretty fucking sure the stress killed me to the point where my body couldn't care for it, so it didn't."

The doctor sighed, rubbing his forehead with a wince. "I doubt that was the cause, and if you're still blaming yourself for the miscarriage, you're not fully emotionally healed yet, either. Here's what I can do to try and ease your concerns, sweetheart.

"We can do weekly blood tests to monitor your hormone levels from here on out. Usually if they drop below a certain number, it's a good clue the pregnancy isn't viable and is likely to terminate itself. Something else to consider is if you lose pregnancy symptoms suddenly, without much warning. I can order an early ultrasound to check for a heartbeat around nine, possibly even eight weeks. If we can see the heartbeat, the probability drops again. After twelve weeks, it drops by over half. Chances are, the first was a fluke, Vine. That's all."

"I can't tell him," Viviana whispered.

Cocking his head to the side with a furrowed brow, the man asked, "Anton?"

Viviana's heart was racing, leaping into her throat with every beat. "I can't tell him and then lose it again. Not now."

"Okay," the doctor said. "I get that. Leave your cell phone number with me and I'll call you directly with the results of the blood work. You don't have to tell him until you're ready. Be here next week, and we'll do a hormone check. Sound good?"

All Viviana could do was nod.

• • •

"Papa!" Demyan screeched so loud Viviana jumped at the counter, nearly slicing open her finger with the knife she was using. "I got to paint with my fingers and Reese gave me his car!"

"His car, huh?" Anton asked. "Are you sure you're allowed to have his car?"

Viviana turned just enough to see their nearly three-year-old shrug. "I don't know. He gave it to me, Papa."

"Well, okay then."

Viviana was pretty sure that wasn't the right answer for Demyan and the car issue, but she didn't correct her husband. By tomorrow, Demyan would have forgotten about the toy, and so would the other boy.

Viviana sighed into the kiss Anton pressed to her neck. "Missed you, baby."

"Good day?" she asked him, keeping her attention on the

vegetables she was chopping.

Because it wasn't a Friday, or the weekend, he didn't need to be at the club until late hours. Viviana was grateful. She needed him close after the news she received earlier, but she still couldn't bring herself to tell him.

"Yeah, it was good. Quiet."

"How'd the meeting go?"

"All right. Ivan just wanted to explain what was expected of all of the employees what with the trial coming up and everything."

"No interviews." Viviana tossed the potatoes into a colander to wash.

"Well, that and more. It's not important. How'd your appointment go?"

Viviana tensed.

"Vine, everything okay?" Anton asked.

"Yeah, the doctor said all was normal," she half-lied.

"So why do you feel like a block of ice all of the sudden?"

Viviana bit her lip to keep from spilling the news of the pregnancy. "I'm not. It's just personal, all right? Jesus, last week you had a fit at dinner with Adrik when I mentioned the word period. Leave it alone."

"That was different, Vine. You were talking about someone else's daughter. You're my wife, it's not the same."

"I'm fine. All is normal," Viviana repeated quietly.

Without warning, Viviana felt her body being turned from Anton's urging. Under his curious stare, she tried to be calm.

"You sure?" he questioned with a raised brow. "Did they check you, or anything?"

"Um—"

"Papa, come see my new car!" Demyan shouted from the living room.

Anton rolled his eyes and grinned down at his wife. "Later?"

Thank God, Viviana thought. "Yeah, sure."

When Anton was out of the kitchen, Viviana finally felt like she could breathe for a second. Hell, she was just glad she managed to delete the message from the doctor she'd received, and missed because she'd been changing Demyan's day clothes into his play clothes, only a half an hour before Anton arrived home. The one that said she was four weeks along and the hormone levels gave the indication everything was good ... and so far, viable.

That's all it was, just one word: viable.

Chapter Twelve

Viviana braked the SUV, throwing it into park before slamming her hands back to the steering wheel. She was so overwhelmed. Torn apart from the inside out and wholly unsure of her surroundings. Never had she felt so totally useless and tattered. Like her soul and heart was a forgotten flag, ripped to shreds and flapping without protection in the tornado that had become her life.

The quiet, sleeping boy in his booster seat in the backseat was the only thing keeping Viviana from screaming her lungs out or punching her fists into a bloody mess. Instead, she balled her fisted hands to her eyes and panted through the tears that fell without permission.

Everything hurt. Everything ached.

Nothing in this poisoned mess was left untouched.

Absolutely nothing.

Why, Viviana wanted to ask. Why hadn't Anton been more careful? Why had he done what he did? Why couldn't she and Demyan have been enough for him?

How could you leave me alone like this?

Viviana didn't have a single clue of how much time passed her by as she sat in the front seat and cried for all she was worth. Not while her heart broke all over again, and the hiccupping sobs turned to chattering teeth and hyperventilating breaths that wouldn't stop catching.

When the sounds of her heartbreak threatened to wake Demyan in the back, Viviana managed to unlatch her seatbelt with shaking hands before she opened the SUV's door. Cool sand slipped into the soles of her sandals as she stumbled out into the warm, May air. Less than three feet from the SUV where her son slept unknowing of his father's absence and his mother's breakdown, Viviana collapsed.

Echoing, wrenching sobs shook her shoulders. Viviana

dug curling fists into the sand.

Shattered and lost—that's what she was without Anton.

Empty.

Broken.

So hollow.

• • •

"Vine?"

Viviana barely registered her name being called over the squawking seagulls above or the lapping waves of water rushing under the pier. The safe haven that was Little Odessa for her had once again been the place she sought out for comfort. It held so many memories sweetened by easier, happier times. Things that left a hopeful sentiment resounding through her emotions instead of the bitterness of the tragedy she was currently suffocated with.

Resting on the beach, her silk dress was surely ruined by the damp sand, her hair was already beginning to frizz and wave from the wet air, but she didn't care. Instead, Viviana watched Demyan, so close to his third birthday, trip through the sand as he watched the water and birds.

The childish laughter coming from Viviana's son was the only thing keeping her sane.

A form dropped beside her on the beach. She didn't give Ivan any acknowledgment as he stared down the shore blankly. Gia, Ivan's youngest daughter, with her summer dress swirling around her bare ankles, skipped past her father. She was only eleven months older than Demyan.

"They've got him placed back at Rikers."

Viviana felt the bile rise into her throat. Anton hated being confined; couldn't stand to sit still. He hadn't been locked up more than a few days the last time before they got him out on bail. But now … What now? With bail revoked, there was no chance for that.

How could he have been so stupid and careless?

"What do I do?" Viviana asked.

"That depends," Ivan murmured.

Dumbly, Viviana shook her head. His answer was far too ambiguous for her worn-out mind to pick apart and understand. "Don't be vague, Ivan. Just get to the goddamn point, okay?"

"I'm here. I should be at Rikers beating off the feds demands for interviews again or at the office working on an appeal, but instead I'm here."

Viviana watched with a small smile beginning to form as the children ran past, leaving pealing giggles in their wake. While Demyan had been acting moody after he woke up from his nap, Gia's tiny presence seemed to make all of that disappear.

"Did you hear me?" Ivan asked.

What difference did it make? "No, not really."

Ivan's hand grasped roughly to Viviana's elbow, shaking her arm. "Stop it, listen to me!"

"How fucking stupid did he have to be, huh?" Viviana turned on her new companion with fire burning in her eyes. Anger suddenly swept through her body with a wrecking ball's force. What little bit of composure she managed to keep after Demyan awoke was all but lost with the simple shake of her arm. "A gun, Ivan. He was out on bail and he was caught with an unregistered, illegal *gun* in his car. He couldn't even—"

"It was my gun," Ivan interrupted quietly, releasing his hold abruptly. Shock fluttered through Viviana's stomach like the beating wings of butterflies.

"What?"

"Mine, not his. I had an afternoon meeting at the courthouse and was late getting out of the house. I needed to drop the girls off at the babysitter because Eva was already gone. I was out of my mind busy, but I stopped to brief Anton on my plans for laying down the motions for a longer stay at the meeting. He was busy, too, handling somebody. I remembered my gun just before I left and tossed it into his glove box thinking he wouldn't even get out of Seven Lights before I got back. I'm sorry."

"Your gun," she whispered.

Ivan nodded, meeting her heated gaze head on. "To the best of his ability, Anton was following the law to keep himself out of the prison during this trial. He has done absolutely everything he could, Vine. I screwed up, not him. Me."

Viviana didn't know what to say. For an entire minute, she simply stared at her husband's lawyer, feeling choked and torn.

"You can't just say it was yours?"

"It doesn't work like that," Ivan admitted. "Either way, he was in possession of a weapon, which in and of itself, is a breach of his bail release."

"But ... but, I need him here, Ivan."

Now more than ever, Viviana needed Anton. She hadn't even gotten the chance to tell him she was ... Oh God, no. Even thinking about the little life just beginning to thrive and grow in her womb only made it worse. Suddenly her heart was cracking and splintering to pieces all over again.

What if Anton was found guilty for the crimes they charged him with?

"What's the sentence possibility?" Viviana managed to ask, her mouth going dry.

Ivan cleared his throat, glancing at the two children standing hand in hand close at the water's edge. What could she do for her little boy with no father to raise him? Would Demyan be who he was supposed to be if Anton wasn't there?

"You know what it is. It'd be life, Vine. Twice over, no chance for parole."

"*Life.*"

"The prosecutor isn't seeking capital punishment. I believe it's because he thinks it wouldn't stick, or a jury wouldn't go for it."

He had lost her at capital punishment. Those words alone brought with them a cold shiver of dread. Viviana had purposely avoided discussing the charges, their specifics, or anything about the trial with Anton. For the most part, she had been far too angry to talk about it. Every time his face was shown on the news, or some reporter showed up at her bookstore, it sent her into another raging spiral.

Public opinion had already decided Anton's guilt. Of that, Viviana was most sure. News reports labeled her husband a trafficker, the man who brought guns into their country and put drugs on their streets. The mothers and fathers of the kids using those drugs or being shot by those guns didn't like that.

Was it true? Yes, Viviana didn't deny that.

But she refused to see him as that man, too. She never had.

Anton was so much more.

A man with as many strengths as he had faults. Someone with a love so deep, so strong he only shared and showed it sparingly to those he felt it was most deserved. Tender with the same hands that had shown others their brutality. Honestly vulnerable behind the ruthless masks he wore. A father in his home. A friend with just a glance. A lover in her bed.

They didn't know *him*.

Viviana wouldn't let anyone poison the man she, or her son, knew. Never.

"Ma!"

Viviana willed away the wetness blurring her eyes as she forced a smile for her son. "Yeah?"

"Is Papa comin'?" Demyan asked over his shoulder.

Fuck, that hurt. What was she supposed to say?

"Later, baby," Viviana lied. "Maybe."

Ivan rested his arms over his knees as Demyan went back to searching the sand with Gia. "We can take him tonight, if you want. Eva won't mind. It'll give you some room to breathe, to think, if you need."

"But what about tomorrow when he comes home and asks for him again? What then, Ivan?"

"That depends," Ivan said.

He'd already told her those words once, and just like the first time, Viviana still didn't understand. She also didn't have the time or patience for word games.

"On what?"

"You have options," he explained gently. "That's why I'm here, not with Anton. We all knew this was a possibility, and we know very well how he's likely going to fair in this trial."

Ivan seemed to leave something unsaid, and Viviana didn't miss it. "But?"

"But we do have a little breathing room here."

"Oh, yeah? Because how I see it, I'm *drowning*."

Ivan swallowed audibly, shrugging one shoulder. "I know. Trust me, I do. Those options I mentioned ..."

"Go on," she urged when he went still and silent.

"Anton was planning to leave the country if we couldn't get the case tossed out before it went to trial, or if we couldn't find Natalie before her testimony. He had identities bought and ready to go for all of you. A place set up where no extradition treaties could send him back. That's still a viable option for you and Demyan, if you want to start over."

Viviana's heart stopped, she was sure it did. "He wants that?"

"He wanted what was best for you and his child. It would have, at the time, kept you all together. If right now, that is what you want, Anton will say nothing. He will let you go, Vine. I have the papers, documents, IDs, and the information for you to access any bank accounts associated with those names in my car. I will hand them over, you can follow the directions on the letter inside to do whatever you want from there on out."

There was nothing about that option that felt remotely okay with Viviana. If anything, it make her feel like a coward just for considering it. New names, a new place, and a fresh start at life didn't sound nearly as sweet as it might have to some.

"No." Her answer came out just as sure and strong as it

ever would. "I spoke my vows and I meant them. I'm not going to leave that man and start all over again somewhere else, hoping I can replace what I already have. I don't want to; I don't want someone else to raise my son. I want Anton. Absolutely not, Ivan, don't bring it up again."

Ivan leaned back to the sand. "Okay. The other option is my own. Anton had no say, I haven't even suggested it to him. He'd undoubtedly kill me just for thinking about it."

Well, Viviana didn't like the sound of that, either.

"Is this the breathing room?"

"Could be," Ivan mused, a little darkly. "But it could make things worse, depending on how it plays out … *If* it plays out, that is. We need a backup plan, one that would have the case put under a microscope, have the charges dropped due to judicial indiscretions, and would force them to release Anton, even for a short time."

"Stop being an asshole and explain it to me," Viviana snapped.

"How far are you willing to go, Vine?" Ivan tipped his chin in the children's direction. "For him, what would you do to bring his father home?"

"What?"

"It's not a difficult question," Ivan said. "A basic human need is love. What we'd do for it, or to keep it, is a whole other matter. I'm simply asking what you would do for yours. There has to be a worth you'd put on it or a limit you'll draw. Is there? What would you do for it? That's all I'm asking."

No, he had a point there.

"Anything."

"Your morals, the values you think you have now … your *vows*," he finished with a pointed look at her. "All of those things, would you toss them aside? Would you risk them, for Anton, or for his son?"

"Of course."

Ivan released a heavy sigh, chewing on the inside of his cheek as he considered her words. "Tomorrow, I'm making a motion to forgo a jury in the trial."

Viviana's head whipped in his direction. Anton had every right to forgo a jury and instead, have only the judge weigh in on his guilt or innocence. It wasn't often that the option was chosen, and she couldn't understand why they would do that at all for Anton.

"What, why?"

"Public opinion is tainted, Vine. He'd never get a fair trial with one."

"And you think a judge and jury of only one is any better?" Viviana asked sharply.

"I think every man has a weakness," Ivan intoned dully. "I think with the right prodding, the right person, that weakness can come forefront and destroy them. Erik is not the only person in our brotherhood who knows his way around a bribe, or a blackmail, for that matter."

Viviana's mind went silent. "Anton's judge ..."

"Is a relatively good man. Divorced, with three adult children. A healthy, spotless twenty-year career as a judge. Certainly not the kind of man who would take a bribe, never mind hoping that you could get close enough to offer one he might want to take.

"But a blackmail," Ivan continued, a bitter smirk growing, "... that is something wholly different. Judge Kander's career may be spotless, but his father's was stained with the scandal of women. Given Kander's divorce was all handled privately with his wife being paid to keep quiet, he very well might suffer from that same adulterous affliction."

"I don't understand," Viviana said.

"What if women were his weakness, Vine?"

She stilled. "What, we just set him up with a working girl and have the possibility threatened that it could go on record? That doesn't sound like an intelligent plan."

Ivan scoffed. "Because it's not. What would that lead to, really? Kander losing his position, his career. A mistrial maybe, but charges could be redrawn the next day and Anton would be right back in prison. We'd be at square one."

"A mistrial isn't an option," Viviana realized, though it

was devastating.

"No, only a verdict. Not guilty, that's all that will be acceptable. They can't retry him for the crimes, and believe that Anton wouldn't make the same mistakes again, so they'll never come close to touching him after. However, if the only option is a mistrial and Anton leaving the country, he'll do that, too. This plan may very well work for both of those options."

"So, then what—"

"You," Ivan interrupted, offering nothing else in explanation.

"Me?"

"Not a hooker, No, *you*, Vine. It would not only be the idea of blackmail, but that perhaps the judge was involved with criminal activity, particularly, involved with the wife of mafia leader. Mix that in with a healthy dose of fear, and we might have winner."

Struck speechless, Viviana balked.

Ivan picked up on her plight instantly. "I'm not asking you to take that man to bed."

"I should hope not," she whispered. "Though it certainly tastes of that, and I don't like what it implies or leaves behind in the back of my mouth. I can see why you didn't bring it up to Anton, now."

Her husband would have been in a right fit, to say the least.

"You said it right. Implies. Suggests. That's all, just enough to make Kander know what it would look like, how it would paint him. Imagine if that judge had to stare back at the gallery and see you sitting behind Anton every day of trial. Think how it would feel for him to receive a package every day reminding him of the position he had put himself in."

When Viviana didn't speak, Ivan sat up straight and stood, brushing sand from his pants. "I suppose it's pretty simple, you can do one of three things. One, be Viviana. The ever faithful, devoted wife of a man America is sure to hate. Stand behind him, give no comments to the hordes of reporters outside the courthouse, and watch them lock him away. Two …" he continued, turning to look down, "You can be someone new. Whoever you want, with your what ifs, your regrets, and your anger."

"Or … *this*," Viviana said, feeling her throat tighten when she couldn't speak it out loud.

"The Bratva boss's wife. Who she is, like she is. No apologies, tough as nails, and whatever it takes. Whichever you choose, you'll find no judgement from me, Vine. I'm only giving you another way."

Viviana wished her heart rate would go back to normal. "But what about Anton? If he found out that I had done something like that, even if it was nothing, just the idea of it … I'm the product of infidelity, Ivan. I would never do that to my husband, ever."

"I know, but this isn't the same, and you're not going to be involved physically with a man, so to speak," Ivan murmured. "Anton might find out, but that's a risk you have to take. If he does, you handle it when it comes. That's not what we worry about, now. How far are you willing to go?"

Again, Viviana sought out her son's presence on the beach.

"It's okay to be selfish, Vine," Ivan added, not missing a beat. "To do it for you, for Demyan. To keep what you have because it's yours. There's only one person who will judge you for it, and that's yourself."

Viviana sneered viciously. "And my *husband*."

"What would he do for you?"

She knew exactly what Anton had already done for her, so that point was moot. Feeling overwhelmed, Viviana blurted out the only words she could think of. "I'm pregnant."

Ivan didn't even glance back at her. "He doesn't know, huh?"

"No."

"How far are you willing to go?" Ivan repeated.

The truth ached as much as it relieved. "As far as it takes."

Chapter Thirteen

"You must be the new girl."

Viviana's gaze flicked to the girl behind her in the vanity mirror. Tall, too skinny, with hair bleached blonde, and her small chest on full display but for the silk robe that did nothing to hide her nakedness, she didn't seem ashamed standing there like she was. Viviana tried not to look bothered by her presence or brazenness.

"Sure," Viviana answered, offering a smile.

Apparently it didn't ring true.

"This your first time?"

Was it? Shit, Viviana forced herself not to bark a bitter laugh. Never in her life had she stepped foot inside a strip club, never mind even considering it. She purposely avoided Anton's strip clubs like the plague that she felt they were. Women who based their worth on how well they could swing around a pole and how many dollars could be shoved into their G-string weren't exactly her thing.

Unfortunately, Viviana didn't have a choice.

And she was not simply there to watch. No, she was there to *dance*.

Anton's trial date was just mere weeks away. It had taken Ivan great effort, and a massive amount of money, patience, and digging to find even a smudge of indiscretion on Judge Kander that was useable in any worthy way.

What Viviana was doing now was simply just a hunch. No one could guarantee the judge would show, no one knew for sure if this was the gentleman's club he occasionally frequented under a name that had absolutely no relation to his.

It didn't help that Viviana and Ivan needed to keep the things they were doing, the blackmail they were planning, as secretive as possible. They couldn't take the risk Anton would find out. Viviana worried how his people would paint her if they ever found out the position she was putting herself in just in the hopes that she might get him back.

It had taken her the entire month she waited while Ivan dug, searched, and fed mouths with money for scraps of personal information on the judge for Viviana to figure out what she had to do.

Everything. Anything.

The guilt, the dirtiness she felt … None of that mattered.

"Hey, did you hear me?" the girl asked.

With a deep breath, Viviana went back to her paled reflection in the mirror. "It is my first."

"Ah," the girl drawled. "Well, take a couple slams of something hard before you go out on stage. Don't let them get too close, and certainly don't let them touch you."

Viviana quirked her brow. "I'm doing a private."

"Ouch. On your first? Jesus, that took me months to get. What lap did you sit your pretty ass down on?"

Anton Avdonin's, Viviana thought with an internal sigh.

"By request of the boss," she said instead.

"Oh."

Just then, a man slipped in between the red velvet curtains, jerking his thumb at the girl. "Sid, you're next. Let's go."

The blonde gave him a nod in response before turning back to Viviana. "I'll see you later, I suppose. What's your name, anyway?"

Viviana reached for the crimson lipstick sitting on the vanity's top. Her name didn't matter. The girl would never see her again, likely. She certainly wouldn't be coming back to this place once her job was done and she left.

But, with all the lies she'd already told to get where she was piling up, what would one more hurt?"

"Just call me Eve."

"Like Adam?"

Viviana smirked. "Just like that."

Eve did take the apple, after all. Sin with a single bite.

How was she any different?

• • •

Ivan's fingers ticked under Viviana's chin, encouraging her to look up. "Hey."

"Hmm?" Viviana felt disoriented and nauseous.

"You okay?"

Viviana shook her head. "That's a stupid fucking question."

How on earth could she possibly be okay? Beneath the thin, thigh-high robe she wore there was practically nothing at all to cover her skin. Nothing but a sheer, lace white thong that contrasted against her olive toned skin, and a matching bra that was as see through as the underwear.

She had come to find out this gentleman's club was not about the flash and dash of the whole scene like some were. It was not about the costumes the girls wore or the routine they put on. It wasn't about the pole or the tricks. It was about the sensuality in their dance. The sex of a woman. The shape of their bodies, the beauty in their movements. Clearly, many took pride in the fact that it was a bit more upscale and classy than the norm.

They weren't strippers, they were dancers.

Viviana didn't give a shit. She still felt like a whore.

She was a mother and a wife. Loved and respected by one man, not many.

Anton would find no respect or love for this.

"Look at me," Ivan said harshly.

Viviana blinked through her reservations and worries. "What?"

He waved a hand at her, keeping his gaze diverted from the way the robe hung off her naked shoulders. It clung to every inch of her skin, showcasing the curves she worked so damned hard to keep below the silky fabric.

Never had Viviana wanted to cover herself up more than right then.

"What?" she asked again when Ivan stayed quiet.

"I know this is … hard."

"No, you most certainly do not know," Viviana spat. "I'm about to go out of my mind."

Ivan's throat bobbed with a swallow, his own nerves showing. "I'm sorry. I only meant to say we can call this off, if you want."

She tossed a glance down the long, darkened hallway situated at the back of the club that led to the private rooms. VIPs were being settled, apparently. Getting their drinks served and whatever else they might need for the next little while. Viviana had called Ivan in last minute just to be sure she was doing the right thing, but she was starting to regret that choice.

"Did he show?"

"Yes, with his second cousin, as the source promised. The cousin stays out on the floor, not in the private room."

Viviana tried to shake the upset that had her stomach rolling. "I need a drink, or a blunt."

Ivan scowled. "You're pregnant."

Just ten weeks. Not even showing. No one even knew, yet. Anton still didn't. Viviana didn't know how to tell him. Besides that, the threat of her last pregnancy and how it ended in miscarriage loomed over Viviana. She didn't want to tell Anton just to take it away from him again. Never mind how it would absolutely destroy her.

"Gee, thanks for the goddamned reminder."

"I'm just say—"

"I know, Ivan. I'm nervous, that's all. I wasn't serious."

Looking about as uncomfortable as he must have felt, Ivan rubbed the back of his neck with one hand. "Haven't you ever … I mean, with Anton, like danced?"

Oh God, was he asking what she thought he was asking?

"That's none of your business!"

"Lower your voice, Vine."

"If I did, which I wouldn't tell you, it wouldn't be the same," she said with a sniff. "That's not what this is, and you know it."

"But it's not any different," Ivan countered just as fast. "You move, you smile, and pretend if you have to. Keep your face out of sight as much as possible, be aware of the way your body looks, how he is looking at you. Be sure to use it to keep his eyes on you, but in the right spots. The server ..."

Viviana felt her tension ratchet up a notch as Ivan trailed off. "What about the server?"

"The judge is going to be a tad more tipsy than normal, so keep that in mind. Only enough to blur his vision a little, to make him sway. He probably won't even notice it, or think anything of it, and the effects will be gone by the time he wakes up in the morning none the wiser."

What kind of alcohol did that? None, Viviana knew.

"You're drugging him."

Ivan smirked, but it didn't look as confident as it usually did. "The server has, yes. She'll also be beyond the curtains, getting the material we need for later. Be mindful of her as well and be sure to keep his attention only on you, even if she shows herself."

Viviana couldn't help it, she had to ask. "Who is this girl?"

"Someone who could be bought, Vine. There weren't many in this club that could, unfortunately. Needless to say, she knows who you are, and me."

That wasn't good. "And?"

"And as much as I hate it, I will handle her before she arrives home, despite her help," Ivan said with a frown. "No one can know; there can be no holes."

"Eve?"

Viviana didn't answer the call right away, but when the name was called again, she realized it was for her. Ivan, just as quickly, had slipped back into the darkness the hallway offered, hiding him from view.

"Your room is ready."

The black, crushed velvet coat trimmed with snow white fur in her arms felt like the heaviest weight. Before she could second guess the situation any longer, Viviana slid on a mask, one she'd never worn properly because she hadn't needed to before now.

The Bratva wife. From an Italian princess to a Russian queen.

As far as it takes. No apologies.

"You good to go, sweetheart?" the man asked.

Viviana simpered a demure smile meant to hide the turmoil she truly felt. "Absolutely."

• • •

Sheer fabric separated Viviana from the small platform that led to a single pole in the middle of a ten-by-ten room. She knew the curtain did nothing to hide her figure behind it. The soft, shaded light kept the private room darkened and personal.

The fur coat she wore in exchange for the previous robe was heavy and warm on her body. Any other time, she would have enjoyed the sensation of that expensive pelt on her naked flesh, knowing that what lay beneath the coat was a gift wrapped in sin that her husband loved to expose and ruin.

But it wasn't Viviana's husband on the other side of the curtain.

The oversized hood trimmed with white fur on the coat shielded most of her face from view, hiding the frown tugging her painted red lips down and the eyes she had screwed shut. With calming breaths, Viviana once again reminded herself of why she was doing what she was doing.

For her children, for her husband, and for herself.

It made it easier. It helped to ease the sting left behind as the dignity and honor she had been raised with melted away. Viviana couldn't help but think of Ivan's earlier question. Had she ever danced for Anton? Yes, she had. But like she had said, it was nothing like this.

That had been a sensual dance of tantalization, seduction, and desire. It had been his fingers trailing the curve in her waist while his mouth burned a hot path between the valleys of her breasts. There had been no stage, no pole, and no

173

lighting. Just the drag of skin on skin, soft sheets beneath her knees, and his hands gripping tight enough to keep her steady. The music had not come from speakers in the wall, but the throaty hum building with a thick, deep crescendo from his chest upwards.

Viviana wanted that dance again. With Anton, always.

So Viviana calmed inwardly, knowing that to get that dance, she'd have to do one that would take more from her than she was willing to give. On the outside, she hid beneath the cloak of obscurity the hood provided before she reached up to hit the start button on the panel. A bluesy melody crawled through the speakers instantly.

Then, she stepped out beyond the curtain.

Keeping her face tilted down enough, Viviana's eyes caught the silver glint of the metal pole and the man in his early sixties that sat just beyond it.

Sickness rolled.

Anxiety built.

The nerves didn't show; Viviana walked forward.

Viviana had been told many times that when she walked, she swayed. The shift her hips, the delicate roll of her shoulders. Somehow, unknowingly, she commanded with a single walk, a fleeting glance, and a bare hint of a smile on her lips. In just those movements alone, she drew attention, she could persuade.

And wasn't that the allure of all women?

The difference between others and Viviana was that she knew the influence of hers.

She also understood how to use it.

When Viviana's hand came in contact with the pole, the coat opening enough to expose the expanse of her barely covered skin underneath, a quiet gasp echoed. As her fingers curled around cool metal, her confidence restoring, another appreciative sound resounded in the room.

Viviana didn't mind that. She was aware of the sexuality she held in her body and how she looked standing in nothing but lace, fur, and skin. Anton never failed to remind her of how lucky he was to have something as beautiful as her at his side, in his bed, and holding his love.

This would be the first and last time Viviana ever used that beauty for her own gain.

Slightly slurred, the judge's voice held the hints of the drugs creeping through his system. "My good God, you've got a beautiful set of legs, sweetheart."

Viviana allowed the camber of her crimson smirk peek out beneath the hood before she turned her back to the pole. "So I've been told."

Chapter Fourteen

Prison was hell. Plain and simple, no need to be dramatic, it just was.

If the inmates weren't attempting to pull some stunt on the guards, the guards were causing shit for the inmates. Sleeping with eyes wide open was a rule, if you could sleep, because the noise at night turned up to a whole new level of things no one wanted to hear. The food was absolute crap, cold and bland on a good day, and sludge every other fucking day. Smoking inside the prison wasn't permitted and occasionally a guard would turn cheek if a few smokes turned up outside in the yard, because smoking wasn't supposed to be allowed there, either.

The African-Americans tended to stick together, much like the Asians did, and the Skinheads were a whole other group Anton avoided like the plague. It was like the Russian roulette version of high school, only a hell of a lot more dangerous. These cliques of people weren't there for the popularity, and they didn't have their tattoos because they thought it was cool. Many of the inmates were of gang origin, or they quickly learned that's what they needed to be to survive once they were inside the penitentiary.

They bartered toothbrushes made into shanks and photographs lined with heroin or speed instead of cigarettes and term papers. The only thing the inmates could count on was a daily schedule of three vomit-worthy meals, yard time, and lights out. There was no who was screwing who to gossip about, simply which man was wearing his pants down below his ass, signaling his willingness to be someone's bitch for protection, drugs, or both.

Yeah, that whole thing of teenage boys wearing jeans down around the ankles? Somebody needed to give a lesson to them out in society on what that shit really meant. It wasn't a style choice, it was a blatant proposition behind these walls.

Anton fucking hated it all.

The only thing the Bratva boss found even remotely manageable about Rikers prison was that it wasn't Sing Sing. Neither correctional institute had much going for them, but Sing Sing was a particular hell even Anton wouldn't survive. At least in Rikers he had a source of protection that came in the form of men who had worked alongside his father, or his step-grandfather. Russian men who had taken a hit for the Bratva organization in one way or another and were now locked up for life.

Behind the walls of Rikers, Anton had respect that was as solid as it would ever get. Men still called him the boss and meant it. He didn't have to worry about his cell mate stealing his shit or trying to pull any nasty nonsense on him at night that would get the fucker killed, because the thirty-eight-year-old armed robbery convict was a friend of a friend outside the prison.

Small world and all that jazz.

Anton still hated it.

With a sigh, he settled back into the metal chair as a buzz rang out in the room. Ivan was escorted into the private conference room reserved for inmates and their lawyers. It was only ever used when trials were upcoming and the inmate needed a safe, private place to discuss things. The room was bare but for the metal table, two chairs that were as heavy as the table, and one wall lined with a two-way mirror.

Privacy, sure. Anton was willing to bet there was a camera behind that glass, plus a couple of guards. Who knew, really? Fucking prison. More than anything, he needed to get the hell out and go home to be with his wife and son.

"Boss," Ivan said, tossing his bag to the table at the same time he reached down to pat Anton on the back of the neck. "How was this week?"

Anton beat off the urge to scowl. "It's prison, Ivan. How in the hell do you think it is?"

"Awful."

"Exactly. Did you ask Vine to have that Armani suit cleaned for me?"

Ivan nodded as he pulled out the metal chair, letting the legs scrape along the cement floor. "Yeah, you'll get it Friday morning at the courthouse. That's the best I can do, sorry."

Again, Anton heaved a sigh, crossing his arms over his chest and feeling overwhelmed. "I hate this fucking place, man."

"I know, but it's not forever."

Yeah, right. "I'm facing murder in the first, conspiracy to commit murder, and a dozen other trumped up charges that are just bullshit, and you want to tell me it's not forever? Give me a break. I'm not fucking stupid. I know what I'm facing here."

Ivan didn't say anything, but like all their meetings over the last month, Anton felt like he was missing something. The lawyer was always frank and honest, he didn't sugar coat a thing. So, when Anton mentioned something like his possible sentence, or the upcoming trail, Ivan's conviction about getting him off on the charges never failed.

Was there something going on behind the scenes he didn't know about?

Anton sure fucking hoped so, but he knew he had to be careful about asking. If there was something in the works whatever it was, the chance of someone, mainly the law, finding out outweighed the need to know the details.

"Hey, what's going on with you?" Ivan asked, bringing Anton from his thoughts.

"A fight yesterday in the cafeteria," Anton lied. "They came a little close for comfort, the guards got in on it, you know. Same shit, different hell."

"You talk to Vine any?"

Anton shrugged. "Yesterday morning. Kurt held my place in line for the phone until I finished eating. It didn't last long, though."

Viviana hated talking to Anton while he was in prison.

The goddamn recorder got on the line every minute to remind the call of how much time was left. Whenever he called, the first thing she heard was that a Rikers inmate with the number four-three-six-two-eight was phoning, and did she want to accept the call.

It was one reminder after the other.

"I miss her like crazy," Anton admitted quietly. "And Demyan."

"She'll be there Friday. Early to avoid the press, so you'll get a moment to chat."

But not his son. Demyan was far too young to be included in something like his father's court proceedings. Viviana didn't have to say it out loud, either, because Anton knew. She didn't want to expose their son to that. There would be many things that would be said about him, and a lot were likely true, but that didn't mean Demyan needed to hear them.

"I haven't seen her in a month," Anton said, glancing at the two-way glass reflecting his strained expression. "It's fucking downright killing me here."

"Her, too."

Anton jerked his head to his lawyer. "What?"

"It's been hard on Vine, too."

That shouldn't have been a surprise, but it was. Viviana hid her anguish and worry over his situation much better than Anton anticipated her to.

"She's not sleeping well," Ivan continued. "Demyan is being difficult because you're not around to keep him in line like you do. Erik took him to the park the other day to give her five minutes to breathe."

"Is he still asking for me?"

"All the time. You're his father and he misses you. He's only three, Anton, but he knows something's not right."

Ouch.

Rubbing a hand over his face, Anton said, "Tell me this is going to be okay, Ivan."

The situation was precarious. The unnamed witness on the

prosecution's witness list who reportedly had verbal confirmation from Anton himself that he had killed Sonny Carducci and had a hand in the deaths of the New Jersey Bratva said more than anything else ever could. Where were they? Likely under police protection until their testimony was needed. Who were they? Anton had a sneaking suspicion, and Ivan's next words only confirmed it further.

"Natalie still hasn't shown up anywhere," Ivan said instead. "Not for work, or even her last paycheck, which apparently came back in the mail because it wasn't picked up. All the people we've sent out for her have come back with nothing. Her place hasn't been touched in a long while, but her landlord confirmed someone's been paying her rent for the last six months."

"Since that night in the club."

That awful, horrible night that nearly ended Anton and Viviana's marriage. Anton still had very little memories of what happened between him and Natalie, but what he did remember didn't fill him with much hope. He could still feel her weight straddling his lap, feel her mouth at his neck, hot breath spilling over his cheek. Something in his drink had muddled him up something fierce, making it almost impossible to think, see, or move.

Natalie drugged him; Anton knew it.

Nothing about those memories turned him on. They didn't do a damned thing for him sexually. Anton refused to believe he had strayed from Viviana, but it would make a hell of a lot of sense if the prosecution could point to a woman and say she knew what Anton had done because she was his lover. It didn't matter if Anton couldn't remember; of course he would say that. At least, that's what the other side would say.

Natalie would have a different story. The mistress's tale, even though she wasn't his.

"I didn't fuck that girl, Ivan. I know I didn't."

"I don't doubt it, but you might have said something, especially if what she had was mixed special to jumble you up and loosen your tongue."

"And it might have been bad." Ivan nodded his agreement. Anton didn't like what that could mean. "You think she was working for them the whole time?"

"Her uncle is affiliated," Ivan said. "But that means nothing if they found something to use on her."

"What are we going to do about it, then?"

"We?" Ivan scoffed, smirking. "Anton, you're going to do nothing. Jesus, for once, just let us handle it. We're still searching for her, and besides that, we've got it all worked out if we can't find the bitch."

"Us?" The flash of guilt that skipped in Ivan's eyes didn't escape Anton's keen notice. "What?"

"Nothing, man. Was there anything else you wanted for Friday?"

The distraction wasn't going to work. "You're hiding something I won't like, obviously. Tell me."

"If I was, and it was only for your peace of mind that I keep it quiet, couldn't you let it go?" Ivan asked.

Anton shook his head. "Given I'm going on trial in a couple of days, no. I want to know everything."

"Maybe it's not that," his lawyer suggested.

What else could it be?

"Viviana, then?"

Ivan shot Anton with a pointed look. "Leave it alone."

"So it is about my wife."

"Anton, I said—"

Anton's fist struck down on the table with a heavy bang before he pointed at Ivan. "Fuck off. You go home to your wife every night. You wake her up in the morning. You hug your daughters. Eva's not angry with you because you might be getting locked up for the rest of your life. Your child isn't begging for you to come home. Don't tell me to leave it alone. If it's about my wife, who barely speaks to me about anything beyond my son and her work day, I would really like to fucking know it."

Ivan drummed his fingers to the table top. "Please don't

make me tell you. She wants to, just not over the phone, and not while someone is recording it. That's all."

"She could come *here*," Anton snapped angrily.

There was no response for that, and instead, Anton found himself searching his friend's face for any clues as to what he was hiding. Why wouldn't Ivan just tell him?

"Is it about my son?"

"No, Anton. Demyan is fine, besides that attitude he's got. When you get home, make sure to correct that shit before it becomes a habit likes yours has."

Something awful settled in Anton's gut. "Is she sick?"

"Starting to be," Ivan muttered under his breath.

Starting to be? What the fu—

Anton's thought process cut off like a metal door banging shut. It was as if a light bulb had flicked on inside his head and it goddamn well hurt. Viviana mentioned to him a week or so before his bail was revoked that she was worried about her still missing cycles given it had been months since the miscarriage.

"Oh, God," Anton breathed. Happiness and anguish swirled like a hurricane through his insides, threatening to send him flying and falling all at the same time. It should have been exciting; he'd wanted another child so badly, after all. On the other hand, the reality of where he was couldn't be forgotten, plus how worried his wife must be because of what happened the last time. "She's ... pregnant?"

Ivan chewed on his lower lip, avoiding eye contact. "I'm gonna get you out, no matter what. Just trust me. Okay?"

Anton choked back the rising emotions. "Okay."

Then, Ivan slipped his hand into his suit jacket and pulled out a cell phone. Ivan skidded it across the table, saying nothing. Anton didn't know how the lawyer managed to get the device through security. They all had to be checked in and left behind when visiting with an inmate.

"Sometimes money still talks," Ivan said vaguely. "You know what today is, don't you?"

"Demyan's birthday."

But Viviana wouldn't let Demyan get on the phone.

"Your son would really like to hear his father tell him happy birthday. That's what he asked for, apparently. Well, he asked for you, but Vine thought this would work all the same."

With shaking hands, Anton plucked up the device. "Thank you, Ivan."

Ivan grinned, waving off the tremor in Anton's words. "Whatever, man. Call your little boy before the guards forget about the money I just shoved into their pockets."

• • •

"Happy birthday, little man."

Viviana felt her smile grow as she watched her son's eyes light up at the sound of his father's voice. It had been well over a month since Demyan last seen his father, let alone spoke to him. The stress the child must have been feeling about it daily was started to manifest physically. From temper tantrums, to taking giant leaps backwards in his potty training, to even his speech and desire to talk, Demyan was clearly lost without his father. Viviana didn't know how to explain it to him, not properly.

"Papa?" Demyan asked.

"Yeah, Demyan. How old are you today?"

Demyan grinned as he attempted to pull himself up higher on the counter where Viviana had turned the home phone on speaker. "Papa! It's my happy birthday, today. I'm *three*!"

Viviana stayed silent as Demyan then went on to speak about everything and anything he could possibly think of to tell his father. Right down to the fact that his mother changed the comforter on his bed to the blue one. He chatted about his new cars, and Rocco, before moving on to his trip to the park with Erik.

Anton took the rambling in stride, saying little and letting the child talk. He always did know how to handle his son so well, even when everyone else couldn't understand the boy.

Then, very quietly, Demyan asked, "Where is you, Papa?"

The change in the room was instant and palpable. As if time had stopped for just a moment, as did everything else. Demyan's heartbreak and distress was clear to hear and unfortunately, his mother could see it, as well. Viviana's heart leaped into her throat at the same time Anton's stuttering breath crackled through the phone's speaker.

"*Are,*" Anton corrected. "Not is, are. That's what you mean to say."

"Okay," Demyan whispered. "It's *my* happy birthday ..."

Maybe Demyan wasn't able to verbalize what he was trying to say properly, but Viviana knew what he didn't finish saying: *and you're not here.* Anton always made such a big deal out of his son's special day. This year was intended to be no different from the last, or the one before.

Until the arrest happened.

"I know it is, little man. Papa just had to go away for a while, but not forever. I—" Anton cut off, clearing his throat with a painful, low curse. "*Ya lyublyu tyebya,* Demyan. I love you, my boy. Papa always, always loves you, no matter what. You are my *malysh.* My little boy. Only Papa's, even if I'm not there."

Demyan looked back at his mother, his blue eyes rimmed with tears and hesitance. Like all children would, he assumed his father's lack of presence was somehow his fault. Viviana wavered on her inner thoughts, trying desperately to get a grip on the emotional chaos she felt for her son, and for herself.

Anton saved her the time and effort. "You have to be a good boy for Ma, Demyan. No more nastiness, no more yelling, or fighting. She misses Papa, too, just like you do. I will not be happy if I come home and your mother tells me you didn't listen to me. Is that understood?"

Demyan nodded bleakly, a childlike frown turning his features boyishly sad, even though his father couldn't see it. Viviana felt her lips crack with a smile.

"Yes, I understand."

"Good," Anton said. "Now, give Ma the phone so Papa can say goodbye."

"But, no, Papa—"

"Demyan, I just said no more fighting."

As hard as it was for Viviana to listen to Anton discipline their child, considering it was the first conversation they had in so long, she also knew deep down inside that it was needed. Demyan refused to listen to her most times, and neither Erik, Ivan, nor their bull Rory could be around twenty-four-seven to give him the male presence he so desperately craved. So, she forced her mouth to stay shut as Demyan screwed balled fists to his eyes and whined.

"But, *Papa*!"

Ten seconds of angry wailing later and Anton asked, "Are you finished?"

Demyan sniffled, toeing the cupboard with his sock foot. "Yes."

"Good. What did I say before?"

"No more fighting," Demyan mumbled unhappily.

"What else?"

"I'm *yours*."

Viviana swore she could feel Anton's smile when he said, "And I love you. Now, go find your mutt."

Seemingly satisfied, albeit sadder than he had been, Demyan reluctantly scurried out of the kitchen in search of Rocco. Viviana felt like cement stuck to the floor, unable to reach out and pick up the phone to take it off speaker, but unsure of what she should say now that her son was gone.

"Vine?" Anton asked.

Hoarse and tired, Viviana replied, "I'm here. Thank you … for that."

Anton sighed. "You should have told me he was giving you issues."

"He's just a child. It's not like I can blame the behaviour on anything but his age and circumstance right now, Anton."

"If you just let me talk to him when I call—"

Viviana felt the heat in her blood flare up instantly. "So he can hear his father is a Rikers inmate? I don't want him relating that to you!"

"You would rather he think I fucking abandoned him, then?"

"He doesn't think that."

Anton scoffed, all dark and hateful. The sound cut straight to her aching heart. "Right, baby. Sure. That's the last thing he would assume."

"You don't understand, Anton."

"No, I do. But I hear how goddamned heartbroken he is and it makes me fucking sick. I know it's my fault. I only want to help. It doesn't matter if it's only thirty seconds, but you have to let me talk to him, Viviana. He's my son, too— my boy. Stop keeping him from me!"

"You're right about one thing," she spat back. "It is *your* fault. Every day I'm the only one reminding Demyan that his father will be home soon. I tell him how much you love him. He sleeps in our bed because he thinks you might come home at night when he's asleep. Is that what you wanted to hear from me, Anton? That he's totally lost and out of control? That I'm just managing to keep hold of my sanity between him, the investigation, and this pre—"

Viviana just managed to catch herself from blurting out that she was with child. Silence covered the kitchen and call. In the background, a familiar voice was attempting to calm the situation.

Rarely did their conversations turn sharp and bitter, now. Sure, there was still a lot of low lying anger simmering below the surface, but Viviana rarely brought it up to Anton. Being where he was, she figured he didn't need to be locked up like a caged animal and pissed off all the same.

And, Viviana wasn't entirely sure she was as angry as she was … Well, like her son, lost and out of control without Anton.

"Vine, please …" Anton started, his plead strained and desperate.

"I'm sorry, Anton. I didn't mean—"

The flower arrangement sitting in the middle of the kitchen table caught her gaze, stopping the words. As Anton promised her when she was pregnant for Demyan, a bouquet arrived for her every morning on their son's birthday. This year, the prettiest tiger lilies had made her heart beat faster and tears fall.

"Friday," he said softly. "You can tell me anything ... *everything* ... on Friday, baby."

The tightening sensation in Viviana's throat increased, making it hard for her to speak, let alone breathe. "Everything," she managed to say. "I promise."

"Ya nye magu zhit' byes tyebya."

The Russian on his tongue was still as dark, deep, and heavy as it always was. The syllables of every word drizzled down like liquid gold to wrap and suffocate Viviana even more. After three and a half years of marriage, and his unrelenting stubbornness about her learning some of his mother tongue, she finally did understand a little.

That statement was no exception.

"I know, Anton."

"Never, Vine," he said forcefully, so sure and strong. In English, the words broke her further. "You know I can't live without you."

Chapter Fifteen

A day later, Viviana slid into Ivan's BMW silently, her tired, red-rimmed eyes shielded by large sunglasses.

"How's Demyan today?" Ivan asked.

"Better after speaking to his father. I'm starting to think hiding where Anton actually is might not be the best choice for him. And obviously it's hurting Anton, too. I hadn't really considered that, but I should have."

Ivan didn't say anything at first, simply flicked the ash of his cigarette out of the window. "I've known Anton for a long time, Vine."

"And?"

"And when he became a father, many things about him changed overnight. He was not the kind of man who found a need to feel guilt because of his actions, but he does now. In Rikers, he's alone with his thoughts to keep him company. His guilt is a constant battle that you only added to yesterday. He knew when he offered you the choice to start over new that it could very well mean giving his son up to another man, maybe, one day. I think for you to keep Demyan from him now, even if it is for a good reason, it's not healthy to Anton. As much as he needs your voice, he needs that little boy, too."

"I haven't been giving him that," Viviana said sadly.

"No, but he's abided by your wishes the best he could." With a wave of his hand, Ivan added, "If we truly consider the time he may still have to spend behind bars during this trial, it could be a while. A couple of months, maybe. Are you willing to keep Demyan from him for that long?"

No, she thought immediately. But it wasn't that simple.

"I can't take my child to that place, Ivan. I just *can't.*"

Viviana's heart rate fluctuated wildly at the thought. Rikers Island was no place for a little boy with its stone walls keeping prisoners locked away. How would Demyan feel if he needed to walk away from Rikers only to realize he couldn't take Anton with him? Would he see his father cuffed? Could he, at his age, understand what that meant?

"I wouldn't want my daughters visiting me there, either," Ivan admitted. "It's not a nice place. Anton hates it more and more every day. But say our plan fails, what then? Do you plan on keeping his children from him until they're old enough to make the trip themselves?"

Children. The one word reminded Viviana of the life still growing within.

"I'm not taking my children to that place," Viviana repeated strongly. Reaching over the console, she plucked up the manila envelope. It had been the entire reason for their meeting and the one thing that possibly guaranteed Anton's freedom. "That being said, failing isn't an option."

Ivan tossed her a cocky smirk from the side. "Good luck, then. It's all on you, now."

Viviana slid out of the car without another word.

The small, cozy coffee shop was just that. Tiny. Quiet. It gave off a safe atmosphere. A happy, calming place with earthy tones and plant life on the counter. Very few people milled about inside, most in corner booths with their heads tucked low reading, or playing on their electronics. At the cash register, Viviana ordered, paid for a chai tea, and waited for it to be served as she scanned the rows of tables, looking for the one person she came here for.

There, at the far back behind a half partition wall, sat the judge who would preside over her husband's case. The same man Viviana had danced for, and who probably barely remembered it because of the drugs that had been purposely placed into his drink to confuse him enough not to recognize her. Tucked safely under her arm were pictures of that very incident, but how far would it be able to take her?

With her tea in hand, Viviana slipped down the rows of tables, the click-clack of her heels tapped down to cheap, linoleum floors. The closer she became to the table, the more her nerves grew. Doubling in size, her heart was pounding as her hands turned clammy.

It's all on you, Ivan had said.

That was a hell of a lot of pressure to have.

Viviana refused to fuck it up.

"May I sit?" Viviana asked as she approached the table, keeping her tone demure and sweet.

Judge Kander's head snapped up away from his tablet at her voice, brown eyes seeking out Viviana's. Confusion and surprise flit over his aging features, but he covered it up with a cough and shake of his head.

"Mrs. Avdonin …"

Of course he would recognize Viviana. Pictures of her, Anton, and their son were plastered on newscasts daily. The trial was high-profile, which put all of them under the microscope. It wasn't such a surprise that the judge knew who she was.

"Judge," Viviana said with a smile. "May I?"

"I can assure you this is not acceptable or appropriate. For your husband, it may very well be detrimental."

"Oh, I doubt that."

"There is nothing for us to speak about," the judge continued, his cheeks turning red. "Being seen with you would not look good for either of us. Please, go. I would hate to hurt your husband's case by needing to report you for this. If you leave now, I will overlook this … indiscretion."

"I've done nothing for you to report me, yet." Viviana made a dismissive noise, glancing back over her shoulder at the few people still preoccupied by their books, electronics, and coffees. "No, you see, I've been very careful, Judge. You can't even begin to imagine the precautions I've taken to speak with you like this."

"Mrs.—"

"Viviana," she interjected coolly. "You may call me Viviana."

"I shouldn't be calling you anything at all!"

"Funny, you had no qualms when you were calling me

sweetheart not too long ago."

At those words, the judge blanched. "Excuse me?"

"Don't you remember?" Viviana asked coyly.

Judge Kander spluttered over his words. "I-I ... but, I—"

"Cat got your tongue?"

Viviana had taken special care to appear a certain way for the meeting. The clothes she wore, a tight, pencil skirt and V-neck blouse, were meant to showcase her curves and the stiletto heels not only made her legs longer, but added an extra notch of sex appeal with their incrusted gems on the spike. The makeup she applied, what bit she had, popped her lips and cheeks with a rosy color, while the dark sunglasses hid the truth and disgust in her gaze.

As the judge went to stand, Viviana tossed the envelope to the table with a careless flair. There was no chance of him leaving the café without her speaking the words she needed to. Eight-by-ten photos slipped out of the package, sliding over the smooth top damningly. The judge's eyes scanned what bit of the photos he could see quickly, color draining from his face.

A particular photo rested at the top. One a bit more sordid than the rest. A still-life photograph showcased Viviana kneeling over the judge on a leather couch in nothing but a white lace, sheer thong and bra. His fist had clenched into the side of her panty, pulling the flimsy fabric away from her flesh.

In his gaze, trained solely on her face, even in his uncertainty and confusion, there was lust. The damning photos did not appear to have been taken inside a strip joint. In fact, they had turned out perfectly. As if perhaps a couple had been caught unknowingly.

That alone was better than Viviana or Ivan could have asked for.

Too bad the poor girl who took them had to die for it.

The judge choked on air. "My God."

"I'm sure you can see the precarious position I'm in, Judge."

"You?" he croaked.

"Only in the pictures," she chimed lightly. "I think we should chat, don't you?"

Again, the judge glanced up, his eyes flitting back and forth between Viviana's.

"How?"

Leaning down over the table, Viviana took her time spreading the pictures out before them. Each one was possibly worse than the one before. She hadn't let him touch her much, sure, but never once had his stare on her faltered during the show.

"I've a better question for you," Viviana said with a smirk. "How could you possibly have not known it was me, Judge, isn't that what they'll ask?"

"But—"

Viviana shook her head, black hair tumbling down. "Ah, ah, ah. Go on, report me. They'll investigate, and rip you apart in the process. I bet they'll be forced to release my husband because no one can be sure who is working for who. Give me ten minutes with Anton Avdonin released from Rikers, and I will have him on the next flight out of America where the judicial system of this country can never touch him again.

"Either way," she continued calmly, "… it's a win for me. My son will have his father, and I will have my husband. I don't care where it is that we have him, so long as it's not behind bars. What will you have, Judge?"

• • •

Waiting in the defense chamber of the New York County Supreme Court building, Anton didn't think he had ever been more edgy in his life. Restless and anxious, he paced along the length of the long, oak table as Ivan read over his opening statement. Because a jury had been dismissed for only the judge, the daily progress of the trial should be quicker. It didn't matter, though; Anton still felt sick.

The morning passed him by quietly, in a strange sort of way. Even the guards at the prison who escorted him to the courthouse hadn't given him much of hard time. Oddly, Anton knew, like everyone else around him, that his whole life was on the line, now.

"You okay?" Ivan asked.

Anton shrugged under the weight of his Armani suit. "Not really. Did you get that motion about the press passed?"

"Yeah. No cameras in the courtroom, but like always, there'll be a reporter or a few taking notes."

"Good."

That was a relief. The last thing Anton wanted was for his trial to be streamed daily, every word, every accusation, and assumption, on the television of anyone who tuned in. Really, he didn't give a shit about just anyone, but he did care for his wife and his mother Sasha. They were already facing enough grief because of his actions, they didn't need to have more piled on. Viviana would likely be at the proceedings every single day, anyway, and Sasha when she could, but the media didn't need any more fuel added to their fire.

"Where is she?" Anton asked.

Ivan closed his files, leaning back in his chair. "Calm down, man. Vine is coming. Despite wanting to be early because of the press, the bastards were out bright and early. You happened to miss the lot of them because they brought you in through the back. She won't be so lucky."

Damn it.

"Is she ...?" Anton trailed off, making a rounded motion over his abdomen.

"Hell no. Not yet, anyway. She's only like ... three months, or something. I don't think she's even told anybody because of what happened last time. It's probably hard on her to think about it all right now. I've got to say, you sure pick the shittiest times to knock her up, man. First time was a bomb, second time you got arrested, and this time—"

"Didn't fucking plan it the first time, asshole."

Ivan sat up straight in his chair, cocking a brow. "But you

did plan this one?"

Anton wished his tongue hadn't suddenly grown two times its normal size. What in the hell was his friend getting at? "It wasn't like that. We were trying before I even got arrested the first time when she miscarried."

"But she got pregnant after the miscarriage, after you knew you might be going to prison, Anton." Ivan drummed his fingers to the table, glancing away. "That might not have been the smartest play on your part."

"Wasn't like that, either," Anton muttered. "We were still trying to move on from the Natalie bullshit, then losing the pregnancy, and weren't careful. I didn't intentionally get my wife pregnant because I was facing serious time. That's just … Jesus, do you think I'm that horrible?"

"I think you're so in love with her that you'd do anything to keep her."

"Not that, Ivan. I wanted another child, but I didn't intend for her to be pregnant at a time like this."

Smiling a little too roguishly for Anton's liking, Ivan shrugged. "Well, whatever you intended, it looks good on you."

Anton's brow furrowed. "How so?"

"The family man. A sweet, charming son. A pregnant, devoted wife. Your family is especially beautiful—one the public may feel they can relate to, in some way. If they can't, they'll certainly want to. You're successful in both personal and public matters. You live in a beautiful home, drive nice cars, and own your own businesses."

"Are you serious?"

Ivan rolled his eyes. "Of course I am. Whether you like it or not, public opinion matters. When you're back out in the world, the last thing you need, or want, is an angry group of people outside your home with their proverbial pitchforks."

"You keep saying when I'm out like it's actually going to happen."

"Because it will," Ivan stated confidently. "Stop worrying. Instead of appearing reckless or uncaring, like the prosecution has been portraying you every chance they get, you actually come across as normal. How could that intelligent, good-looking, pregnant woman have possibly married a mobster, Anton? How could the man they say you are possibly have a child as sweet and innocent as Demyan?"

"You just said she hasn't told anyone about the pregnancy," Anton pointed out.

"Vine can't hide it forever. Sympathy plays a factor, also."

"The judge will be impartial beyond even what a jury would be, Ivan."

"Perhaps," his friend mused. "But I do believe you might find this particular judge will be partial to us, Anton."

The implication there was not hidden, by any means. Anton wasn't entirely sure what he should say, or ask. Before he could gather his thoughts, Ivan continued.

"After all, a jury would get to hear you be slandered over and over. So does the judge, but he's looking at the facts. And what is it they have, exactly? A DNA match that's only thirty-five percent, from the father's side; not nearly close enough to be a sure thing, given your biological grandfather could have had a dozen more male children we don't know about before Nicoli wacked him. No weapon or ballistics for Sonny's murder. A shell casing was found in the burnt out restaurant where the Belovs were found, but no gunshot wound was ever located on the bodies. Yet, they're still calling it a murder. You may have been seen near the area that night, but so were a lot of other people. Those things mean nothing. They add up to absolutely nothing. If anything, they create plausible, reasonable doubt."

"Witness testimony," Anton pointed out. "Natalie will say I told her what I did, which outweighs the rest."

"If the witness shows," Ivan replied, unfazed. "They cannot use her testimony without her presence. You have a right to confront your accuser."

"Are you saying you've found her?"

That would be incredibly good for Anton, but especially bad for Natalie.

"I'm saying we're watching and we have some time before they'll call her to the stand. There might be a lead on that, anyway."

"Yeah?"

Ivan shrugged, but didn't look up from his papers. "Something came from Jersey. Thank your new friend Adrik. He's got a lot to lose with you in prison, so ..."

Anton licked his lips, shoving his hands into his pockets with a heavy sigh. This was the most information he had safely been able to pull from Ivan, but he wondered how much more he could get. There had to be more, considering everything. They weren't ones to leave holes where something might slip through. Not anymore, not after all of this had happened.

"What about the judge?"

Ivan's confident mask finally cracked in the form of a fleeting frown.

"Will I not like this?" Anton asked when his friend stayed silent.

"I think, if you really need to know, you should ask Vine," Ivan finally said.

Well, that didn't bode well, either.

"Are you telling me my wife is involved in whatever schemes—"

Ivan held up a single hand. "I'm telling you not to ask her unless you're willing to understand what she did for you."

• • •

"Papa!"

Viviana felt tears spring to her eyes as Anton turned on his heel at the sound of his son's voice with a choked gasp. The decision to bring Demyan to the courthouse was one she wrestled with, to the point where she had little to no sleep the night before. No one expected or knew she was bringing him, as it ended up being a last minute thing that morning. One that made her especially late, and put her front and center for the media outside.

The sounds of their camera shutters clicking down repeatedly as Viviana and Sasha attempted to shield Demyan from the photographs was still haunting her memory. The tiny fists of her son had grabbed so tightly to the strands of her hair hanging loose around her neck. He stayed clinging to her shoulder, his favorite blanket tossed over his head, so confused and scared of the people, their questions, and the flashes of light.

Viviana had continued to wave the reporters off, saying nothing.

They weren't important. Let them have their pictures. They didn't matter.

Demyan dropped from his mother's arms to the floor and his sneaker-clad feet barely made it two steps before Anton was meeting him. Shaking and laughing at the same time, Demyan was wrapped in his father's embrace. Anton buried his face into the boy's neck and held tight, lifting him off the floor at the same time Demyan's legs wrapped around his father's middle.

"Oh, Demyan ... My little boy ..." Anton's whispers were hushed, turning relieved and pained at the same time. With one hand, he smoothed down the dark hair at the back of Demyan's head. Standing in the middle of the room, as if no one else was there watching, Anton rocked his son, gentle murmurs of Russian mixing in with his English. "I miss you so much. So, so much, Demyan. Papa is so sorry."

Viviana forced the tears blurring up her vision to stop. It wouldn't be long before Demyan needed to leave. They didn't have a great deal of time and she drew the line at having him inside the courtroom. Sasha already agreed to skip the first day of proceedings to take the child back home.

Sasha came to stand at Viviana's side, expelling a shaky breath. "I've not seen him in so long ..."

Viviana nodded her understanding to her mother-in-law's unspoken words. Neither had she, really. Rikers didn't only scare her for her son's sake, but for her own, as well. Not once had she worked up the nerve to make the trip with Ivan, never mind going it alone. Anton hadn't asked her to come, so she felt he must have understood what she couldn't, or wouldn't, say.

"Go on," Viviana urged Sasha, willing the quake in her tone to leave. "Say hello, and spend some time with him before you leave."

After all, Viviana would have all day with Anton. Hours to watch him, though they wouldn't be able to speak during the proceedings. There would be short breaks for an occasional recess, and a longer one for lunch. She would have her time, but Demyan and Sasha wouldn't.

Sasha didn't need any more encouragement to greet her only child. Their embrace, much like Anton's had been with Demyan, was just as heart-wrenching to witness. Only quiet murmurs passed between mother and son, the same apology falling from Anton repeatedly. The guilt he must have felt over the war his family faced was beginning to show. Viviana hadn't expected that and it hurt.

"God, Ma," Anton started to say, his jaw tightening. "You didn't have to come."

"I know, but I wanted to."

The guard standing just outside the doorway caught Viviana's gaze. With a nod, the man reached in and grasped the doorknob, closing the door soundlessly and offering the family a bit more privacy. Because there were no windows in the room, and only the one entrance, he didn't need to be inside, but he couldn't leave his post.

Either way, she was grateful for his actions.

Anton let Demyan down to the floor. Instead of exploring the room like he usually would, the child stayed at his father's side, his hands clasped into Anton's pant legs. It almost seemed he thought if he let Anton go, he might disappear.

Viviana ached a little more.

Had she made the right choice bringing him?

Would it scar Demyan further when he left his father behind?

"This was unexpected," Ivan said quietly beside Viviana.

"He's going to have a hard day," Viviana explained.

"Demyan?"

"No, Anton." Viviana offered an apologetic smile. "I didn't want him going back there frustrated, or worse, angry because of today. It might be good for Demyan to see him, but Anton needed it, too. Maybe he'll take that back instead of the trial."

"Papa," Demyan said, tugging on his father's pants.

Anton was down on one knee instantly, answering Demyan with full attention. Their son attempted to explain he had to leave Rocco at home, though he wanted him to come. The soft smile playing on the edges of Anton's lips mixed in with the happiness shining behind wet eyes told Viviana all she needed to know.

She made the right choice. The rest didn't matter.

Chapter Sixteen

"Bye, bye, Papa!"

Anton hid his sadness with a wave, hoping those wouldn't turn into famous last words for him and his son.

"Not bye, Demyan, just I'll see you soon," Anton said.

Demyan, holding tight to his grandmother's hand, gave a fierce nod.

The door wasn't closed but two seconds before Anton crossed the distance between him and his wife. That ten feet of space had been teasing him ever since Viviana walked into the room. She'd mostly kept her distance, giving Sasha and Demyan their space and time.

Now, he just fucking wanted her.

The moment Anton's palm came touched Viviana's reaching hand, heat siphoned up his arm, snaking over his skin and straight into his veins. Air sucked through his teeth, like the hissing sting of heartache beating through the organ in his chest. Their fingers laced as Anton drew his wife into his arms, taking in the sweetened scent of her floral perfume that always soaked into his lungs like the best drug.

Closer was better. The beats of her heart thumped against his chest. The lingering pain of letting his son go slowly started to subside. There, with Viviana's face hidden against his neck, Anton felt the first of his tears begin to fall.

"Vine," he said, her name alone in his mouth sounding a hell of a lot like a prayer. "Thank you, baby."

"No, no. He needed that, so I brought him along. He'll probably be so confused tonight, but I just—"

Anton shushed low, tugging Viviana's warmth in closer. Wordlessly, she tilted her head up enough to press silken lips to the underside of his jaw, her fingers dancing along the front of his suit jacket. The action caused a shiver to crawl from the base of his spine up to his shoulders, while a familiar pressure built in his groin. Tingles sneaked over his skin. Want and need warred a battle through his insides.

"Jesus," Anton half wheezed. Surprised would be an understatement. They hadn't touched in so long, and it only took the most innocent of grazes for his entire body to react like it had. "Baby, baby ..."

Again, Viviana kissed his jaw softly, fisting his jacket. Ghosting her mouth along his cheek, she stood on the toes of her heels to meet his burning gaze long enough for Anton to see the love and devotion staring back in her eyes.

As badly as he needed to see that, it was just as much overwhelming.

The wetness on his cheeks betrayed the tears he'd tried to cover up. Always so strong, Anton didn't want his wife to see him weak. Pride played no part here, though. With Viviana, there was no hiding.

"It's going to be okay," Viviana said, quiet and firm. "It is, Anton."

Dumbly, Anton could only nod. "Okay."

Ivan's previous words earlier that morning were still on the forefront of his mind. Anton wasn't ready to ask Viviana how she knew this fucked up situation would, or could, work out for them. Or worse yet, he wasn't entirely sure he was ready to accept whatever role she may have played.

Viviana didn't give Anton time to consider his thoughts further, because in the next moment, her lips were pressing to his with an almost bruising force. Sweet like honey, and bitter from the anxiety still edging at the corners of his mind, the feel of her mouth on his overtook everything else. Nothing mattered but the nip of her teeth to his lip. A heady groan tumbled from his chest into the room as his fingers weaved into her hair. Soft, sleek waves that smelled like home, and love, and *her*. Heat flooded his veins while blood flooded his cock.

Before Anton realized what happened, his back was hitting a wall with a thump.

A throat cleared behind them, embarrassed and surprised.

Anton swallowed back the building lust, cringing as he remembered the last presence who hadn't actually left the room when the others had. Viviana, on the other hand, hid her mortified pinked cheeks against his hands cradling her face.

"Ivan," Anton said under his breath.

"Yeah, I'm going to pretend like my eyes don't need a serious bleach cleaning," the lawyer replied dully.

It wasn't the first time Ivan had seen or heard something between the two, but he hadn't ever been so close. The one thing Viviana and Anton never lacked was passion. Obviously it still burned as bright as it ever did. Being apart only fueled that need.

Over his wife's shoulder, Anton met Ivan's knowing gaze. With a tick of his chin to the side, he asked, "Could you …?"

Ivan frowned. "Maybe, man, but no guarantee."

Jesus, Anton didn't care. It wasn't like he needed a great deal of time to do … What in the hell was he planning on doing? Didn't matter, he realized. Anything with Viviana was perfect, even just holding her, but he needed to do it alone.

"*Try*," Anton growled.

"Anton!"

Viviana's admonishment only earned her a smirk from the lawyer across the room.

"It's all good, Vine," Ivan said. "I should go … grab something from my car."

"That's what, twenty minutes?" Anton asked.

"Just about."

Good enough, Anton thought. "And the guard?"

Ivan shrugged. "That's the maybe. This is your space in the courthouse for the duration of the trial while you're in this building. You can't escape without going right past him. Someone needs to be in this room with you at all times."

"Someone is," Viviana said pointedly.

"Exactly," Ivan responded with a wink to Anton.

Without another word, Ivan made his move to leave the room. Anton followed his lawyer's steps with a watchful eye, not missing Ivan's hand slipping up to flick the lock on the doorknob before the door clicked shut behind him.

Anton sighed when after the man was gone, no knock immediately came for the door to be reopened. "That's better."

"About Demyan." Viviana had his full attention again with just their son's name. "You were right. I was wrong to keep him from you, no matter my intentions."

Anton sniffed away the remaining tears still lurking along his lashes. "Nah, baby. I understood, really. But I was going out of my mind thinking he needed me, and I wasn't there."

"He never forgets about you, Anton," Viviana said, reaching up to brush away the wetness under his eyes. "Talks about you every single day. He's got your picture in his room, and he watches all those videos of you and him on my phone over and over. He's got his papa, all the time. Whenever he wants you, you're there. I promise, you're the first thing I talk to him about in the morning and the last thing he hears before bed."

"But it's not *me*, Vine."

Biting the inside of her cheek, she agreed. "I know, but until this is over, it's the best we can do for him."

"And what about us?" Anton asked.

"We haven't been doing well, huh?"

"Not going on like we have. Pretending, whatever you want to call it." In all truth, it fucking sucked. She needed to know that. "If you're pissed off at me for all of this, I need to know. I want to, Vine. Just talk to me about something more than your day. Tell me if our kid is being a brat. Cry, I don't care. But don't pretend for my sake, if that's what it is, not anymore."

"Okay."

Anton raised a brow. "Just okay?"

"Yeah, Anton. Just okay."

A brief, uncomfortable silence passed before Anton asked, "Are you ready for this day?"

"No, I'm terrified," she confessed sadly. "That fear

doesn't rule me. It can't. I need you home, especially now."

Yeah, that Anton knew. With the pregnancy, Viviana must be facing more stress than normal. And thinking of which, she still hadn't told him about it. Anton wasn't about to let her go one more minute dealing with that alone.

"Vine, I know about ... Well, I just know."

In his embrace, she practically turned to ice. Color drained from her pretty face, pink lips popping open in shock. That wasn't exactly the reaction Anton was expecting.

"You *know?*" Viviana asked, the air in her voice disappearing. At his confused nod, she added, "And you're ... okay with it?"

Anton's confusion only rose further, as did the ache in his heart. The choice to have another child had been shared equally between them, but he knew those feelings might have changed for Viviana after everything they had dealt with, and were still handling.

"Do you not want to have the baby? I mean, it's not the greatest time and the last pregnancy didn't end well—"

"The baby," Viviana interrupted. "You're talking about the baby."

"Is there something else?"

"No," she rushed to say. "No, of course not. That was really the last thing on my mind today is all."

Anton laughed, relief sweeping his senses. "The last thing? You're *pregnant.* You must be sick half of the time, tired the other half, and sick and tired of keeping it a secret, aren't you?"

Viviana hummed a sound that had his insides waking up all over again. "I am."

"Pregnant." Needing to feel more of her skin against his, Anton slipped his hands up under the white blouse she wore, laying both his palms flat to her smooth stomach. Electricity danced along the edges of his fingers as he swept them over her flesh. "With my baby."

"Yes, Anton. I'm sorry I didn't tell you right away. There was so much going on, and I was scared of losing this one, too. I had an early ultrasound at nine weeks to check for the heartbeat. They could see it. That helped. I'm thirteen weeks along now, so we've passed the first trimester. That helped a hell of a lot more."

"No way, baby. No apologies. I'm so fucking excited, you don't even know."

The smile Viviana graced him with was the most honest and open thing he'd seen in so long. Again, Anton found his lips caught in hers while his hands stayed pressed to her midsection. Their second kiss was much slower than the first. Tantalizing and promising. So hopeful and loving. He took his time exploring her mouth with gentle flicks of his tongue, needing to taste and savor the beauty of his wife.

"I've missed you, Vine. I love you."

"Always," she echoed.

What happened then between them was as fast as it was rough. Anton removed his hands from Viviana's body just long enough to bend down and grasp the backs of her thighs. She seemed to expect his move, finding purchase on his shoulders to hold her steady as he walked her backwards. At the long, sturdy table that was certainly not meant to be used in the way Anton planned to use it, he sat his wife down at the very edge.

Viviana's thighs opened further under gentle urging. Born from a want that had been building from the moment Anton knew his wife was in the same room as he, the desire swirling in his gut grew.

It was the first time Anton took a serious inventory of her outfit choice for the day, as he'd been so focused on just her that he hadn't noticed at all before. The royal blue skirt she wore was tight to her body, falling just above her knees. The blouse kept her covered, but with the pop of three buttons under his hand, her olive toned skin was exposed to his mouth.

Anton nipped a gentle path along the hollow of Viviana's neck, and down to her collarbones. The sweetest gasps rolled from her lips in perfect tune with the shifts of her hips that rocked into his groin. Frantic and rushed, he was all too aware of just how much time they didn't have. That anyone might knock on the door. That the guard might hear the sounds he created just by touching his stunning wife. It was only urged on further, needier, by her hands skimming between the opened front of his suit's jacket, sneaking beneath to try and flick open the buttons on his dress shirt.

The buttons didn't slip through the loops as fast as she wanted them to. Viviana's frustration showed when she tugged roughly on the tail of his shirt to pop open the buttons quicker.

"Careful," Anton warned.

"I need to feel you," Viviana said, her voice airless but full.

Viviana drove her opened palm from Anton's navel, up over the railroad path of his abdomen, to the spot on his chest where his heart lay beating beneath. It was mixture of the softest touch with the strongest pressure. A sensation he hadn't been expecting to feel at all. It damn near brought him to his knees.

All over again, Anton's body was reacting to his wife's close proximity. Not just the obvious, no, but the things she couldn't see. Like the way his pulse picked up, beating fast and hard straight down to the shaft of his hard cock. Or, how his lungs seemed to ache with every expansion, but it hurt so fucking good. The heat of her skin pressed to his, tapping straight in to his blood and bones.

God, this girl owned him.

Just like she always had.

So, when her fingers curled against his chest, her fingernails digging in to claw down, Anton could only sigh. He felt everything, and it reached everywhere. Viviana always did know how to get him moving faster, after all.

The skirt she wore was bunched up over her hips, exposing simple, black cotton beneath. Anton wasted no time reaching in between the creamy, smooth contours of Viviana's thighs to lay his palm flat at the seam of her core. With his fingers hooking under the side of her panties, he slipped in one digit between the fleshy, soft folds of her sex, giving no notice of his intrusion.

Abruptly, Viviana tensed and cried out. Anton caught her next lower, sultry moan in his mouth, shushing to keep her quiet while he worked a tender beat with the second finger he added. Slick, warm arousal coated his fingers and Viviana's pussy. That's what Anton wanted, to have her ready, and so wanting for him. It'd been so long since he took her, and the last thing he desired for her to experience was any discomfort.

"No time," he heard her say. "We don't have—"

"Like fuck," Anton muttered through his teeth.

Using his free hand, Anton pushed Viviana back until she lay flat to the table. Leaning over her form, he opened her shirt, pushed aside the black lace of her bra, and took her pink nipple into his mouth. Beautifully, her back arched like a bow. Anton bit down roughly around the taut peak.

"Shit," Viviana gasped.

"Mmhmm." Anton grinned, releasing his bite. A perfect set of his teeth marks stared back imprinted into her flesh. Face to face, he reveled in watching her lips part and eyes roll back. "You're going to feel that all fucking day, baby. You're going to feel all of me when I'm done with you."

Anton pumped his fingers deeper, seeking for that spot to make her shake. When Viviana's eyes flew wide open, her head falling back to the table, he knew he'd found it. One of her hands grabbed onto his wrist like a vise while her other reached back to hold the edge of the table. The faintest sheen of perspiration marked her skin. The silken, hot walls of her pussy clamped down around his two fingers as he thrust up into her G-spot again.

Viviana came with a broken cry, the sweetly tart wisps of scent from her sex finally starting to waft through the room.

"There we go," Anton soothed, stroking with his fingers to coax her orgasm out as long as he could.

Who knew how long it would be before he touched her again. Viviana looked so fucking amazing laid out underneath him, too, with her skirt gathered up and her blouse opened. Like maybe they weren't where they really were, and what was happening around them wasn't actually happening. After all, they'd done this so many times before. For a short time, he could pretend.

"God, baby, look at you."

There was a quake in Anton's voice that Viviana didn't miss. Those melted, milk chocolate eyes of her locked on to his damningly, soaking up every inch of his face with a simple sweep of her stare.

"We have to hurry," Viviana said.

That might have been right, but it didn't mean Anton wanted it to be. He said nothing when she fumbled with the button and zipper of his pants. Her shaking hands pushed the fabric of both his pants and boxer-briefs down in a frenzy. There was no question in her desire, only the hot, tight grip of her palm wrapping the steel-hard length of his erection in satin.

Anton barely had time to remove his fingers from her body, keeping her panties swept off to the side with his thumb, before Viviana was pulling him closer. She didn't seem to need his help guiding her home, so he cupped her cheek with one hand. The moment the head of his cock rubbed against the slit of her pussy, Anton choked. The cold grip of something he was unaccustomed to feeling gripped him fiercer than ever.

Fear.

"Anton?" Viviana asked, glancing up.

A shudder crept up Anton's spine. What was stopping him from taking Viviana?

"Not the last time," he said through an audible swallow. The statement was vague at best, but his wife seemed to understand, responding with a faint nod. "Never, Vine."

"Never."

It only took a single, well-aimed flex of his hips and Anton was buried to the hilt in the heaven that was his wife. At the same time, he let go of the hold he had on her panties. Using both his hands, Anton grabbed hold of Viviana's wrists and pulled her up from the table to meet him. Their mouths crashed together with a strength Anton never felt before. Teeth clashed as her tongue swept alongside his. The muffled moan that escaped from his chest mingled with Viviana's gasped cry of his name.

What control Anton thought he had, was suddenly all but gone with a snap.

It was the heat, the wetness, and the tightness surrounding him.

Pulling away from her sex, Anton didn't make it halfway out before he was slamming back in. Viviana's nails cut into the skin of his hands, marking him like he loved. Something brutally swift came down on him harsh and strong, taking the wind right out of his chest. Anton filled her, stretching her open as her thighs dropped from his waist and widened further so he could get her deeper.

Like hell just picked him up and dropped him off in the best goddamned place.

"Fuck, Vine ... Fuck, I *can't* ..."

No, Anton couldn't do a damned thing. Even thinking was a lost cause. The only thing he understood was his cock was covered in her, slicked up with the arousal he wanted smeared on his mouth, and suddenly he was balls-deep inside her walls again. The trembling lips pressed to his opened at the same time her eyes opened wide. Fire burned in her gaze like the passion boiling at the very pit of his stomach. Over and over their hips met, the drag of skin on skin taking him a little higher, and a little lower.

Viviana brought their connected hands up, turning her face away from his view just long enough to press her lips to his knuckle. Then, she bit him, too. Air cut through his teeth, but her mouth was already back on his, their hands falling back down to the table.

"Faster," Viviana pleaded, holding his stare, refusing to let go.

It should have been slow, soft, and sweet.

It wouldn't be anything like that at all, and Anton knew it.

Brutal and dirty, it was how they always were; how life had made them.

When they were done, Anton would clean her, fix their clothes, and hold her like he'd wanted to. In the courtroom, he'd take a moment to kiss his wife, holding her chin between his forefinger and thumb to keep her gaze like she did him, just to remind her. While the prosecution laid the groundwork for a case that had to fail, he'd stare at nothing but the bite mark on his knuckle.

That's what Viviana did for Anton.

No one could do it better.

So, he let her.

Chapter Seventeen

Viviana fumbled to answer the ringing cellphone in the darkness of the bedroom, not wanting the noise to wake the sleeping child beside her. It took three swipes of her hand over the top of the bedside table before she finally grasped a hold of the vibrating, screeching device.

"Do you know what fucking time it is?" she asked when she brought the phone to her ear.

"Oh, good, you're awake."

Ivan sounded as sarcastic and cocky as he always did. Viviana was starting to wonder how in the hell her husband managed to put up with his best friend and lawyer for as long as he did. Then again, Anton had a similar attitude, so maybe that was why their bond was as strong as it was.

"No, I'm not—"

"Do you have someone to watch Demyan?" Ivan asked suddenly.

Viviana wiped the sleep from her eyes, glancing at the clock blinking a time that shouldn't be legal for someone to wake her up at, given the week she just had. The first week of Anton's trial had been nothing more than the prosecution repeatedly dragging her husband through the mud. It was hard to sit there in the galley listening to it all.

It was harder keeping her act up. The one she held for Anton, the one reserved for the public, and an entirely different one that reminded a certain judge of the position he was in.

No, Viviana had no patience for late night phone calls that sported Ivan being a fucking smartass.

"Ivan, it's—"

"Only one in the morning, so get up," Ivan interrupted.

Viviana screwed her lips shut with a huff, chancing a look at her sleeping boy. "Listen, Demyan is in my bed. I'm not in the mood for this tonight."

The next words Ivan spoke chilled the room by several degrees.

"We found her, Vine."

"*Her?*" she asked quietly, knowing he'd get the point.

"Yeah, we fucking got her. One of Adrik's men followed that lead and it led straight to her. We owe him a lot for this. It's going to be done by the morning, and it'll all be over."

The cellphone dropped out of her hands to the bedspread. Viviana didn't dare pick it back up for fear what Ivan said might actually be true. Natalie was the last piece to their puzzle. The one thing that could still put Anton away, even with the judge being blackmailed.

There were things the justice system could not ignore. A witness giving testimony, for one.

Quickly, Viviana plucked up the phone again, running on adrenaline and heartache. Their phone call couldn't be recorded as they had used burner phones for as long as she could remember. They switched them out every couple of months just to be safe.

"Where is she?" Viviana demanded lowly.

Ivan replied, "At the club. You want a drive, or no?"

No, she didn't need a drive. And she wouldn't want someone seeing the breakdown on her way home, either.

"You could leave it alone, Vine."

"What?"

"Leave it alone," Ivan said again to her surprise. "Forget about it and let us handle it. You've already forgiven what might have happened between her and Anton, whether it did or didn't occur. You've moved on. You don't have to come."

Ivan made a valid point, sure. Unfortunately, there was more to it than he could ever possibly understand. Anton was so adamant that nothing could have possibly happened between him and Natalie that Viviana wanted desperately to believe him. But, the truth of the matter was simple. He didn't know.

Anton couldn't know for sure, he didn't have the memory

to make his words fact.

Even so, there was a bleakness to Anton's voice whenever he spoke about it. A cloudiness hazed his eyes. Viviana knew guilt was the first emotion to plunder through his system in regards to how it hurt her.

It wasn't only Viviana that needed to know the truth. Anton did, too.

"I have to know if that woman was with my husband," Viviana said softly.

"You're sure?" Ivan asked.

There was no hesitation in her thoughts. No flowery explanation in her words. Just honesty, as plain as it was.

"Yes, I need to."

• • •

Viviana pushed through the obnoxious, smothering crowd inside Seven Lights at a little past two in the morning. There was thirty feet of dancing, drunk, and far too happy people in her way before she would be able to disappear up the metal staircase that led to Anton's upstairs office.

While her husband was incarcerated, a few of his guys had really stepped up to take care of the club after the feds were finished tearing it apart during their searches. Viviana had no interest in the place, and even if she did, she wouldn't know what to do with it. The same guys handling the club business also made sure the other businesses Anton had a hand in was running properly, too. Even though Viviana technically owned those businesses, they were for all purposes, her husband's. She didn't have the first clue how to run a strip club, restaurant, or bar. Not a one. They didn't ask her to, either.

"Vine!"

Over the loud music, drunken voices, and laughter, Viviana heard her name called again. She followed Ivan's voice through the throng of people, feeling her heart beat faster the closer she came to the stairs. There were so many bodies inside the club she had to wonder if the building was over its fire code.

Seven Lights always was popular in Brighton Beach. With Anton's arrest, it was even more so.

No one seemed to notice it was Viviana pushing her way past them, though. That, or they were too drunk and enjoying themselves to care. She'd tried to dress the part of being at a club to dance, at Ivan's suggestion. Even though she hadn't wanted to. Taking the time to get dressed up and do her makeup had wasted precious time that would have been better spent getting this over with and going home.

Finally at Ivan's side at the bottom of the stairs, he leaned down to say in her ear, "No one noticed a thing when they brought her in through the back."

"She's up there right now?" Viviana asked. Jesus, there was a whole building full of witnesses! "Are you fucking stupid?"

"This isn't our first scene, girl. Besides, with the cops they had watching Natalie, it was like picking up a penny out of a fountain. I guess they weren't even inside the motel they had her shacked up in, just waiting outside like a bunch of fools. She was a sitting duck. Simple, or so says Adrik."

Viviana tried to wave her worry off, but it was already settled in way too deep. "How'd his guys find her if ours couldn't?"

"Adrik has a few official contacts we could really use on our side, too."

"Is she actually awake?"

Ivan rolled his eyes. "For now."

Yikes, that was cringe worthy. Viviana wasn't sure she wanted to know what that meant.

"I don't want to see—"

"It's clean. Nothing like that. Anton wouldn't want it that way, anyhow. Messy means we'll have more to clean up later. That's unacceptable. Come on, Vine, if you're so fucking intent on doing this."

When she paused, Ivan asked, "You do want to, don't

you?"

"Very much," Viviana admitted.

Ivan frowned. "So what's the hold up?"

"What if it did happen? You were right earlier, I have forgiven him. I'm perfectly happy to move on and not know because of it." Viviana blew out a quiet sigh, her stress rising. "Did I just come here to punish myself? Because I believe him when he says he couldn't have done it, but that doesn't mean it didn't happen. If I find out it did, will that change my opinion?"

"I don't think you came here to validate what you already feel, Vine."

"Oh, no?" she asked, trying hard not to scoff. "Please, feel free to tell me why I did, then."

"Because you wanted to hear her say it," Ivan replied simply. "You know how you feel about it, and so does Anton. Your reaction now, if you find out he did fuck her, won't be any different from when you first thought he did. What's the difference, really? Nothing. You only want to hear her say it. Either yes, or no.

"You want the confirmation that he can't give. And you want to ask why, like any normal person would. Those are the answers you haven't been given. Humans are the most curious of creatures. We have to know everything, pick things apart to understand the hows and whys of it all. You want to be satisfied in your information and there's nothing wrong with that. It has very little to do with forgiveness, Vine."

Oddly, what Ivan said made a lot of sense. It was something she hadn't considered, but it felt right.

"Okay," Viviana said, feeling her emotions lockdown and ready for the battle ahead.

Ivan waved at the stairs. "After you."

• • •

Natalie sat across from Viviana with a fleece blanket tossed over her shoulders. With a stony expression and blank, eyes

215

staring at the wall, she looked tired. If it weren't for the slight tremor rocking the girl's shoulders, she would almost appear unbothered by her current situation.

Viviana knew better.

"Are you scared?" she asked Natalie.

They were the first words Viviana had spoken to her since entering the office, and the effect they had were shocking. Natalie flinched, eyes fluttering closed as she grimaced. "I've been scared for a long time."

Viviana nodded. That she could understand. "Your uncle is here as well."

"To kill me," Natalie said with a sniff.

"No, to show respect for his boss. Something you wouldn't understand." Viviana rocked back on her heels, resting her elbows to her knees. "You see, Viktor has caused Anton issues once before. Slapped me around a little when he was supposed to bring me to my husband safe and secure. Their business relationship hasn't been the same since, or so I've been told. Viktor has a lot to prove. You'll certainly help that."

"But I will die."

Viviana made a dismissive noise, though her heart clenched painfully. There was no denying the fact she didn't like where this had all led them, and where they had yet to go, but it was the ways and rules of their life. Something Natalie hadn't followed.

"Did my husband really tell you he killed Sonny and the Belovs?" Viviana asked quietly.

Natalie glanced up from under her damp lashes, the mess of wetness on her face shining in the overhead lights. "Yes."

"What did you give him?"

"Vine," Ivan stared to say.

"Shut up, Ivan." Viviana didn't even turn to look at him. "Natalie, what did you give him?"

"I ... I don't know," the girl confessed.

Confusion ran rampant. "Excuse me?"

"They said it wouldn't do any harm, just make him more

agreeable. That's how they said it: agreeable. The feds, I mean. I wasn't told what it was, only how to use it."

"They'd do anything," Erik said angrily. "And what could he say, huh? Nothing, because it was probably all burnt out of his blood by the time they thought to check. Fucking ridiculous."

Viviana had to agree, but she forced herself to bite her tongue and not respond. That wasn't the discussion she wanted to have at that time. The question burned inside her mouth, so she let it out, knowing full well the answer might kill her further. "He wasn't agreeable before?"

"No."

"But he was after?" Viviana pressed.

Natalie blinked, the blank expression returned while tears slipped from the corners of her eyes. "I'm a pretty girl, or so I was always told."

Sure, that was true. Natalie wasn't anything to scoff at. "Your point?"

"Men look, they always have. I've never had a problem catching a man. It should have been easy. All I needed to do was get close, make him pay attention, catch his eye, and move in. The agents assumed because Anton wasn't having a public affair that he must have been keeping it on the low. Someone inside. Or maybe even more than one. God knows he's got enough girls working for him to do it, right? You were always around, I don't think they even knew."

"Knew what?"

Natalie shook her head frantically. "It should have been easy!"

Without warning, Viviana reached out and grabbed Natalie's face. Her fingers squeezed painfully tight, nails digging into the creamy toned flesh of the girl. With a jerk of her hand, Viviana forced Natalie to look at her. More of the girl's tears fell at the rough handling.

"Knew what?" Viviana repeated through her teeth. "You will answer my questions without unnecessary rambling or I promise, this won't be easy for you, girl."

"How much he loves you," Natalie whispered.

Momentarily, Viviana's grip loosened in her surprise. "Why did you do this to us?"

"They hounded me, nonstop. Showing up outside of my apartment, where I shopped for groceries, and even sitting outside my older brother's job." Natalie swallowed thickly, her tears falling freely, now. "I wasn't sure if I was more afraid of the feds, or someone in the Bratva finding out they were following me."

"They knew that," Viviana assumed. "Used it to get you."

"I—"

Anger washed through Viviana like a wrecking ball. Who did this girl think she was? Whatever excuses she was ready to spit for her choices, no one wanted to hear. Viviana's fingers dug in again, causing Natalie to quiet with a painful whimper.

"You should have come to my husband. If you had told him the truth, he would have helped you. We might not be law-abiding citizens, but we take care of our family when they take care of us. You didn't do any of that, Natalie. Instead, you very nearly ruined my life. You took my lover from me. You took my son's father from him. How dare you?"

"Pl-please ..."

"Don't beg me," Viviana hissed. "A smart woman—a worthy woman—would never beg for anything. But since you're obviously neither of those things, it shouldn't surprise me."

When Natalie stayed silent, but for her tears and occasional sniffling, Viviana sighed. She was so tired. Exhausted from the time, from her anxiety, and her troubles. An ache had started to settle somewhere deep inside. She no longer wanted to be in front of this woman. Talking more seemed useless, like wasting her time and breath.

"You don't matter," Viviana said with quiet conviction. "You didn't matter to my husband when you were trying to catch his eye. You didn't matter to me, as I never thought you were a threat. Hell, even the feds overlooked you in the end. What a stupid, awful girl you are. I want to feel badly for you, but I can't."

"Vine," Ivan said from the corner. By the tone of his voice, it wasn't meant as a warning, or even a question. Just an acknowledgment.

Not one of the other six men in the room had spoken since Viviana's arrival. They allowed her to do as she pleased. She was grateful, but now she was done.

Viviana released her hold on Natalie and stood. "One more thing, Natalie."

The girl wouldn't meet Viviana's gaze. "What?"

"Did you fuck my husband the night you drugged him?"

Natalie sucked in a ragged breath, pink coloring her cheeks. Throats cleared around the room, surprise lighting up the noise as they stilled in their respective positions, all waiting for the possible answer. Of course some of the men knew Viviana would ask, but maybe they hadn't expected her to be so blatant or crass about it.

She wasn't one to pretty a damned thing up.

"I thought—"

"I don't want your nonsense," Viviana snapped hatefully. "Just tell me the goddamned truth. Either you fucked him, or you didn't."

"I didn't."

This time, it was Viviana's turn to freeze in her shock. Something surged into her throat—her heart, likely. "No?"

"He can't remember, then?" When Viviana didn't respond, Natalie smirked bitterly, turning her face down. "No, we didn't, but certainly not because I didn't *try*. Unlike most men, I understand the word *no*."

Viviana refused to react to that. None of the rest was important. She had the one answer to the only thing she had needed for so long.

"Ivan?" Viviana asked under her breath.

"Yeah?"

"Make it fast."

Outside of the office in the upstairs hallway, Viviana found herself grasping tight to the metal banister overlooking the dancing people like it was her only lifeline. Over and over, her breathing hitched, sometimes stopping completely. Wildly, her heart beat out of control.

Relieved. My God, the relief was as painful as it was good.

She heard nothing as last call was shouted out. She thought nothing as the bass was turned up louder on the floor below, pounding beats into the wide open space. She tasted nothing as her own tears finally fought their way out, creating rivulet lines down to her lips.

Behind her, a woman was set to die if she hadn't already.

For Natalie, Viviana felt nothing.

But for Anton, and for herself, she felt everything.

Ivan had been right. The reaction she felt now wasn't any different.

She still cried. She still broke.

Chapter Eighteen

"This man is allowed the expectation of a fair and *speedy* trial, sir," the judge said firmly. "I have read the investigators' reports regarding the witness's disappearance, and while it was sudden and suspicious, there was absolutely no sign of foul play. This is your third request for a stay. Already, Mr. Avdonin has spent a month and a half waiting for his trial to continue while remaining in prison. I'd say he's waited enough."

"Exactly," Ivan muttered under his breath.

The judge shot Anton's lawyer a look that silenced him. "I'm not suggesting he's innocent."

Anton wisely chose to stay quiet during the entire exchange. Between Ivan, the Assistant District Attorney, and the judge, they had the arguing thing handled. He didn't need to get in on it, by any means. It probably wouldn't help his case if he did. He was just lucky he was allowed out of Rikers to be a part of the meeting between everyone.

"Well you can't suggest my client is guilty for anything when there's nothing to say he caused Natalie's disappearance, either. Phone recordings from the prison show nothing. I'm sure they've got their snitches inside working the angles, but nobody's speaking. You said it yourself, Judge, the investigators found zip." Ivan shook his head, leaning back in his chair with a cool disregard for the attorney sitting next to him glaring daggers. "The reality is simple: my client did nothing in regards to that missing woman, and without her lies, their case is falling apart at the seams."

"My case is—"

"Enough," the judge interrupted sharply.

"Your case is crap," Ivan said, ignoring the judge's warning. "DNA on cigarettes my client doesn't even smoke that isn't completely conclusive. Witnesses that say they believe it was my client near the restaurant where the Belovs were found dead. Even your motive is shaky! What an intelligent attorney would do right about now is request for the charges to be dropped because they know they can't win. Then, maybe when they had something more concrete, they'd come back to it. But, you're not smart, are you?"

Anton snorted under his breath, suddenly interested in the white crescents on his fingernails. Ivan was one hell of a lawyer. Not only was he condescending, but he was patronizing as fuck. In the courtroom, he was as professional as any attorney could be, but outside, he chewed up the prosecution verbally every chance he got. The fact of the matter was simple, the A.D.A. was nothing more than a young, upstart attorney looking for his first big win.

There was no way on earth that win would come from Anton.

"What about the possibility of a deal?" the attorney asked.

Ivan barked a laugh. "For *what?* My client is innocent."

"And I'm God."

"All right, I've had enough of this damned nonsense in my chambers," the judge said. "My decision is final. You're stay is refused. The trial will resume Monday morning at nine."

"Anton?" Ivan asked, turning to look at his friend.

Anton shrugged. "Works for me. I'd like to get home to my pregnant wife as soon as possible."

The A.D.A. scowled while the judge flinched. Anton was more curious over the judge's reaction.

What was that all about?

"Before we finish," the A.D.A began.

Frustrated, the judge turned his angry gaze on the man. "What?"

"I'd really like to have the video tapes of Natalie Berezin's interviews with the federal agents accepted into evidence. They're as good as an official statement. She was sworn—"

"Absolutely not!" Ivan shouted.

"Mr. Lavrov, be quiet."

Anton's fingernails weren't so interesting anymore and there was no way in hell he could stay silent. "That woman was not my mistress, let alone my lover. I don't have lovers, and I'd like for you to find even one woman on this goddamned earth and bring her to court to stand in front of my wife and say we had a sexual relationship while I was married. So you can say she was sworn in, and that it's official all you want, but there's no way for my lawyer to challenge the lies she told."

"That's what you deny in her deposition? The depth of your relationship?" the A.D.A asked, shocked.

"That's what I know she told and what I know is a lie," Anton retorted hotly. "Whatever else she said I told is beyond my knowledge and memories."

Ivan rested back in his chair, a little smugly. "My client made my argument to have that evidence overturned just fine, I think. What more do I need to say other than he's right? Without Natalie's presence, he's unable to confront his accuser. And if it is allowed in, I will parade friends, family, coworkers, and anyone else I can find through the witness stand to say repeatedly she didn't have a relationship of any sort with my client that went beyond her position as his employee. If she lied about that, what else did she lie about?"

"She didn't accuse him," the A.D.A said, ignoring Ivan's rant. "She gave witness testimony to his guilt."

"But it's the same thing," Judge Kander said quietly. "Ivan is correct. Miss Berezin is technically accusing the defendant of a crime, or in a way, saying he gave her direct knowledge of his involvement because of their relationship. Consistently, the defendant has rebuffed her claims as falsehoods. Argue the details all you want, the end result will be the same. It's not allowed in. You should have known better than to try."

Well, that was the end of that, wasn't it?

Apparently not.

"However, if you can prove to me the witness's disappearance was caused because of something the defendant is affiliated with," the judge continued, shooting

Anton a look from the side, "... I'll allow it in."

Ivan smiled. "Well, I guess it's a good thing they won't find anything, huh?"

• • •

In the courtroom, only Ivan sat beside Anton at the defendant's table. At first, the press and media construed that as an unequipped legal team, given the high profile nature of the case and the charges he faced, but Anton knew better. Behind the scenes, Ivan's entire firm worked on Anton's case, though they kept quiet about it.

Hours had been spent pouring over the prosecution's joke of evidence. The best of the best in DNA experts were brought in to examine and rip apart the thirty-five percent match on the cigarette butts found at the Carducci crime scene. Ivan dedicated an entire group of paralegals just to work on reading over case transcripts from similar trials where the defense teams had won. What led to the win, how had they done it, and what could be gained for Anton's trial.

Oh, Anton had a legal team behind the scenes. No doubt about it. But in the courtroom, it was only Ivan.

For a lawyer who was so convinced his client was going to walk out free of the charges he faced, Ivan didn't leave a single damned thing to chance. Anton was grateful. It gave him something to ask about during the breaks in proceedings. With his wife at his side, it allowed them conversation that felt hopeful, not tarnished with the fear of prosecution.

As the judge ordered, the trial resumed that following Monday. The prosecution used that entire week of proceedings to finish parading their witnesses and laying their evidence down for the judge to consider. Interestingly enough, their motive and case direction had changed. Without being able to use Natalie's reasoning for why Anton killed Sonny Carducci and the Belovs, they had little to go on.

Now, it was just greed, they said.

Because Sonny had done Anton wrong. Well, that wasn't a

total lie.

Because the Belovs stepped into his mafia's territory. Well, that wasn't exactly a lie, either.

Unfortunately for the prosecution, everything about their case had holes that needed filled, now. They might have had the reasons, but they didn't have the whys or the hows of it all. Instead of focusing on the holes, they attempted to dance around them.

When the prosecution finally rested on that first Friday of September, Ivan took his chance to zone in on every hole and misconception, every little inconsistency the other side refused to acknowledge, and he opened it up.

He opened it up wide.

The degraded DNA on the cigarettes was an easy enough thing to argue with an expert specialist brought in to explain the actual statistics of the match's probability. At thirty-five percent with the amount of Russian heritage in New York, he told the court, there could have easily been another few hundred or more men in the state who owned that sample. To pin it down to just Anton, and say it could only be his, was laughable and unrealistic.

Reasonable doubt.

Anton lived for those two words. They were, essentially, what held his freedom.

Suddenly, Anton was made aware that public opinion was beginning to change. Even though he didn't have access to see the legal shows or read the papers covering his trial, mostly because he didn't want to, Ivan and Viviana kept him well enough informed about it all.

The question was asked, was he guilty? It was likely. But had the prosecution done their job? That was the more important question. The people didn't think they had. Anton knew better than anyone it wasn't the people who decided for him, though. It was only the judge.

Hadn't Ivan said the man would be partial to them?

Anton still wasn't quite sure what to make of that

There was a great deal of speculation about whether or not

Anton would take the stand on his own behalf. It was a choice Ivan offered to him, and his lawyer was open and honest about the benefits and downsides. Eventually, Anton chose to say no. For one, he had done what they were accusing him of, and for two, neither he nor Ivan wanted to give the prosecution a chance to question him on the many things Anton refused to speak about when they and the federal agents tried before.

However, what Anton never expected, and wasn't informed about, was that his wife would take the stand. Anton barely held himself back from punching Ivan in the back of the head when he called Viviana as his final witness one week after he began his case. Sitting in his chair, teeth clenched and fists hiding in his lap, Anton practically vibrated in his rage.

"Ivan," Anton hissed under his breath when his lawyer sat back down at their table. He didn't let the anger in his tone simper for a second. The damned lawyer wasn't even standing while Viviana was sworn in. "What in the fuck—"

"Trust me," Ivan murmured. "Anton, you have to trust me."

Throughout the trial, Viviana had been Anton's solid ground. She sat only five feet behind his defense table, close enough for him to turn around and reach out to hold her hand if he wanted, although it wasn't allowed. Even so, it was close enough that he could smell her sweet rose perfume hinting around the edges of his senses, calming him when something pissed him off. She was close enough to whisper his name and make every nerve in his body react to the sound of her silken voice in a large, hostile room.

Every single day she was there. Without fail.

Now, she was much too far away and in a place Anton never wanted to see her.

Standing in front of a deadly quiet room, Viviana appeared composed and unbothered by the sudden attention of one-hundred or more pairs of eyes all on her. For the most part, she'd always dressed to hide the growth of her pregnancy, but today the knee-length pencil skirt and white blouse showed off her twenty-one week swell beautifully. Add in her delicate hand cradling low along her midsection, and Anton was pretty sure every gaze in the room was trained on the tiny roundness Viviana held.

There was no quake in her composure, no crack in the mask.

And God, she was so painfully fucking beautiful to Anton.

Beating back the rising emotions and worry, Anton rested back into his chair with a shaky breath. Ivan still hadn't moved from his spot, either, reading over papers in front of him.

Once she was sitting in the witness chair, the eyes of the people around them, were drawn to Viviana's beautiful face instead of her stomach. Ivan went through the usual round of questions. Her name for the court records. Her relationship and affiliation to Anton. A brief history of their marriage. Ivan even asked a few things about Demyan, and her current pregnancy.

"You are the niece of the deceased Sonny Carducci, correct?" Ivan asked.

Viviana barely glanced up through her lashes as she answered, "Yes."

"Were you close with your uncle?"

"No."

"Why was that?"

Viviana cracked a smile, one that left a bitter taste in Anton's mouth. "It's hard to be close to a man who wants to kill you."

A pin could have dropped and it would have echoed.

Ivan tilted his head to the side, sighing. "Your uncle, like your father, was affiliated with the Cosa Nostra, correct?"

"They never openly admitted that in court records," Viviana replied softly. "So I can't confirm for sure that they were."

"But you know what you witnessed growing up," Ivan prodded. "You know what you heard, and what you've been told that are fact."

For the first time, Viviana tensed. "Yes."

"And what was that?"

"They were not affiliated, they were it," she answered.

"The ruling Cosa Nostra family in New York."

"Yes. There's a difference between affiliation and being a member. As far as I understood, my father had been the boss of his family from the time he was in his early twenties. My uncle then took over his position years later."

"After your father's death," Ivan finished for Viviana.

"Right after."

"What do you know about the incident surrounding Roman Carducci's death?"

Finally, the prosecution stood. "Objection. Relevance to Mr. Avdonin and this case in particular?"

Ivan sneered to the side. "Anton isn't the only person on trial here, like it or not. The circumstances we're discussing lays out Sonny Carducci's character. This is the first family member willing to openly speak about the deceased."

The judge seemed all too interested in the wood grain of his gravel as he muttered, "I'll allow it."

"Vine?" Ivan asked, repeating his earlier question.

"I know he killed my father," Viviana said quietly, refusing to look up again.

"Objection! Speculation, that was never proven and the deceased was never charged for that crime."

"Mrs. Avdonin," the judge began hesitantly, "... please refrain from speculating on events—"

"I was on the phone when he murdered my father. I heard him kill him. I heard what happened afterwards. That's not speculation, that's fact," Viviana interrupted coolly. "I listened while he taunted my father, when he forced him to his knees, and then when he pulled the trigger. And after ... would you like to know what happened after, too?"

No one said a word. Viviana had turned in her chair to face not the courtroom, but only the judge. Even the A.D.A sat back down in his chair, speechless. Judge Kander's eyes widened right along with his mouth. Anton's fists had squeezed so tight in his lap, his fingernails were beginning to break the skin. This was not the kind of information Viviana should be sharing. It was more than just dangerous for her to.

"Um … No, thank you," the judge stuttered. "Mr. Lavrov, move to something different, please."

"Not a problem," Ivan said, grinning. "Mrs. Avdonin, was that why you say your uncle wished to kill you?"

"I was a liability. No witnesses," Viviana responded, turning back in her chair. "Those are the expectations of that lifestyle."

"Yet, here you are."

Viviana shrugged. "Someone got him first."

Ivan continued with his questions, moving on to different topics revolving around Anton, the bomb incident, and Viviana's memories of that day. She didn't have many, and like Anton knew, couldn't accurately deny or verify his presence at the hospital for that day, or most of that night. There had been staff from the hospital brought in earlier in the trial for the prosecution who said Anton never was there, and there were others brought in by Ivan who swore up and down Anton never left his wife's side.

It was a he said, she said, and Viviana didn't add or take away from it.

Again, reasonable doubt.

Ivan questioned Viviana on many things, from asking if she'd ever found a gun or drugs in the home she shared with her husband, to delving deeper and asking if Anton had ever shared information with her about his alleged trafficking business. On both accounts, Anton never did—he was always careful in that regard, and this was exactly why.

Then, there were the questions everyone was waiting for, the ones Ivan never asked. He didn't even dance around them, or suggest he might bring the topic up. The Belovs. Anton couldn't figure out why. Never once did Viviana lie, though. She didn't have to with the way Ivan phrased his questions and directed them on certain topics.

So, when Ivan thanked Viviana and ended his questioning, the prosecution stood. Anton watched his wife visibly tense at the onslaught everyone knew was sure to come.

"Do you still recognize your maiden name, Mrs. Avdonin?" the A.D.A asked. "Or use it, in any capacity?"

"Carducci? No."

"Why is that?"

Viviana frowned, her gaze skipping to Anton's momentarily. "When I married my husband, I took all the parts of him, including that one."

The A.D.A rounded his table, training his sights on Viviana like a predator. Anton had all he could do to stay seated and remain silent. The last thing he wanted, or needed, was to watch his wife be attacked in the way this man would do to her.

"It has nothing to do with the fact that Nicoli Avdonin is your biological father, correct?"

Viviana didn't even blink a lash. "I never knew that he was my biological father until much later in life and by then he had already passed on. So, no. I would say not."

"Who were the first people you admitted the truth of your paternity to?" the man questioned, picking at his fingernails with disinterest.

Again, Viviana tensed, swallowing nervously. "From what I can remember of that day, I believe it was two federal agents who accosted me in my hospital room while I was still heavily medicated and in a great deal of pain after the bomb incident."

Well done, Vine, Anton thought, wishing his wife could hear him. Not only had she answered the question, but she'd done it in such a way that it didn't exactly look well on the agents for the time they chose to question her.

"Was your husband there at that time, Mrs. Avdonin?"

Viviana blew out a breath, shrugging one shoulder. "While I was half asleep, high on morphine, and he was also exhausted? No, I think he was wandering the halls to keep awake. But it's hard to remember through the fog that day

THE SCORE

created. Anton doesn't sleep when he worries. I do recall Ivan coming in before the agents left, though, if you were going to ask."

"I wasn't," the man stated dully. "And these agents ... what else did you tell them?"

"I'm not sure what you—"

"About your father, specially. Roman, I mean. Not Nicoli."

"Again, I'm not sure what you mean."

"They questioned you on the circumstances of his death, did they not?"

"They did," Viviana confirmed quietly. "I told them the same story I told everyone for my own protection."

"That Sonny had nothing to do with Roman's death."

Viviana nodded once. "Sure."

"Yet, today you changed your stance on that. You were questioned twice before that on the matter, and kept to the same story. They offered you protection from your uncle, if that's what you needed. Today, suddenly it's different, and no one is offering you protection—"

"Is there a question here?" Ivan interrupted sharply. "Because otherwise, he's standing on a soapbox I'm getting tired of."

Anton's desire to punch Ivan lessened.

The A.D.A shook his head. "No, just observing."

"Then move on," the judge barked.

"Fine," the man drawled, turning his attention back to Anton's wife. "Viviana ... or can I call you Vine, as your husband's lawyer did?"

"Viviana is perfectly fine," she replied shortly.

"Oh, Vine is only reserved for those you know well, hmm?"

Ivan's pen dropped from his hand. "Objection!"

"Withdrawn."

The judge raised a brow, scowling in the A.D.A's direction. "Mr. Penny, don't start playing games with witnesses in my courtroom, or your questioning will end."

"Vine is reserved for those who know me," Viviana said firmly, ignoring the outbursts around her. "And you're certainly not one of them, sir."

God, Anton loved his fucking wife.

The A.D.A went back to questioning Viviana on the day of the bomb, repeatedly challenging her memory of Anton's presence. He even went as far as to challenge the dosage of her medication, claiming it wasn't enough to affect her memory, let alone cause it to diminish. Viviana, very sweetly with her eyes drawn down to her stomach, asked if the whack she took to the head when she hit the pavement could have done it instead.

The man didn't respond, but then again, he wasn't the one being questioned.

When he finally decided he was going to get nothing from that, he moved onto Viviana's knowledge of Anton's businesses, his affiliation with the Bratva, his family history, and so on. For forty minutes, the man slammed accusatory question, after hostile claim at Anton's wife. With each one, Anton felt his back straighten a little more, his muscles tighten like coils ready to break.

There was only so much a man could take, after all.

Viviana, however, took it all in stride.

Then, one question really pricked at him ...

"Did your husband ever tell you he thought Sonny Carducci should die?"

Viviana stilled in her chair, looking up from under her lashes. "Yes."

"And what did you say, Mrs. Avdonin?"

"I agreed, I imagine. I can't remember for sure, but I know how I felt about my uncle and the danger he posed."

"Did your husband ever tell you he killed Sonny?" the A.D.A asked.

"No."

"Mrs. Avdonin, let me remind you that you are under oath. When your uncle was murdered, you were not married to your husband and wouldn't be for another month.

Whatever was shared between the two of you in that time period was in no way protected by spousal—"

"I'm aware of that," Viviana interjected, keeping her tone calm. "And as I said, no, Anton did not ever tell me he killed my uncle. Not before we were married, and not after."

"Did you ever ask?"

Viviana's mouth drew a thin line. "No."

"Why not?"

"Why would I?"

"Is that an answer, or ..." The man's words drifted off as he glanced at the judge for help.

"Mrs. Avdonin, please answer with a yes or no statement, not with a question."

"I didn't need to ask," Viviana stated.

"Why not?" the A.D.A repeated. "Surely you were curious, knowing the strife between them. You must have felt safer, knowing Sonny was dead, after all you've claimed. Wouldn't you want to know if your husband was the reason for that?"

Viviana shrugged, meeting the man's gaze head on. Her honest, frank answer shocked the room into stillness all over again. "Because, sir, I didn't care."

The A.D.A seemed too surprised to delve into that one, but really, Anton figured it was self-explanatory without Viviana needing to elaborate. "Has your husband ever said anything about the death of Sonny Carducci?"

"Yes."

"And?" the man prodded.

"He told me it was over. That we could go home."

With a frown, the A.D.A took a moment to consider her words. "What did he mean?"

"Speculation on the witness's part," Ivan put in from his side of the room. "Hearsay, for lack of a better term."

"Rephrase," the judge ordered.

"Do you know why he said that?"

Anton grew cold all over, his nerves ratcheting up to a whole new level.

"Sure," Viviana replied. "Sonny's death was all over the

news. I'd just survived a bomb we were pretty certain was set by order of my uncle. If anything, he was giving me comfort in the knowledge that it wouldn't happen again. And it did."

"So not a confession, in your opinion."

"My husband doesn't need to confess anything."

"Are you sure about that, Viviana?"

Viviana smiled. "Positive."

After exhausting every route he thought he could possibly take on the Sonny front with Viviana, the A.D.A moved on to the topic Anton was most afraid of.

The Belovs.

Viviana refused to answer from the very first question. Anton felt as if his heart was going to leap into his throat if the way it was beating was any indication. Like a drum, the goddamn thing thundered and he was pretty sure even Ivan could hear it sitting next to him.

"Viviana, answer the question."

Very quietly, Viviana said, "Spousal privilege, Mr. Penny. I'm not required to."

"Ma'am, you relinquished that privilege when you sat up there and opened yourself up to your husband's lawyer and my questioning. You lost the spousal privilege when you talked about your personal conversations with your husband regarding Sonny Carducci's death, your husband's business, and the Bratva organization …"

"One death has nothing to do with the other," Viviana stated quietly.

"Judge," the A.D.A began.

The judge looked so overwhelmed and confused, he didn't know what to do.

Finally, Ivan stood. "I never directed any question towards the witness regarding the Belov family, their associates, their manner of death, or even the friendship between the Avdonin family and theirs. Not once did I open Viviana up to even the possibility of those questions. Repeatedly, she has claimed spousal privilege to investigators, federal agents, and anyone else who has asked about the Belovs. She has a right to use it if she hasn't given a response on it for record. In fact, as her lawyer, she hasn't even spoken to me about the death of the Belovs."

The A.D.A pointed at Viviana fiercely. "She's sitting up there testifying about the charges facing her husband!"

"But not the Belovs," Ivan replied calmly. "Not once did she talk about them."

"Spousal privilege—"

"Mr. Lavrov is correct," the judge interrupted, blinking down at Viviana from his spot above her. Understanding had dawned on the man's features, and he almost seemed like he didn't believe it. "I understand your frustration, Mr. Penny, but she is not required to give information on that aspect unless you can open her to the topic of the Belovs and their affiliation with her husband."

"What about her affiliation to them? Or did that suddenly change, also?"

The judge shot the A.D.A with a look that would burn. "Are you being smart with me?"

"No, I'm just—"

"Ask about *her* affiliation, or move on."

Frustrated, the A.D.A turned back on Viviana. "Were you friends with the Belovs, Mrs. Avdonin?"

"I wouldn't call us that," she muttered. "Tatiana Belov wasn't fond of my husband's affections for me."

"She was jealous?"

"She never told me that."

"But you two were seen having an argument on the night of your husband's birthday?"

"Yes," Viviana replied. "She made it clear she thought I wasn't the right kind of woman for Anton, and I made it clear her opinion wasn't needed."

"Did you dislike Tatiana Belov or her father?"

"I didn't know her father well, but I wasn't particularly fond of her, no."

"Why?" the A.D.A asked.

"You could say we were raised with different values,"

Viviana said, shrugging.

"The night of the fire that killed the Belovs, where was your husband?"

Viviana repeated the spousal privilege, but it seemed the man expected that.

"Where were you, Mrs. Avdonin?"

Viviana met Anton's gaze from across the room and he knew without a doubt she could see every ounce of worry and pain swimming through his veins with just a glance. Not once did she have to lie, so far, but that one question brought his wife into very dangerous territory.

"With my husband," Viviana answered, not taking her eyes off Anton.

"Where with your husband?"

Anton's relief at the wrongly phrased question was earth-shattering. Viviana opened herself up to questioning on the Belovs, if the A.D.A hadn't been so damned frustrated not to realize it. Instead of pointing it out and asking her where her husband was, he asked where she was with him.

Sweet fucking relief.

Ivan's hand was suddenly clenching so freaking hard on Anton's wrist to keep him seated in his chair, that Anton didn't even realize it until he felt his bones creak from the pressure.

"Told you," Ivan whispered.

"You're a fucking asshole," Anton mumbled back.

"A fucking asshole who probably just won this case."

"Viviana, please answer my question."

With a single slant of her head, Viviana dismissed the man's probing. "I plead the fifth."

There was silence, and then there was more arguing. This time, Ivan didn't need to say a word. Viviana had every right to keep the A.D.A from questioning her on a topic that very well might incriminate herself in a crime, even one she had unwillingly participated in or knew about. Beyond that, if he couldn't ask about her, he couldn't get her to talk about Anton's involvement.

It was in no way an admittance of guilt for Viviana, or of Anton's, and by law, it couldn't be seen that way.

"Jesus Christ," Anton breathed.

Ivan nodded, tightening his grip on his friend's wrist again. "He's almost done, man."

Agitation covered the A.D.A's features as he moved back to his table, sitting down with a glare. "You talked about your son, Mrs. Avdonin, can I ask you a question on that, or will you find a way around it, too?"

"Objection!"

"Withdrawn."

"Ask," Viviana said, unbothered.

"It's been months since your son has seen his father, correct?"

"Two, actually. I brought my son to visit his father on the first day of the proceedings, but I haven't felt comfortable exposing him to this again."

"That must hurt him and his father," the man observed.

For the first time, an honest show of emotions flitted over Viviana's face by way of tears that shined in her eyes. "It does, but I won't confuse my child."

"You mean to say you don't want him to hear the truth. That his father is a murderer."

"I mean, the man you claim my husband to be is not the man Demyan knows. I will not have you, or anyone else, tarnish my son's love for his father. And that love—it's beautiful."

The A.D.A stopped his questioning.

Chapter Nineteen

"Fucking fantastic, Vine," Ivan said, holding her face between his hands. "You did absolutely perfect."

Viviana nodded, but she still felt weary and unsure. Being up on the witness stand was far more nerve-wracking than she thought it would be. Being under the prosecution's constant stream of questions, not knowing where the man was going to take it next, was horrifying.

Then, there were the eyes. God, so many fucking eyes watching, judging …

"Everyone was looking at me," she whispered.

Viviana didn't realize it until Ivan began rubbing his hands up and down her arms, but she was shaking.

"And what was that shit he tried to pull about Demyan at the end, anyway?"

Ivan sighed. "Probably just a cheap shot at Anton. If you won't let your son see his father, then how must you really feel about Anton's actions? That kind of thing."

"Did I give the right answer back?"

"You did it all perfectly," Ivan repeated.

"Mr. Lavrov, one minute until the recess is over," a guard informed from the side.

Viviana flinched at the idea of going back inside the courtroom.

After her testimony, Ivan must have seen the anxiety that built up in Viviana because he asked for a five minute break to consult with his witness before closing statements began. The judge easily agreed, seemingly tired and finished with the trial himself.

"It's almost over," Ivan told Viviana quietly. "Don't let Anton see you nervous or worked up, Vine. Especially at this point. He's done incredibly well going on your lead alone. If he sees you're stressed out, it won't be good. It gets him anxious and I won't be sitting beside him while I do my closing statement to reign him back in."

Bleakly, all Viviana could do was nod.

"Ready to get this over with?"

"Yes," Viviana said. More than ever, she wanted to say. "Then let's finish it."

Closing statements were a two hour long process that simply recapped the entire trial in a short amount of time and with less words. Viviana sat behind Anton in silence, keeping her eyes drawn down to her stomach where her hand rested, feeling the movement of the baby. It helped to keep her calm.

The prosecution side focused on the things they had and knew. The witnesses at the hospital the night Sonny was killed who were adamant Anton wasn't in Viviana's room until the next day. The thirty-five percent DNA match on the cigarette butts at the Carducci crime scene. The witnesses who put Anton near the Belov crime scene, his affiliation with the owner of the ruined restaurant, and so on. They also focused on the obvious, public strife between Anton and the victims.

Ivan, however, focused in on the reasonable doubt. He was quiet and sure as he talked about the things the prosecution hadn't proven, the evidence they didn't have to show. Like the prosecution, he named his own witnesses, the ones who put shadows on the prosecution's witnesses' testimonies. His mannerisms and voice stayed confident as he recapped his own case, having never changed direction once in the entire trial.

By the law's standard of reasonable doubt, he stated, Anton was owed freedom.

It was as simple as that.

But was it, really?

Even with all Viviana and Ivan did, blackmailing the judge and getting rid of Natalie, was it enough? The fact of the matter was simple, no one knew. The judge could just as easily give a guilty verdict and take the chance of the photos going public. It would likely result in Anton getting a new trial, and possibly even being released for a short time. That would be the best outcome, next to a not guilty verdict. If Anton was able to get released, Viviana was going to get him the fuck out of the country in a heartbeat.

"Vine?" Ivan asked, pulling gently on her elbow to get her attention.

"Let's go."

• • •

Anton's mouth ghosted along Viviana's knuckles, touching down on each and every one to lay a tender kiss. After the closing statements were finished, the judge took to his chambers to deliberate. There was still an hour or so left in the day, so Viviana had a short while with her husband in the defense chambers before Anton was taken back to the prison.

"What were you thinking?"

"I was thinking I was a good distraction, and an opinion people wanted to hear," she answered.

"They're going to investigate you, now," he pointed out.

"Let them. They'll find nothing, Anton."

"Still fucking crazy."

"It worked," Viviana said. "You know it did. Are you angry with me?"

"Proud," he murmured. "Worried. Never angry."

But he would be, she knew. He would be so very angry with her.

Viviana made the decision weeks ago to tell her husband the truth about the judge situation and the blackmail that followed. Even if the judge found him guilty, Anton would eventually find out. She wanted to be the one to tell him, not Ivan, or anyone else.

She just couldn't do it yet.

"How's my baby?" Anton asked softly.

With one hand, he reached between their chairs to feel the hard swell of her midsection. Despite the baby's activeness in the courtroom earlier, it was now quiet and unmoving. Anton had yet to feel the child's kicks and movements. It broke Viviana's heart knowing how badly he wanted to, and all that he was missing.

Like finding out the gender of the baby ... She still hadn't told him that, yet, either.

She did bring the little black and white photos of the baby's ultrasound pictures for him to see, though. From the pictures of the feet, to the curvature of the baby's spine, he'd been so enamoured with the tiny little pictures. At her next appointment, she remembered to record the sound of the heartbeat for him to hear.

"Good. Heartbeat is still strong. Everything looked good on the ultrasound, like I said."

Anton smiled, sweeping his thumb back and forth. "A new year's baby. Do you think you'll make it that long?"

The baby was due on the first of January, but that was only an estimation given Viviana didn't know the day she conceived and didn't have a last period to go on.

"We'll see. Probably not, though."

"Is two enough, baby?" Anton asked, cocking a brow at her. "Or is it awful I'm already thinking about the other bedroom that's still empty?"

Did Viviana want more children? "Slow down, Anton."

Anton sat back in his chair, tension writing lines over his strong features.

"What's wrong?" Viviana asked.

"It's almost over," he replied. "And it doesn't feel like it."

"Doesn't it?"

Anton shook his head. "Not to me. I don't know why."

Viviana's guilt pounded away at her insides. "Everything is going to be okay."

"You keep saying that."

"And I mean it."

It would be another four days before the judge came back with his verdict.

• • •

Not guilty.
Not guilty. Not guilty. Not guilty.
Not ...
Guilty ...
Viviana's hand was secured tightly in her husband's, just as it had been when the judge slid his verdict across his desk with a frown. The courtroom had exploded in noise from every side. The judge smacked his gravel over and over until the people settled down enough for him to speak.

Viviana still wasn't sure Anton believed it as she pulled him through the crowd outside, ignoring the reporters, the cameras taking their pictures. Behind them, she could hear Anton's lawyer making a statement, and the A.D.A arguing from the steps that regardless of double jeopardy, this wasn't the end of everything.

Ivan had made it clear to her when they got word that the verdict was in what she needed to do. Get him out of that courthouse, he'd said. Take him somewhere quiet. Let him breathe, Vine.

She could understand why, now.

Anton was deadly silent behind her. Whether it was from shock, or confusion, he was too quiet. He'd not said a word. Not when the judge told the prosecution their case had lacked real depth, or the evidence required to put a man behind bars for the rest of his natural life. Not even when the judge then went on to say he believed Anton's guilt was likely, but he didn't have the proof to say it for sure. And certainly not when the judge wished Anton good luck, and granted his freedom.

Nothing.

Not a word.

"Vine ..." Anton started to say behind her.

Painful. Oh, Jesus, he sounded like he was in pain.

"Just a minute, babe. We're almost gone," she told him, squeezing his hand.

"Okay."

Down the steps they went, eyes following their every movement. She took him across the parking lot to the car he adored so fucking much. Viviana decided on the Bugatti for two reasons. It was the only show of wealth she allowed in the entire trial. They had been very careful not to appear overindulged, or dripping in money to the public. And for two, Anton loved that car.

Fast with an engine that roared like a thousand hooves of horses beating to the ground, and memories of a sweeter time, it was exactly what Anton would need. Something to get them gone, to get him out of his head.

Viviana turned and pressed the keys into his palm. "Drive."

Anton blinked. "Drive?"

"Wherever you want to go. As fast as you need. Drive."

"I want to go home," he told her, his brow furrowing. "Our son ... My mom ..."

"Okay, then home it is. But you get to drive."

Viviana didn't think she'd be able to, what with her hands trembling like they were.

Despite claiming he wanted to go home, the moment an exit for the highway came into view, Anton changed lanes and took it. In seconds, the Bugatti was shifting from one gear, and then slamming into the next. Over and over, they swerved in and around other cars to pass them at a rate of speed that pushed Viviana back into her seat from the force.

She wasn't afraid, though.

"Jesus," Anton growled.

"Talk to me," Viviana said from the side, barely glancing over at her husband.

Clipped and short, Anton's words strained to get back his clenched teeth. "I thought ... just, wasn't sure."

"You thought you'd be going back," she assumed.

Anton nodded, his grip on the steering wheel tightening to a white-knuckled grasp. The hand on the stick shift slipped it into the last gear without even hesitating and the car lurched forward, moving faster. Without a word, he turned on the car stereo. The CD they hadn't taken out from the last time they drove the car starting blasting through the speakers, pumping bass into the floor.

"I told you it would be okay, Anton."

"Not everything is black and white," he replied.

"Ivan and me, we handled it," she tried to explain. "I'll tell you everything. I wasn't going to let you—"

Anton slammed an open palm to the steering wheel, cursing severely under his breath. "Shut up, Vine."

Hurt and surprised, she asked, "What?"

"I don't want to know. Okay? Just shut up, and don't tell me whatever you think you need to tell me. My wife doesn't get herself involved in business. She doesn't put herself under the scrutiny of investigators. She doesn't keep things from me, like the fact that she was going to be a witness in my trial!"

Anton didn't even know what Viviana did and already he was pissed off.

"What in the fuck were you thinking? The Italians are going to be in a fit over your statements. I'll be smoothing that shit over for years!"

"Anton, relax."

"Vine, I said—"

"It wasn't business. It was *you*. You're not business to me. And I spoke to Conrad. It's fine."

Anton's head whipped in her direction, his eyes blazing. "You spoke to the Italians without me?"

"Erik and Ivan went with me, and Aunt Lucy was there. It wasn't an official thing, Anton."

"Like that fucking matters!"

All right, Viviana had taken just about enough of his yelling.

"Stop it. Stop shouting at me. You couldn't do anything behind bars, so I handled it. I'm fucking capable of having a meeting with Conrad and my aunt without setting off a war inside the city. In fact, I did. No one was killed over a short dinner. The trial is over. We're fine."

Anton snorted. "You have no idea."

"No, Anton, you don't."

"I ..."

Anton clamped his mouth shut and glared out the windshield. This was not how Viviana expected their first conversation to go outside of the confines of the court. Anton should have been relieved and thankful for his freedom. Instead, he was frustrated and snapping out at the closest person he could. Unfortunately, that just happened to be his wife.

"You're still stuck in your head. Thinking when you turn around, you're going to have to go back. Aren't you?"

"God, I just don't understand," Anton whispered. "He said it. I might as well be guilty for it, they just didn't prove it. Was it really that fucking simple after four months in hell?"

"No," Viviana said quietly. "It wasn't."

Anton said nothing in response, but the engine roared from his foot pressing down to the gas pedal again. Minutes of silence later, and he turned off the highway onto a dirt road that looked like nothing more than an access for ATVs outside the city limits. Surrounded by trees, it was secluded enough to keep the Bugatti out of sight once they were a little ways in the road.

Anton slammed the car into park and opened his door. Viviana stayed in her seat and watched her husband's breakdown from the passenger seat. Roughly, he tugged the silver tie loose around his neck, tossing the article to the ground. The same thing happened to his suit jacket before he was loosening the top two buttons on his shirt. Raking his fingers through his hair, Anton squatted to the gravel, his chest rising and falling rapidly, and stared at the ground.

When he didn't move, Viviana decided to get out of the car, also. She rested against the hood of the Bugatti, feeling the cool September air breezing right through her thin cardigan.

"Fuck, fuck, fuck." Anton breathed deeply, still staring at nothing. "It's over, yeah?"

"Yeah, you're not going back."

From her spot, Viviana could see Anton was holding back his emotions and fighting himself on the inside. No one was around to see him, though, and she was pretty sure she knew what he needed then.

"It's okay to cry. Or scream. Whatever you need. It's fine."

Anton did just that. From the echoing sobs that shook his shoulders, to the tears he wiped away with his clenched fists. Vivian understood that more than anything, being free to live his life with his wife was what Anton wanted the most. He hadn't believed he was going to be able to do that, no matter what they told him.

Viviana tried to move forward to comfort him, but Anton held up one hand to stop her from coming closer. His breathing was still verging on hyperventilation. Both of his hands had dug into the gravel. There was something heart-wrenchingly painful about his breakdown, but Viviana let him have it.

Then, Anton turned quiet. Standing, he swiped his hands over his suit pants to get rid of the dust. Thinking he was ready to leave, Viviana slid off the hood of the Bugatti.

"I'm sorry," Anton said under his breath.

"For what?"

"Yelling at you. I shouldn't … You didn't deserve that. I don't know what's wrong with me."

"It's all right. It's been a stressful day. I get it," Viviana said with a shrug. "You ready to go?"

"No, not yet."

Anton didn't say another word before crossing the distance separating him and his wife. Viviana found her back pushed into the hood of the Bugatti once more. Anton's hands gripped tightly to her waist as he plucked her up like she didn't weigh a thing and sat her down on the car. Over and over, he kissed her mouth with soft kisses.

"Sorry. So sorry, Vine."

The guilt Viviana was trying to swallow clawed at her throat. "Stop, please, Anton …"

Instead of taking her request for him to quit apologizing, Anton seemed to think it was for him to stop touching her. Viviana felt the loss of his hold and kisses instantly. She grabbed at him and pulled him in close once more.

"Don't stop that," Viviana ordered, staring Anton straight in the eyes. "Never that."

Anton sighed into her hair as she rested her face against his neck. She could smell the lingering soap on his skin. Even seeing him every day during the trial, Viviana only now realized his hair was an inch and a half longer than what it was before. Secured back in their embrace, both turned quiet. Ignoring the guilt she felt, Viviana played with the longer strands at his neck, scratching her fingernails up along the back of his scalp.

It wasn't long before Anton's hands were wandering on her sides again. Over her stomach he stopped momentarily, the tension in his shoulders relaxing. Anton pulled at her blouse until her small, swelled midsection was exposed. The cold air had her skin pebbling, but Anton's warm kisses as he bent down and pressed his mouth to her stomach lit her body up with internal fireworks.

"You're beautiful when you're pregnant, you know?"

Viviana smiled, tugging gently on his hair. "So I'm not otherwise?"

Anton's chuckles rocked between them. "You're always beautiful, baby. But, it's not the same. Seeing you grow and feeling the baby move. I've missed so much of this already."

"We've still got a little while to go," Viviana assured. "You didn't miss everything. Not the important bits, anyway."

Anton traced circles over her stomach with his index finger. "Beautiful," he repeated.

The deeper, huskier tone his voice took on reminded Viviana how long it had been since she heard her husband lustful and wanton. A shiver crept up her spine when Anton kissed below her navel, his tongue striking out to taste the spot he kissed.

Viviana didn't stop him when Anton spread her thighs to

step in between and drove her skirt up higher around her waist. She didn't stop him when he tugged her panties down around her ankles, either, letting the already soaked fabric drop to the ground. Between the kisses he landed to her lips, Anton whispered the sweetest, most loving things.

Things Viviana had waited too long to hear again.

She was self-seeking. Dirty in a way her husband couldn't possibly understand because she wouldn't stop him at all. Even knowing once she told him the truth about her actions and choices regarding stripping, the judge, and the blackmail, Anton wouldn't want to touch her again. So she didn't stop him, because it very well might have been the last time he did.

All of Anton's touches were deliberate and tender. Nothing like the rough, focused want he usually poured over his wife during their most intimate moments. While he unbuckled his pants and shuffled them down with the boxer-briefs he wore underneath, his hot, wet mouth stayed on hers the entire time.

Viviana reveled in the feeling of his warmth saturating her body as he took her with gentle, slow thrusts. Anton didn't need to give her time to adjust to his cock, she was already more than ready for him. Needing to center herself to something, to stop the sway-like feeling taking over her senses, Viviana held tight to Anton's jaw with both hands.

Their gazes locked like missiles and she watched every emotion flit over his face; watched his lashes fan his cheeks with every blink. As his breath washed over her mouth, Viviana's picked up. Every stroke took her higher and every time their hips met, the tip of his cock hit the perfect spot to make her gasp.

Anton was usually so vocal with his dirty mouth and desire when they fucked. This time, though, it was only heady groans falling from his chest while he hooked her legs tighter to his waist and her soft moans urged him on.

In no time at all, Viviana was so close to her orgasm she could feel the starting effects of it running through her blood like a cloying poison. She didn't get the chance to fly, though.

Where her flats pressed to Anton's back, she felt him tense with his own release just before his cock spilled in thick streams deep into her sex. Anton's eyes shut as he held her tight to his cock, keeping her filled with him while he shook.

"Jesus Christ," Anton mumbled.

Never had her husband come before her.

Viviana felt the orgasm she'd nearly had start to slip away at the same time Anton pulled out of her body. She didn't have time to react before he was on his knees, grabbing her hips and pulling her body to the very edge of the Bugatti's hood. Then, his mouth was covering her sex.

Sharp flicks of his tongue diving into her tight channel drove Viviana insane. She held tight to the metal of the car, her fingernails scratching against the expensive paint. With every swipe, she knew he wasn't only tasting her, but himself as well.

It was another first for them both. Anton had never tasted his wife after he'd come inside her, but he didn't seem to mind. It only turned Viviana on more to know their mingling fluids were what was coating his tongue. It left streaks of wetness on his cheeks as he looked up between her thighs with a desire fueled gaze that sent her spinning out of control.

When his thumb grazed her clit, and his tongue drove up inside her pussy again, Viviana let the fast rushing orgasm take over. As good as it felt, it also made her ache. Keeping his hands on her body, Anton rose to kiss his wife once more. Viviana couldn't hide how much she enjoyed the taste of her own sex on his tongue as it slipped into her mouth.

Anton said nothing as he fixed her skirt and his own pants. Grabbing the forgotten jacket off the ground, he cleaned them both as well. Viviana was still trying to come back down from the high her emotions were running on.

"We're being selfish," Anton murmured.

Viviana turned to look at him, confused. "Why's that?"

"People are probably waiting for us."

"They can wait a little bit longer. We're not moving until you're ready to."

Anton swallowed thickly, kissing the top of Viviana's head. "Yeah, but I can't wait much longer to see my son. It's been too fucking long as it is. I owe that kid so goddamn much."

Viviana knew she couldn't keep what she'd done from her husband any longer. "I need to tell you something, Anton."

Chapter Twenty

Anton wouldn't meet her gaze when he asked, "What's that?"

"This morning before I left, I told Demyan his father was coming home."

"You couldn't have known."

"No matter what, you were," Viviana said firmly. "Today didn't make a difference to the end result. If you went back to prison, we had it set up that the judge's decision would be thrown out due to scandal and you would likely be released for a short time before they could bring charges again."

"Vine …"

"You know I love you, right? Like crazy love you. Nobody else is worth to me what you are. Do anything for you. Drive myself insane, or hurt you to save you love you, Anton. I love *you*."

Anton's jaw clenched. "Whatever this is, I'm not going to like it, am I?"

Viviana shook her head, tears rising. "I'm sorry."

"What kind of scandal?" Anton asked.

"One involving a woman."

Anton's eyebrows knitted together in his confusion. "That wouldn't work, Vine. So it looks bad, big deal. He's not the first man to be involved in that kind of thing."

Viviana bit her lip and forced herself to speak. "It would if that woman was me."

Instantly, Anton jerked away from his wife as if he'd been burned. It hurt like hell, but she let him do it. Pain and betrayal filled his blue eyes, darkening them with anger and disbelief.

"*No*, baby."

In a rush of breath, Viviana told Anton everything. From the day Ivan approached her at the beach, to the plan itself, to how she followed it through at the strip club. Even as

251

Anton stepped further back from her, far enough away that she couldn't reach out to touch him, she kept talking. The words might as well have been vomit, for Christ's sake. She couldn't stop them.

By the time she was able to stop, Viviana wasn't the only one crying.

"You did ... Took your clothes ... Allowed another man ... Why ..."

"I wasn't with him. I didn't do that, or anything like that, Anton. I just—"

"Stop talking."

Anton struggled to find words, his gaze darting back and forth like a deer caught in the headlights. His fists had clenched into tight balls at his sides and from his shoes to his shoulders, he shook. Viviana knew that look, she knew what was happening. Anton was pissed. Finally, the anger burst out of him in a shout that made Viviana flinch.

"Get in the fucking car!"

Viviana slid off the hood without a word, stumbled on the gravel and all but fell into the passenger seat. She slammed the door closed without him telling her to. In two steps, those clenched fists of his snapped into the Bugatti's hood with a force that rocked the vehicle. Viviana could see his knuckles had split open from the impact but that didn't stop him from punching the car again.

Over and over he hit the metal, cursing at a level so loud and clear Viviana could still hear him even with the doors shut. Blood streaked over his hands and wrists, staining his dress shirt. Anton shouted out his rage until his voice turned hoarse and his breaths came out ragged.

Oddly, Viviana wasn't afraid of him, though.

After all, he'd been the one who ordered her into the car. Now, she knew why.

Outside the vehicle, Anton's anger had simmered enough that he stopped hitting the hood and yelling, but his gaze was locked on Viviana's.

"You let a man touch you," she watched him mouth.

"I'm sorry," Viviana whispered.

Above everything else she did, Viviana understood that because she had given another man access to her in a private way, it was what hurt and angered her husband the most.

"You let him *see* you."

"Anton, please try to understand ..."

"My wife! You're *my* wife! Is that what you wanted, for me to think of you like your mother? Like a whore? Is that what you are? I don't need or want a whore for a wife, Viviana."

Viviana choked on the accusation, slamming back into the seat like he'd struck her with his hand instead of words. Sobs caught at the lump forming in her throat.

"I've never—"

"You took your clothes off for another man!" he roared.

"For you, Anton!"

"Fuck you," Anton spat. "Don't you even ... Just, fuck you, Vine."

• • •

The sharp tasting smoke from the weed Anton was smoking curled into the air in a thick stream of grey. In the night sky, it made its own cloud against the black backdrop. Sitting up on the stone side of the bridge, Anton watched the water of the creek rush below him.

It'd been seven days since he last seen his wife.

The hardest fucking seven days of his life.

He hadn't even gone home, just made her drop him off at his club and that was that. He didn't speak a word, even when she begged him to, even when she cursed at him to look at her, to come home to their son. No, nothing. Anton couldn't.

It killed him to know his son was practically in arm's reach, but Anton couldn't bear to be in that house. He knew why, also. It wasn't safe for him to be there. Even though it disgusted him to feel the way he did, Anton wanted to hurt Viviana. Make her feel on the outside like she'd made him feel on the inside.

Bloody, torn, and battered.

Used. Abused.

Betrayed.

Anton now understood how his wife must have felt when first confronted with the idea of his possible infidelity, even if that had proven to be untrue as he always believed it was. It certainly wasn't the same thing, to be sure, but it still fucking hurt like hell.

Never had Anton put his hands on Viviana to hurt her. Never had he thought about using his strength against her to make her feel pain, or make her cry. But, for a moment, he'd wanted to. Some mafia men were open about the opinions they had regarding wives who stepped out of line. One thing fixed the situation: a bullet.

As if the woman was nothing more than a bitch of a dog that needed put down.

For that split second, while he had stared at his wife sitting on the car with the lingering taste of her come in his mouth, he understood why those men felt that way.

It scared the living fucking hell out of him.

For once, Anton understood how he saw his wife. He'd always called Viviana his. To anyone, everyone, she was his. It was just that simple. No explanations. *His.* Like property. The thought was awful. Even if he loved her, and he did with everything he was, he still felt like he owned her.

Brutal honesty was something Anton was known for, but this was the first time he was giving some of that rectitude to himself. He didn't own his wife. If he couldn't hold back the violence he felt over what she did, he needed to take himself out of the equation. So he did just that.

But he couldn't bear to explain to anyone.

Who the fuck was going to understand?

Who wouldn't look at Viviana after knowing and call her exactly the same thing he had, a whore?

Anton refused to see anyone at his club, also. His men came and went, but they didn't make it beyond the downstairs. There was shit he needed to work through in his own head, and the last thing he wanted to even think about, let alone discuss, were those men and their issues regarding the Bratva.

Because the club was open for regular business, his new servers were there, too. Anton couldn't help but watch the beautiful, young women and wonder. A darker part of himself thought it'd be so fucking easy. They'd be all too willing. And hell, maybe he hurt Viviana with the clusterfuck that was the Natalie situation, but actually choosing to sleep with another woman because he wanted to would downright kill her.

Like she'd chosen to take off her clothes, dance naked for a man, and allow his hands to touch her while she did so.

Anton couldn't do it, though.

Couldn't even think of another woman in a way that would make his dick twitch.

Fucking useless.

"Anton?"

Anton didn't turn at the sound of Ivan's voice, but he tilted his head to acknowledge his old friend. Earlier in the day, Anton finally made one call out from his club's office to Ivan, asking the man to meet him there. Taking one last hit off the joint, Anton inhaled the burning smoke before tossing the roach into the water.

"Did you go home, yet?" Ivan asked, climbing up on the ledge to sit down.

"Nope."

"Are you going to?"

Anton nodded, feeling the sweet effects of the weed starting to edge in around his mind. "I love that woman. So fucking much."

"Yeah, I know," Ivan murmured.

"No, you don't. I love her so much I considered taking her life to keep her from doing anything like that to me again," Anton confessed. "What kind of man does that make me, Ivan?"

Ivan stared out in front of them and cleared his throat.

"That's ... I don't know."

"Awful. It makes me a fucking monster. She could call me any name, hit me, ruin me, and take my son from me, but that ... that broke me. I think I went insane for days, man."

"Did you get the media card I sent over?" Ivan asked quietly.

Anton felt the bile rise into his throat. "I saw the pictures."

"And?"

"I destroyed the card."

"That's not what I asked, Anton."

"I needed a couple of days to think," Anton snapped. "Especially after seeing them. Fucking disgusted me. Everything disgusted me. She's my wife! You could have used anyone but my wife, Ivan!"

"No, I couldn't have," Ivan argued firmly. "And you know it." When Anton stayed silent, Ivan sighed. "Your mother cried when you didn't come home that day."

"Mmm."

"And your wife nearly had a nervous breakdown."

"Nearly? Shit, I did, Ivan. I fucking *did*."

"Yeah, well, aside from your selfishness, you could have taken into consideration Vine is under immeasurable stress, pregnant, and caring for your toddler son alone. She could have run when you gave her the chance, but she didn't. She fought for you—you don't have to like the way she did it, but she did."

"Fuck off."

Ivan took a breath, resting his hands into his lap. "I convinced her to do it, man. Used guilt to talk her into it with Demyan, and given she was pregnant, she just added onto it herself. Another woman wouldn't have worked, and I know you fucking hate me for it, but I needed the backup in case we didn't find Natalie. Please try to understand why I did it this way."

Anton figured that a long time ago. It was why his anger had simmered in regards to his wife to practically nothing at

THE SCORE

all and turned to Ivan, instead.

"For the record, I didn't bring a gun with me." Anton turned and moved off the stone ledge, standing straight on the empty, dark bridge. "Because if I did, I would have put a bullet between your eyes, Ivan, and I would have enjoyed it. I need to trust you to do what's right for me, and what you did nearly fucking killed me."

"I did what you asked me to," Ivan muttered.

"I did not ask you to turn my wife into another man's whore!"

Ivan was off the ledge and standing toe to toe with Anton in a flash. Both men huffed their anger, glaring through the darkness.

"Shut your fucking mouth," Ivan hissed, his fist landing in the middle of Anton's chest. He barely even felt it through his rage. "That woman is no man's whore. She did what she did for you and you know it. Even though she felt disgusting, knowing how you'd feel and how you'd see her for it, she still did it to make goddamned sure you had your life. Even if it meant you wouldn't share it with her, she still did it. Do not call her that, Anton. Don't do that to that woman. She loves you."

Anton felt tears slip from the corners of his eyes, but he didn't make a move to wipe away the emotion.

"And yes, I did do what you asked me to," Ivan continued. "You asked for a backup plan. For a way out if we couldn't win. I did that. I'm sorry it wasn't the way you wanted, and that I brought Vine into it, but it would have worked if you went back in. No one knows. No one will ever know what happened."

"I know she's not," Anton muttered heavily. "A whore, I mean. That's not Vine. It's not my wife, and she loves me, I know, but you nearly made me see her like that. What you did, Ivan, it just … I had that woman on a pedestal and when she fell from it, it didn't just break her. I'm so angry with you for what you did. You and me, we need to take some time away from business and friendship for a while, at least until

257

I'm good with you again."

"At least you know what you need," Ivan replied calmly. "Whatever you want, Anton."

"I don't like you a whole lot right now," Anton said quietly.

"Seeing as how you're not behind bars, I'm okay with that," Ivan admitted, frowning.

"I've been two seconds away from kicking your ass all week."

"The first hit is free, Anton. Every single one after that, I'm going to hit back."

Anton was fine with that. He took the first hit with brutal force, knocking his friend straight to the ground. Blood spilled instantly from the broken nose Ivan now sported. Anton didn't need more than one hit. He just needed to get the anger out, the anger he'd felt was misdirected towards his wife. Anton stood above his friend and shrugged, sticking out his hand to offer the man a way up from the ground. Ivan took it while wiping away the blood with his free hand.

"Didn't need more than the one," Anton muttered.

Ivan huffed under his breath. "Go home, Anton."

"I am. I need a fucking drive."

• • •

The Oceana house was dark when Ivan dropped Anton off in the driveway. His friend handed over a set of keys to the house before telling Anton to get himself in check before he went back to work again.

Anton agreed.

Inside his house, all was quiet.

Anton found Clarissa drinking a cup of tea at the kitchen island.

"Hello, Anton. I guess I should say a belated welcome home."

"Sure. Thanks. Where's my wife?"

"Sleeping. It's well after eleven. If you're here to hurt her in some way, you can leave, Anton."

Anton barely held back his shock. "Pardon me?"

"I loved your step-grandfather. Knew his mind and heart in ways you couldn't possibly understand. The only thing he loved more than his family and his Bratva was a girl he couldn't raise himself. I watched that girl break to pieces all week over you. I imagine something happened, and I don't care much to know about it, but I won't watch her hurt like that for another week."

Anton felt a need to apologize, and he didn't even know why. "I'm not going to hurt her."

"Good," Clarissa muttered into her cup. "Also, your son is in his room, likely playing with his toys again. Viviana needs rest, and that child just won't go to sleep until his little body shuts down and forces him to. If you could handle that, I'd be grateful and so would your wife."

Like an idiot, Anton nodded. "Okay."

"And call your mother first thing in the morning. That poor woman is going out of her mind."

"Okay," he repeated.

"You can go now, Anton."

"Thank you, Clarissa … for everything."

The maid smiled. "Don't screw it up, Anton."

Demyan's bedroom door was wide open, but someone had placed a safety gate in the doorway to keep him from getting out. Sure enough, inside the lit up room was his son, playing with Rocco and his matchbox cars. On his nightstand was a plastic cup, still half-filled with red juice. Demyan's familiar blue eyes were tainted with the darkness of someone who needed sleep, and he didn't even notice Anton standing just beyond the safety gate. Even Rocco, almost asleep, didn't notice his shadow. Why wasn't his child sleeping?

Hadn't Viviana said their son was sleeping in their bed?

"Demyan, what time is it, little man? I think it's your bedtime."

Demyan's head jerked up at his father's voice. "Papa …?"

Fuck, his boy didn't even seem like he believed what he

259

was seeing. Anton watched fat tears slide down his son's cheeks. All over again, his heart broke. Finally, Rocco woke up to the commotion, giving a quiet bark in welcome, but that was all. Anton ripped the safety gate from the doorway when he couldn't get the latch to work under his shaking hands.

"Come here, Demyan. Come to Papa."

Demyan was up off the floor before Anton blinked, his little hands reaching, making grabbing motions towards his father. "Up, Papa!"

Anton cradled his son, holding him tight and saying nothing for minutes. His chest ached when tiny fists wrapped into his T-shirt and refused to let go. "God, I missed you. I'm home, little man. I promise."

"Papa's *malysh*," Demyan whispered.

"My boy," Anton echoed. "Always, Demyan."

"Ma?" Demyan asked.

"Yeah, we'll go get Ma." As he walked down the hallway towards the master bedroom, still holding his son, Anton asked, "Why aren't you sleeping, Demyan? It's bedtime."

"Papa comin' … Ma said," Demyan told him, his childish voice groggy.

Anton's heart rate picked up at that revelation. Viviana had told Anton she let Demyan know he would be home soon. To know his son refused to sleep because he was waiting for his father was an awful feeling.

God, he was a shitty husband and father. Selfish as fuck.

That ended immediately.

"I'm sorry, little man. But, Papa's home now, so you have to sleep, Demyan."

"Sleep. S'bedtime," his son mumbled.

"That's right. It's bedtime."

"With Papa and Ma."

Well, Anton wasn't about to deny his boy that. "For tonight. Tomorrow night, it's your bed."

"M'kay, Papa."

Chapter Twenty-One

Silently, Anton pushed open the door to the master bedroom, his gaze instantly zoning in on the sleeping woman he'd missed so fucking much. Viviana wasn't even curled up on her side of the bed, she was wrapped in blankets on his side. Anton didn't even make it two steps inside the room before his wife was sitting up in their bed, a choked noise falling from her lips as she caught sight of Anton holding Demyan.

"Please don't take him …"

Anton shook his head, stopping whatever crazy thought she had before she could finish it. "He wants to sleep with his mother and father tonight. I thought it'd be okay, if it's fine with you, baby."

Viviana blinked, sniffling. "He won't sleep at all. Clarissa basically yelled at me to go lay down. I've been up with him all week."

Shifting the already sleeping boy on his shoulder for his wife to see, Anton placed Demyan on the bed with his mother. "He's sleeping, now."

"That's good. He needs it."

"And so do you," Anton murmured.

Viviana sobbed, turning her gaze down to their son. Anton knew that look on her face—shame. "I'm so sorry."

"Don't. I don't need to hear it, honestly. I know you are and that's enough. I was so fucking angry all week, and I just couldn't get rid of it. I was scared to death if I came home, I was going to hurt you. I love you. I should never, ever want to hurt you, Viviana."

"You're home, now," she said softly.

"I am, and I'm not going anywhere. I should have called, or something. I know. I was being selfish."

"No, you needed space. Time to think."

Anton shrugged. "In a way. What I needed more was to

calm down; I wasn't in control of myself. Anger can be just as much a drug as it is a poison. Nothing gives me the right to call you names—and you're not, Vine."

"Not what?"

The word stuck in his throat. "A whore, or anything like that. I know you're not. I know you're faithful, devoted, mine. I know all of those things. I shouldn't have said that word and put you in the same sentence. I'm sorry."

Even in the darkness, Anton could see the tears she refused to acknowledge. "I've only been yours. I'm only ever going to be, Anton."

"Yeah, I know. Listen, I don't like what happened, and I'm really not okay with it, but I get it. I understand why you did it. But I don't ever want to talk about it, Viviana. Ever. I've had to think about it all fucking week and that was enough. So after tonight, don't bring it up to me. Don't you ever do it again, either, no matter what happens to us. If you do, baby, if you do that to me again ..."

He couldn't even finish the thought running through his mind.

"Okay," Viviana said, nodding. "Ever. Never. I get it. Is that all you needed to say?"

"That's all I can give you right now, Vine. And I love you."

Viviana moved on the bed, making room for Anton to climb in. Between them, their son was snuggled in tight, snoring away. Over his prone form, Anton skidded his hand along the blankets until he found his wife's.

"But I wanted to hear you tell me why, Viviana. From your mouth."

"I couldn't not have you," she said brokenly. "What was I going to do without you?"

Yeah, he figured that out a long time ago, too.

"Love you," Anton repeated. "I've been wanting to tell you that all week."

"I love you, too."

"I know. That's what kills me, baby."

• • •

Light filtered into the bedroom, and Anton groaned, not feeling as though he'd slept nearly enough. Childish giggles sounded from his left, making Anton turn to see what had his son so happy.

Demyan, on his side with his back turned to his father, poked his sleeping mother's stomach and laughed again. Anton's brow furrowed as his vision cleared of fatigue. He couldn't figure out what in the hell his son was doing until Demyan poked Viviana's rounded midsection again. Under the thin shirt she wore, tiny movement responded back to the poke.

"Demyan," Anton whispered, admonishing his son while trying to hide his humor. "Don't poke Ma, that's not nice."

He reached out to pull his giggling son into his side, then pressed his opened palm to Viviana's stomach. Under his palm, his baby kicked. It was the first time he'd felt the baby move and his heart swelled at the sensation.

Damn, he loved his wife.

"Not Ma," Demyan said, staring up at his father and grinning. "That's baby Ana. Ma says so."

Baby Ana.

Oh, hell.

They were having a little girl. The girl Anton wanted.

A girl. Sweet in pink, her daddy's little princess, and beautiful.

Ana.

Anton was so stuck on realizing his second child was a girl that he barely recognized the squirming dance his son was doing in the middle of the bed. But when Demyan began grabbing at his groin, Anton snapped out of it.

"Go pee, kiddo."

"Okay!"

Demyan didn't waste time crawling off the bed and disappearing into the master bath.

With his son out of sight, Anton let his hand travel up from Viviana's midsection until he stopped at her cheek. Sleeping, she looked so peaceful and at rest in the morning light. Anton rolled his thumb along her cheekbone, soaking in the love that still suffocated every fiber of his being.

"Love you, Vine."

Viviana smiled, letting her husband know she wasn't really sleeping. "Do you?"

"Like crazy. In a way that says there's got to be something fucking wrong with me. So, Ana, huh?"

"For your grandmother, and me, sort of. I liked it. She seems like an Ana."

Anton moved across the bed, kissing his wife until her pretty brown eyes opened wide to stare into his. The feeling of her lips on his reminded Anton of every reason why he loved his girl.

"Is Ana a good name?" Viviana asked when Anton pulled away.

"Ana's great, baby." Anton found his wife's hands with his own, intertwining their fingers before he tugged her into his chest. "And so are we."

"Yeah?"

"Yeah. New day, you know. Do you always let him poke your stomach like that? Because when I used to do it—"

"You're a grown man, Anton."

"So? Demyan seemed to like it."

"This baby isn't Demyan."

"Well, she seems to like it."

Obviously realizing she wasn't going to win the argument, Viviana rolled her eyes and giggled. "You're ridiculous."

"Yeah, but I'm your kind of ridiculous."

"Good thing."

Anton knew they had a ways to go, but oddly, this didn't feel like an end.

It was a beginning.

"We're okay," Anton said in the morning light, wanting his wife to know again. Viviana graced him with a smile. "We always were, baby."

"Always," she echoed.

Nearly four months later, Ana Christina began to make her show into the world five days before her due date. Unlike the birth of their son that went without issue, Ana's was not the same. Anton could tell that from the very beginning when his wife woke him not long after he'd fallen asleep early that night, swearing she couldn't do it alone because the minor contractions were so awful already.

She took hours, Ana did. They weren't easy hours. They were the kind of hours that ripped every bit of strength Viviana had left away and left her weak and exhausted. For a second child, a second birth, the doctors were confused. Viviana's body should have responded better, it should have understood what it needed to do. Instead, she struggled through contraction after contraction, never dilating enough for pain medication until ten hours turned into twenty, and those twenty turned into thirty-two.

The entire time, Anton felt so lost. Viviana could handle pain. Of that, Anton was most sure. This wasn't the same. It was brutal. Her whimpers, her tears. They tore him to shreds. It hurt him even more when she begged him to promise no more children. She didn't want to do it again.

Anton made that promise, though.

Unable to help his wife, all the while watching the monitors around them, Anton was unsure of what he was seeing. And then the baby heart monitor, the one keeping track of little Ana's heart, stopped showing life.

Suddenly it wasn't about waiting anymore, it was about rushing.

Ana was born in to the world late in the evening of December twenty-eighth. She'd been without oxygen for minutes. Her cord had somehow detached. From the very start, she showed not only how much of a fighter she was, but that she was also trouble. Once they got her breathing, she started to cry. Anton was pretty sure his daughter cried nonstop for the first three years of her damned life, but he didn't care.

Anton loved his dark haired, brown-eyed daughter from the first second he laid eyes on her. She looked just like her mother, but with blue-black hair like his. Five tiny fingers on her small right hand curled around his thumb inside the incubator and just like that, their home was filled, all pain and fear from the day forgotten.

Ten tiny fingers.

Blue-black hair.

And the brownest, prettiest eyes.

"Papa?" Demyan asked as he stared into the incubator, confused.

"That's baby Ana," Anton tried to explain.

Demyan made a face. "No, that's not baby Ana."

Anton chuckled. Attempting to explain to Demyan that his baby sister wasn't his mother's stomach was not an easy thing. The kid was so damned stubborn about everything. Just like his father. Not to mention, it was clear he was also jealous. Viviana and Anton expected that, though. It was normal.

"No, that is baby Ana."

"That's yucky."

"Demyan, don't call your sister yucky."

"That's yucky," his son repeated seriously.

Viviana giggled from her spot in the rocking chair three feet away. She was still healing from the C-section and walking could be an awful experience. "It's the sibling kind of love already. If we're lucky, yucky will be the nicest thing he calls her."

"Vine," Anton groaned. "Don't jinx it, baby."

Over his shoulder, Anton met his wife's gaze and caught her smile with his own. They'd had a rough few months together. Hell, they had a rough fucking year. Eventually Anton learned what he needed to do was put his mind and thoughts to the side, and let his heart take back over.

Trust was rebuilt.

Those cracks in the foundation were filled.

Anton learned he didn't have to feel like he owned her, to own the best parts of her. Viviana gave them willingly, in any case.

They were okay.

So okay.

God, he loved his wife. Like crazy. Like nobody understood.

Viviana's smile turned into a knowing grin. "Love you, too."

"Still kills me, baby."

Because he could be a lot of things. A monster. A man. Overwhelmed. Exhausted. Loving. Unsure. Her husband. Their children's father. The Bratva boss. He could be so goddamn bad, or so fucking good. Sometimes love hurt, sometimes it suffocated.

Sometimes it just consumed.

She didn't care. Viviana loved him, anyway.

Yeah, it killed him. But in the best way.

Epilogue

15 years later …

"Demyan! That's disgusting. In the freaking pool? Where I swim? Daddy didn't have that put in for you to screw whoever-the-heck in it!"

"Ana, get in the house right *now*."

Anton sighed, resisting the urge to bang his head against the hallway wall as his walk came to an abrupt stop. Sure enough, the telltale shriek of an embarrassed female and splashes of water followed Ana's angry tirade and Viviana's warning.

"Ugh. He's only been home a week. He's awful, I can't stand his stupid ass."

"Ana Christina, I swear!" Viviana yelled. "Watch that mouth of yours."

"But, Ma, he's—"

"Ana, I said enough. Demyan, take your friend home."

"Oh, that's not the kind of girl I'd call a friend, Ma. Friends don't let other friends screw them in the pool."

Anton screwed his eyes shut and sucked in a deep breath. At only nineteen, his son was without a doubt, the carbon copy of his younger self. Demyan liked very few things, but they were simple things. Good music, vodka, fast cars, guns, women, and football. Demyan also tended to talk more with his fists than his mouth when it came to guys. Hence his presence at home for the next month.

A suspension from his university's football team summer camp riled the young man up enough to send him home to think. Anton knew his son was just trying to find some solid ground. But, was his behaviour and attitude most days entirely exasperating? Yes.

"Holy crap, you're just going to let him off with that?"

Ana asked, sounding disgusted. "He brought some piece of *pizda*—"

"All right, I've heard all I want to out of you," Demyan barked. "Fucking little brat."

"Demyan *Anton!*"

It didn't matter who was shouting Demyan's name in anger, they still stressed his middle name like that was the exact reason he acted like he did. Hoping to all hell his wife had a hold of the situation outside, Anton slipped into his office and closed the door soundlessly. The last thing he wanted to do was get himself caught up in the middle of that chaos.

Growing up sibling-less hadn't exactly given Anton the best idea of what his children would be like as they got older together. Nearly four years apart in age, he figured Demyan and Ana would be as tight as knots. Instead, it seemed like the only fucking thing his kids did was fight.

They simply had to be within yelling distance for the slander to start getting slung.

I love my kids. I love my kids, Anton chanted internally to himself as he sat down at his desk. It was a mantra he learned to favor over the years.

The computer's screen flickered to life, the page automatically refreshing to show the emails that had been missed for the morning and late afternoon. Despite keeping a low profile as an active boss in the Russian Bratva at his age, Anton still played his part. In essence, he was a vor for life. There was no escaping it, he just didn't play such a leading role, anymore. Others, like his son, were starting to take center stage in more ways than one. Demyan still had quite a few years to go before he would take that stage alone, but his day would come.

Going through the emails and responding, Anton barely noticed the time passing him by until a familiar two knuckle rap sounded on the outside of his office door.

"Come in, Demyan."

The door opened and the first thing his nineteen-and-a-half-year-old son greeted him with was a roguish smirk that brought back memories of Anton's younger years. Raven black hair hung over mischievous blue eyes. His lips quirked up in a grin. Demyan was broad shouldered, six foot, three inches tall, and built like a brick house. A sight to see for sure.

He didn't lack female attention, by any means.

Sometimes the kid used that to his benefit far too much.

"You know better than to call your sister names," Anton scolded, keeping his eyes on the computer screen. "If you can't play nice with Ana, I'll send you back to the other side of New York. Neither your mother, nor I, want to listen to you fight like cats and dogs, Demyan."

"What would I even do over there?"

Anton's gaze flicked up to meet his son's. "Work, and not for the Bratva, either. You enjoy that far too much, and I'm starting to think you could use a bit of pride elsewhere."

"Oh, I've got pride where it counts, Papa."

"Mmm, not that kind, smartass," Anton replied blithely. "Don't push me."

Demyan rearranged himself on the leather couch, tossing his legs over the side of the armrest before flopping back to stare at the ceiling with a heavy sigh. "Even when I do go back, they're not going to let me play first string next season because of the fight."

Football was the only thing Anton didn't have in common with his son.

"You could always quit football if you're not getting what you need from it."

"I'm getting more than enough, it's the goddamned guys who think that it's okay for them to push my fucking buttons. They only pull that shit because of my last name." A dark chuckle echoed from Demyan before he added, "They don't even know what that name carries, or what I could do. Not really."

Anton shrugged. "We all have to follow the rules, in one way or the other. You broke the football team's policy about fighting with teammates, so now you handle it like an adult."

"You're lecturing me on the importance of following rules?" Demyan scoffed, shooting Anton a look from the side that was filled with disbelief. "Really, Papa? That's rich coming from you and all."

There were some chains Anton refused to bite onto, and that was one of them. There came a point in his life when he realized his children would know exactly who he was and what had happened in his past.

When his son had asked, Anton didn't lie. It wasn't such a surprise that Demyan barely blinked an eye about it, either, considering he'd been so close to his father growing up. The kid always did have a healthy curiosity for the life around him, sticking his nose into situations where he didn't belong. Demyan was a lot like Anton in that way, actually. It was even worse because his son was a goddamn natural.

Demyan would make one hell of a boss one day.

Anton found himself constantly drawing the similarities between him and his son. From chasing pussy from the time he was old enough to want it, to stealing his father's Mercedes. He even dabbled in a few harder drugs, which brought his mother to tears. Demyan pulled every stunt his father had once done twice over. Sometimes even worse. On more than one occasion, Demyan frightened the fucking wits out of his father doing some of the shit he did, giving Anton a damn good feeling of what it must have been like to be his own mother and father.

If anything, Anton found himself respecting Daniil and Sasha even more.

There was an open door policy between Anton and his son. Always had been, and always would be. Demyan needed a safe place to go to, so Anton was it—a cornerstone. Sometimes it led to Anton learning things he didn't want or need to know, but at the same time, Demyan was never afraid to come to his father if he needed something, or just wanted to talk.

He made his son a vor on his eighteenth birthday, just the same as he had been.

All the while, Anton let Demyan live, he let him grow, disciplined him when he needed to, and taught him what he knew had helped him the most. More than anything, Anton knew Demyan needed to make those same mistakes he did long ago, otherwise his son wouldn't be who he was. Anton was so proud of who his son was, now.

No regrets, Anton mused with a glance at his carefree, albeit frustrated, son. Viviana asked Anton once to be a father first to their children, and the boss second. Somehow, he knew he managed to do just that, though the two things mingled at times. It was impossible to avoid.

"Who raised you with that disrespect in your mouth, huh?" Anton asked over the computer. "Surely not me, Demyan."

"Sorry," Demyan muttered. "So hey, listen—"

"No, you listen. Was that the redhead your sister caught you with in the pool?"

Demyan's blue eyes blinked with shock before a mask of indifference fell in its place. "So what if it was? I'm always safe, we're good."

"No, we're not good, Demyan. Being safe doesn't always equate to a whole hell of a lot. Mistakes happen more often than not. So help you God if some girl shows up on our doorstep pregnant with your child and you get strapped down with a woman you don't want or love. I can't leave you alone for thirty minutes and you've got naked females running loose in my house. Jesus, we only went to the store for steaks."

"Technically, she was—"

Anton held up a single hand. "Who pays for this house?"

"You."

"Who lets you live in it when you don't feel like cleaning your apartment?"

"You," Demyan said unhappily.

"Exactly. And your mother, but that's beside the point." Anton sighed, rubbing a hand over his face, annoyed. Going back to his computer, he began typing out the final email he hadn't finished before his son interrupted. "The point, is that you know the rules here, too. None of those girls you run around with are to be in this home, not unless—"

"I'm prepared to keep them," Demyan said quietly. "Yeah, I know."

Anton's hands froze over the keyboard. "Excuse me?"

"I said I know."

If Anton was hearing his son correctly, Demyan was telling him something incredibly important and huge for him. "And?"

Demyan chewed nervously on the inside of his cheek, pushing himself into a sitting position on the couch. It wasn't long before the jittery jump of his knee started, giving away how anxious he truly was. Anton didn't think he had ever seen his boy so completely overwhelmed before.

"My God, spit it the fuck out, Demyan," Anton said.

"Wasn't the redhead," his son mumbled.

Anton turned slowly in his chair, bringing it out to the side of the desk where he could see his son face on. "But you've been with her a lot lately, yeah?"

"Casey?" Demyan made a dismissed sound under his breath, shrugging those broad shoulders of his and refusing to meet his father's stare. "Sure, but it's not like we're serious or anything. Shit, we're not even fucking. She's a good friend of mine, I guess. Some innocent fun when I'm bored. People assume; I let them."

Anton didn't like where this was going. "Does she know that, though?"

"Sure. I can have a female friends and not *be* with them, okay? I do know how to do that, even if you think I don't."

"Well, okay then."

That was enough for Anton. He didn't need to know any more about this Casey. As long as she wasn't screwing around with his boy, she wasn't knocked up, and Demyan wasn't leading her on, Anton didn't care what they did together.

"What about Sofia? You two had a thing there for a while, didn't you? Is that over for good now, or what?"

Adrik Vasin's daughter had grown into a beautiful young woman. One that caught Demyan's eye when he was a newly turned eighteen and fresh out of his parent's house into his own life. Anton knew the two new adults had played around on more than one occasion, though he turned his cheek to it. They were old enough to make those choices and it wasn't in Anton's home, after all, so he didn't much care as long as it didn't affect his Bratva or business.

Mostly, Demyan liked Sofia for who she was and the values she sported. Demyan admitted as much to his father, and given the way she was raised—with Bratva values—she appealed to Demyan for that reason. Unfortunately, that was one of the only reasons she appealed to his son. She was Russian, a beauty, a little on the wild child side, and related to Demyan's life in a business sort of way that gave him a solid outlook on what could be his future.

But, she wasn't someone he loved. Sofia also didn't love him.

"We worked better in bed than we did out of it. She's wild. Tripped me up when I was bored. Good for that, you know."

Anton cringed, not wanting to hear that story for a minute. "Jesus, Demyan. I really like the arrangement I have with Adrik. You know how particular he is over that girl. Please don't go using his daughter for a toy and getting yourself shot. I'd hate to have to kill my friend because he taught you a lesson about respecting a man's daughter."

In his usual dismissive fashion, Demyan laughed off the warning. "Sofia and I are good, really. We're done and she's fine with that. Hell, she's the one who ended it. I think she's messing around with one of her bulls, so I'm the last man Adrik will be coming after. Don't worry about it, Papa."

"I feel like I'm missing something here," Anton admitted.

Demyan frowned, raking both his hands through his hair as he rested his elbows to his knees. "My friend, she didn't leave. Mom sent me in to let you know she was still here, and maybe staying for a while."

Again, Anton simply stared at his son in a mixture of shock and confusion. "Yeah?"

"She um ... surprised me, kind of. She didn't tell me she was coming. I don't think anybody knows she's here, yet. Ivan is probably freaking out, or if not, he will be soon."

Suddenly, Anton's mind was catching up to speed lightning quick. "Oh, Demyan, *no*."

"What am I supposed to do, huh?" Demyan asked, finally looking back up at his father. Wetness shined behind his blue irises but he blinked it away just as fast. "I didn't ask her here. Ana didn't get a good look at her, thank fuck, because that would have only made it worse. Mom just ... I don't know about Ma, really, but she didn't look especially pleased about it."

"Might have helped if Gia wasn't naked."

Demyan snorted. "Right. She wasn't. That was just Ana being her usual self."

Gia ... it was always about her when it came to Demyan, Anton thought with a shake of his head. Turning to stare out the window, his mind ran wild. Gia Lavrov was Ivan's youngest daughter. Nearly a year older than Demyan, they had spent their childhood and most of their teenage years stuck to one another. Demyan insisted he remembered her even when she was young, but Anton wasn't sure if that was his son actually having the memory, or creating what he wanted.

Because Demyan so badly wanted Gia.

She was the only girl Demyan would drop anything and everything for. Anton had seen him do it, and watched him hurt when he was shut out time and time again. Those walls his son built up around his heart and soul only grew higher and tougher over the years. It was no wonder Demyan couldn't find a woman to ground him.

Demyan might have touched many women, but he only loved one. Just Gia.

Anton couldn't help but wonder if she was setting his son up for nothing but heartbreak again.

"She's supposed to be getting married next month, son."

"I know," Demyan whispered, sounding pained at just the thought alone. "God, I know, Papa. I *do*. She was the one who came here, okay? Texted me ten minutes after you guys left and said she was outside. A taxi dropped her off."

"Just like that?" When Demyan didn't answer, Anton asked, "Does Ivan know she's here?"

"I don't think so, but maybe. I didn't really ask much of anything when I saw her."

Then, Anton had another thought. One that was as sobering and difficult to understand as Gia herself being there. Demyan could have just as easily gotten Gia to his apartment across the city and Anton and Viviana would have been none the wiser about her arrival. He could have stayed away with her and not said a word until somebody figured it out. No one would have known for a good while. It wasn't unusual for his son to come and go as he pleased, and Gia was a twenty-year-old adult.

"You meant to be caught," Anton said softly.

Demyan wet his lips, hands wringing between his spread legs. "And if I did?"

"You know I have to call Ivan, now." A single nod answered him back. Anton felt a lump lodge in his throat, painfully so. "Why would you do that? He's my oldest friend, Demyan. This will break his fucking heart to find out she's been running around with you whenever she was able to."

"Just say you didn't know."

Yeah, that wouldn't work. If there was anything Anton was known for, it was keeping a close eye on his family. Ivan would know. There would be no excuse he could use worthy enough to pass off the fact that Anton had knowledge his son had been meeting up with Gia for over a year. Beyond the point when their rocky teenaged relationship had ended, and then picked up where it left off after she had met her boyfriend who only two months later became her fiancé. Mostly, Anton thought Demyan and Gia weren't anything serious, seeing as how they couldn't keep it together the first time, and nothing would come of the confusing, secretive thing they had going on now.

Evidently, Anton should have known better.

Demyan sniffed, wiping his cheek off on his shoulder as he said, "She'd never tell him herself, even now with her calling the wedding off. She's always so worried about what Ivan would think, or what her mother would say. They never wanted her to be with someone affiliated."

Wait—Gia called the wedding off?

"Wasn't the Bratva the whole reason you two went south in the first place?"

"Things change."

"They do, but that's a pretty big thing to change overnight," Anton said under his breath. "It wasn't overnight, though, was it? This wasn't a onetime thing with you two, and you know how your mother and I feel about that. There are boundaries you shouldn't cross, Demyan, and a relationship between other people is a big one to leap over."

"What should I have done, then, let her marry that idiot because everybody else wants her to? I know he's Mr. Fan-fucking-tastic and all. She doesn't love him—she loves me. That's not fair to Gia."

"You mean it's not fair to you," Anton corrected. "Not everything is about you, Demyan. She wanted to marry that boy. Suddenly that's changed, too?"

"No, she never did. It just took her a while to figure out that the rest didn't matter, she wasn't going to make a happy future with someone who was fine enough for now. She still wanted *me*."

Anton forced his mouth to stay shut so he could think. A ragged exhale left his lungs before he rested back in his chair and rubbed at his forehead, feeling the headache beginning to throb there.

If anything, Anton was incredibly proud of his son. He wouldn't tell Demyan that, but he was. The one thing Demyan wanted, he hadn't let go of. And even if it ached to get to the end result, he was clearly prepared to do it.

"This might not work out the way you want it to," Anton

said warningly.

Demyan nodded. "But it might, though. And if it gets me her, I don't give a shit about the rest. I'm willing to take that risk. I love her like nobody else."

Anton sighed. "Yeah, you always did, huh?"

"Like crazy."

"Are you really ready for what that means, though?"

"I've just been waiting on her."

The familiarity in Demyan's conviction was Anton needed to hear. After all, that had been him once, too.

• • •

Viviana leaned in the doorway of her daughter's bedroom, letting her mind run a million miles a minute. Ana pretended her mother wasn't there. That wasn't unusual for the girl. Sometimes it was just plain annoying, but wasn't that always the way with teenagers? All they ever seemed to do was test their limits. God knew Anton and Viviana's kids sure tested theirs enough.

Ana was fifteen, so she still had a bit more pushing room for a few years. Viviana didn't turn cheek to the innocent charade her daughter had going on, either. Sure, Ana was a straight-A student, on the swim team, and barely stepped out of line, but she could be one wicked fucking thing, too. Sometimes it was just the simplest curve of her pretty lips quirking up into a grin that told her mother all she needed to know.

Ana could be a hellion, no doubt about it.

With almond shaped eyes that pooled with a melting, milk chocolate color, shiny, straight ebony hair, and add in the fact that at her young age she was already five foot, seven inches tall with curves abound … Well, Ana caught the gazes of the boys her age, and a few older ones. That seventeen-year-old neighbor boy Anton caught Ana jogging with the previous weekend when she was supposed to be exercising alone was a perfect example.

Really, Viviana tried not to think about it. She trusted her daughter. But, even if she didn't, Ana toted one hell of an overprotective father and a big brother who was heavy on the fists when it came to boys that might be staring for too long. Daddy's little girl didn't quite do their spoiled daughter justice.

Ana, from the day she was born, wanted for absolutely nothing. Anton made damn sure of that, regardless of Viviana's worry he would somehow turn their child rotten. To her father, Ana did no wrong. As for Viviana, she knew without a doubt her daughter was, essentially, the Bratva princess. And already, there were too many eyes watching the young girl, the daughter of one of the most infamous Bratva bosses, just to see what she might do ... or better yet, who she may pick if that was the life she wanted to lead.

Those were too heavy of expectations for a girl of only fifteen, so both Viviana and Anton did their best to shield Ana from it. Viviana had no clue if they were succeeding or failing.

"So ..." Viviana trailed off with a pointed cough meant to draw her daughter's attention away from the tablet in her hands. Ana tugged the ear buds from her ears and look up with a huff. "About earlier, I wanted to let you know what's going on with that."

Ana quirked up a brow. "You mean Demyan getting his dick wet in more ways than one?"

Viviana stared up at the ceiling, wishing the pulsing headache would go away. "Ana, please."

"Fine, sorry. What, now?"

"Did you, um, happen to see who the girl in the pool was?"

"No. You pulled me back into the house and she ran under the cabaña. Why, Ma?"

Chewing on her lower lip, Viviana frowned. She figured it would be better if she just spat it out and got it over with. "It was Gia."

Ana's eyes widened as her mouth dropped open with an

audible pop. That was about the extent of Viviana's feelings, too, really, but she had to be more objective for her son's sake. The situation was delicate enough as it was without adding to it.

"Before you say anything, your brother is going through a crappy time right now. This isn't going to be easy on him, or her, and it's certainly not going to be easy on your father or Ivan when that all goes down. What I need is for you to keep that attitude of yours in line for a few days until this all blows over. Can you do that?"

Dumbly, Ana nodded. "Isn't she marrying Mark, or ... What's his name again?"

"Matt," Viviana said quietly. "He's a nice kid."

Matt Taylor wasn't anything to scoff at. He was handsome, sure. Well-to-do on the financial side of things, but so were Gia and Demyan, given their fathers' statuses in the Bratva. What Demyan was that Matt wasn't, was affiliated with the mafia. As far as Viviana knew, Gia wanted to stay clear away from that mess. She didn't want to be a mob wife, even though she had clearly been in love with Demyan since they were kids.

When it came to being a vor, that was something Demyan hadn't been given much of a choice in. What he had been given, however, was the chance to live how he wanted while he did it. Demyan was going to college, taking his time to grow up, make mistakes, enjoy his life, and learning the ways of his future in the Bratva all the while. Sometimes it was difficult, worrisome, and confusing, but she knew Demyan wouldn't have his life any other way.

Gia couldn't seem to accept that, or at least she hadn't, before.

What changed?

It hurt Viviana something awful to watch her son struggle and fight for someone who kept pushing him away the closer he came. But, if Demyan was anything, it was stubborn. Giving up was not in his nature.

"He's like a doctor or something, right?" Ana asked.

"No, he's still got a couple of more years in college to go, but he will be."

"Huh. So are you asking me to leave Demyan alone?"

"I'm asking for you to be nice to your brother for once."

"Sure, Ma."

Then, Ana smiled one of those private grins. Despite the nastiness that was occasionally shared between Demyan and his little sister, the two loved one another. They merely showed that love differently than other siblings. Mostly in a way that drove their parents totally insane.

"You know, I always wondered if they would happen again."

Viviana stared down at her daughter, confused. "Demyan and Gia?"

Ana shrugged. "Yeah. I mean, he holds her hand."

"Do they?" Viviana had never seen that before. She noticed a lot between the two over the years, but rarely that, and when she had, it was mostly when they were children. "When?"

"Sometimes, in private. Under the table, or passing by in the hallway. Where he thinks nobody sees. Just reaches out and grabs her hand, you know?"

Viviana smiled, hiding it with her hand. "Like Dad does with me."

"Kinda."

Happy with the way the discussion had gone, Viviana left Ana alone. Eventually, after walking aimlessly through the halls, she found her way into the master bedroom, closing the door quietly to shut out the rest of the house.

The window at the far left of the bedroom offered a view of the entire backyard. Down below, she could plainly see her son relaxing back on one of the rocking lounging chairs. Gia's tinier figure wearing a flimsy summer dress was curled into his side and resting on his chest.

No one would be able to see them from down below, Viviana knew. Their position on the other side of the large cabaña kept them out of view. Oddly, the way Demyan's hand smoothed down the golden waves of his lover's hair, his lips moving against Gia's cheek to signal he was speaking something, Viviana felt like she was intruding.

Her son was a lot of things. He could be moody and particular, or uninhibited and carefree. Like his father and the men who came before him, he was dangerous and magnetic. A natural born leader in his mafia driven environment, and an easily free, happy soul in his family life. At times, he could be a philanderer, as much as Viviana hated to think about it, although he never brought those women home for her to meet.

Demyan was also a wanderer; unsettled, never at rest, and constantly searching for something—someone—to finally tie him down.

Had he found that?

Oh, Viviana hoped so. She desperately wanted to believe Gia was what he had been looking for.

"How long?" she asked quietly.

Anton cleared his throat behind her. She hadn't acknowledged his presence when he entered the bedroom not long after she did. "Does it matter?"

Viviana lifted a shoulder. "Maybe."

Despite the vagueness to her question, and his, she knew Anton understood. Nineteen years of marriage gave them the ability to speak few words and still get the point across. Not all of those years were easy, nor were they spent in a blissful, ignorant happiness, but they were the most real and true years of Viviana's life.

She wouldn't give them up for anything.

"Like this?" Anton asked, coming to stand at her side so he too could look down. "About a year."

Viviana frowned. "Like this how, Anton?"

"She's been engaged for a year, if that helps any." It did, much more than Viviana wanted to say. Anton blew out a harsh sound, shaking his head. "Everything is a choice, Vine. Was it wrong for him to be chasing after a girl that obviously wasn't his, for him to run around with her behind the backs of others, and to continue having that relationship when he knew it should have stopped? Yes, but I think he did what he had to."

"Did we do something wrong?" Viviana asked.

Anton's head whipped to the side, those blue eyes of his blazing with surprise. Viviana simply stared back at him. Life was beginning to weather her husband in the best of ways at his age. Lines creased around the edges of his eyes, relaxing him when he smiled. The faintest hint of salt was starting to pepper his dark hair. That rough, well-cut physique he always had never changed, though. Broad shouldered, definition in all the spots she could touch, and rock-solid from top to toe, he was still amazing in the physical sense. To look at, Anton was, without a doubt, the most handsomely distinguished man she could remember at his age. To touch and to love, he was the very best.

"I don't know, did we?" she asked again.

"No," Anton said. "If anything, we did well. We let him be tough if he needed. We let him be weak if he wanted. We taught him respect, and he gives it back to us in return."

Viviana sighed shakily. After everything that had happened in their life, even the suggestion of being involved in an affair was not acceptable. They raised both of their children to have a healthy respect for the relationships other people had, to know it wasn't for them to intrude on.

"Why like this, though? It's not okay."

"Because everything is a choice, like I said. Demyan had to start making different choices that were for his benefit, instead of ours, or hers. They may not have been choices we agreed with, but they were his to make. He wanted something, so he took it. That was all."

"You're not angry?"

Anton's mouth quirked up in the barest ghost of a smirk. "Nah, not with him. God, he's been watching that girl ever since he was two, you know? He couldn't help she was so against the lifestyle he lived, or the things surrounding him. Demyan just ..."

"What?"

"Waited her out, baby. Took his time to get what he knew would be his eventually, just like I did for you."

Anton finished his statement by offering her a sentimental grin before saying, "Like any good man would. Sure, he took her when she wanted him to, when someone else had claim, but she let him do that. That's no excuse, it's still not right, and he'll surely have to apologize to Ivan for doing wrong with his daughter, but he still waited her out. The way Gia wanted him to. Demyan didn't make some grand gesture, he didn't shame her like he could have when he had to watch her tumble off with somebody else. There was none of that. He let her be, and waited for her to come to him.

"That's a good man, and we raised that man." Anton reached out to grasp Viviana's wrist, tugging lightly to draw her into his side. The warmth of his familiar, spicy scent soaked into her lungs like a drug as she buried her face into his chest and allowed herself to be suffocated in it. "So no, I'm not angry. I'm frustrated, tired, and my head hurts, but I'm not angry."

Comfortable in the embrace, she asked, "How long have you known?"

"A while."

Viviana should have been angry with him for that. Allowing something inappropriate to continue after he had knowledge it was happening wasn't like Anton at all, but maybe because it was Demyan, he looked away.

"Do you think everything will work out?" Viviana asked, her voice muffled by Anton's chest.

The chuckles he released rocked their frames. "Eventually. I talked to Ivan for a good hour."

"And?"

"And nothing. She called the wedding off this morning, told her father exactly where she was going, though she didn't say why specifically. Ivan pretty much worked it out on his own and he let her go. He didn't have to, he could have called and gave me a heads up, but he didn't. Like us for Demyan, he let Gia have her choices and make them how she deemed fit for her."

Viviana was confused. "So, he's not angry, either?"

It seemed like Demyan and Gia's misdeed was overlooked.

"No, because Ivan just wants his child to be happy. He does want to speak with Demyan, and I'll be there to mediate it all, but that's small compared to everything else. If anything, Demyan owes him a frank discussion, and maybe an apology if Ivan asks for it. Our son knows his place, so rest assured he already expected all of this."

Anton's hands slipped in under Viviana's chin, drawing her face away from his body so he could look down at her. With the pads of his fingers rolling along her jaw in tender motions, he leaned in close to skim his nose along the apple of her cheek. Softly, a hum built in the back of his throat, soothing away the residual emotions that were making Viviana weary and unsure.

"Look at our son," Anton said, nudging his nose under her jaw. "See what we did, baby."

Sure enough, when she stared out the window again to look down on her son, Viviana was filled with an unexpected sense of peace and finality. Demyan, with his hands cupping Gia's smiling face, had tossed his head back in his laughter. Their legs had tangled together on the lounge chair that rocked with the movement of their bodies. It was sweet, though it wasn't. Honest, though it hurt. And true, though they had a ways to go.

Love was never easy. Sometimes it played an awful, dirty game.

But, it was an awfully great thing to have, too.

Gia's hand came down to smack at Demyan's T-shirt covered chest, and the laughter outside abruptly stopped. Viviana couldn't see her son's face then, but she could see his lover's. Gia wore an expression churned with happiness and chance, mixed heavily with waiting and relief. With a predator's grace, Demyan was lifting his back off the lounger in one fluid motion, inadvertently pushing Gia back. When his body loomed over hers and Gia fisted her hands into his sides, Viviana turned away again.

Anton's lips touched down to the side of her mouth, and Viviana smiled into the kiss. "We did well."

"We did," Anton said, his confidence and pride shining through strong. "I know he's always been a little difficult, and God knows he's made it tougher at times than it needed to be, but Demyan comes out on top. We did that. We get to sit back and enjoy it, now, that's all."

"Let's let him have his story, is that what you're saying?"

"As beautiful or as ugly as it may be, we have to let him have it and trust it will work out. Somebody let us have ours. All of our scores are settled, and we made it through just fine. Time to step aside, Vine. Think you're ready for that?"

Viviana smiled, letting Anton's mouth seek and explore the expanse of her neck. "Are you?"

With you, always.

ABOUT THE AUTHOR

Bethany-Kris is a Canadian author, lover of much, and mother to three very young sons, one cat, and two dogs. A small town in Eastern Canada where she was born and raised is where she has always called home. With her boys under her feet, a snuggling cat, barking dogs, and a spouse calling over his shoulder, she is nearly always writing something ... when she can find the time.

Find Bethany-Kris at:
Her website www.bethanykris.com,
or on Facebook at www.facebook.com/bethanykriswrites,
on her blog at www.bethanykris.blogspot.ca,
or on Twitter - @BethanyKris.

Sign up to Bethany-Kris's New Release Newsletter here:
http://eepurl.com/bf9lzD

MORE BY BETHANY-KRIS

The Russian Guns
The Arrangement
The Life
The Score
Demyan & Ana
Shattered

Filthy Marcellos
Filthy Marcellos: Lucian
Filthy Marcellos: Giovanni
Filthy Marcellos: Dante

Watch for more at www.bethanykris.com

www.ingramcontent.com/pod-product-compliance
Lightning Source LLC
Chambersburg PA
CBHW072346020726
47506CB00004B/1028